Tent City

A Novel

Amy L. Bernstein

Published by Open Books

Interior design by Siva Ram Maganti

Cover image © Shutterstock AI Generator

Praise for *Tent City*

"In an uncomfortably familiar present, Amy L. Bernstein shows us how fine the line is between economic safety and essential survival. She puts us at the precipice of—and allows us to peer over the edge into—a community's struggle against inexorable pressures. Bernstein's thrillingly perceptive story asks "Where does individual and collective responsibility start and end?" and imagines for us what happens when we don't have answers. Captivating and horrifying, *Tent City* is everything a novel should be."

—Amy Goldmacher, *Terms & Conditions*

"Bernstein writes with compassion and empathy while unflinchingly facing hard truths. *Tent City* is a cautionary tale about the uncertainty of our collective future and the choices we make today."

—Liisa Kovala, *Like Water for Weary Souls*

"In *Tent City*, Amy L. Bernstein demonstrates fiction's power to drill to the heart of the human situation, sans sugar coating, without pulling any punches. The world she shows us is not dystopian. Rather her characters, young, middle-aged, and older are ordinary people making the most of the hands dealt them. As we see their lives play out, we learn the fragility of human experience, and we examine our place among our brothers, sisters, parents, and friends."

—Stephen Woodfin, *The Warrior with Alzheimer's*,
a Kirkus best book of the year

"I have spent my life judging the distance between American reality and the American dream."

—Bruce Springsteen

Contents

Part I

The First Spring

Chapter One

Hero_Foreclosures.com

JUST LISTED!

100k sq. ft. shopping center, Remington County near Willing. Ideal for mixed use or conversion. Visit our website for an extensive list of foreclosed properties.

Not a single one of the natural or manmade features drawn so distinctly on an 1872 map of the town of Willing, in Remington County, remains visible in the twenty-first century. The Tong River that once ran like a crooked seam through the town, cleaving it in two, was dammed and paved over by 1915. The sawmills and textile mills hugging the Tong's shores were gone before that. Gone too were the smoke-stacked candy factory, the spice factory, and the smelly tannery that rose up in fits of fevered industry as the town's borders expanded. All the jobs generated by the organized dismantling of all these large commercial properties dried up ages ago—the bricks carted off to begin life anew in service to less grand enterprises.

No matter. Sylvia Bird King never studied an 1872 map of Willing. And when the time came 15 years ago for Sylvia, then pregnant with twins Jeannie and Zeke, and her husband Carson King to buy their first house, Willing's old industrial sob story wasn't on the radar. And that house, oh that house: love at first sight. The house itself was a spacious but standard-issue center-hall colonial. But the yard told a different story, a story about success and prosperity that reflected the perpetual gleam in the couple's eyes. Three acres of undivided land, the largest undeveloped plot of residentially zoned land in all of Willing—longer than two football fields combined. History and nature had conspired to create an enormous, level carpet of grass running the full width of the rear of the Kings' house and then many hundreds of yards beyond the back deck, stopping only at a dense stand of pin oak trees, which in turn lead downhill to a forgotten stream that was once a tributary to the Tong. Carson insisted upon keeping the expanse weed-free and uncluttered. No children's swing set or climbing castle. No garden gnomes or rose bushes. The yard was adorned simply by virtue of its own sweeping green expanse. The Kings called it *the manor grounds* and considered it their economic insurance policy: land that could be subdivided and sold at an enormous profit someday. A day they knew was bound to arrive, as if foretold.

On a recent April morning, the yard is in fine form, as usual. But it is also beside the point. Sylvia and Carson, wrapped in blankets, drink coffee on the east-facing deck, as they so often do, the morning light glinting off the glass-topped table lightly coated with pollen dust. Both have eyes glued to phones. Neither takes in the hopping robins and the first fresh green grass of the season glistening with dew.

Carson argues with a text. "We're not doing that. Not letting Bruno and Jorge go."

Sylvia pursues her own train of thought. "If I don't sell the Walters property this week, they'll pull the contract."

"We're over-budget on these damn houses," Carson growls. "But it's just a blip. Vin and Dizz, over-reacting again."

Sylvia glances briefly at her husband. "I need you to get Jeannie after soccer this afternoon."

"Again?"

Sylvia shoots him a look. "I'll trade you one Jeannie pick-up for a trip with Zeke and his friends to the monster truck show on Saturday."

"But *I* want to go to the monster truck show. Guy time."

"Fine," she says. *Checkmate.* "Then you can do both."

Carson's phone rings. "Yeah, I'm heading out to the site now. We'll talk about it when I get there. Listen, Vin, you and Dizz gotta start playing the long-game!" He waves absently at Sylvia and disappears inside the house.

Sylvia looks out across the lawn, cup halfway to her lips.

Between one rapid eye blink and another, everything in her line of sight shifts. The great lawn is now blanketed by rows and rows of pitched tents—a sea of colored nylon pyramids and plastic stakes drilled into the soft earth, threaded with thin, taught ropes. Sylvia blinks hard, her phone falling by her side. She looks again: Tents everywhere. Shadows move inside the tents, as sunlight hits the opaque structures. And a sound comes from nowhere, yet is everywhere, a loud rush of air, almost voice-like in its insistence. Sylvia looks away, eyes welling with tears for no reason. No one is nearby to confirm or deny this vision—or what it might mean. The people who know her best, who wouldn't hesitate to tell her she's crazy, are inside, getting ready for the day.

Sylvia stands and scoops up her phone. *No,* she thinks. *I have no time for this…menopausal bullshit…or whatever it is.* She turns quickly toward the sliding glass doors, just in time to catch twins Jeannie and Zeke—earbuds jammed in, the better to tune out parental instructions.

"Bye," the twins chorus, then disappear. Sylvia waves at their backs—lanky, brown-haired Jeannie, and curly blond Zeke, always in a hurry now.

Her phone rings as she turns back to face the yard, reassured by the ordinary, featureless expanse of green.

"With all due respect, Mr. Walters, our agreement says the end of the month," Sylvia tells her caller. "I still have a whole week. I'm doing absolutely everything I can, believe me. Please… No, I'm not… I don't need…Thank you…You too."

Terrible clients, the Walters. A realtor's worst nightmare: fussy, always changing their minds. And what expectations! Unrealistic—even in the best of markets. Irritated, Sylvia turns back again to the yard for solace, a slight catch in her breath. *It's just stress.* But reality is once more out of sync, the vast acreage again transformed—a full-on encampment now. Among the tents, fires burn inside metal drums. Laundry dries on strung-up ropes. A soccer ball and a child's doll lie on the ground just feet from the deck. Sylvia shakes her head briskly before dashing inside to grab car keys, purse, and the extravagantly expensive lavender coat with flower-shaped buttons she bought recently, just because it's spring, and because the color contrasts nicely with her thick, brown, shoulder-length curls.

Get a grip.

Chapter Two

As Sylvia heads east toward the puffed-out Walters place for a brokers' open house—surely the push that is needed to get a deal done—Carson is going twice as far in the opposite direction. He's driving out to a partially built block of new houses on a rise at the very outskirts of Willing, which will, once completed, be called Willing Enclave. Carson's idea, deemed (by him) simple but elegant. If only he didn't have to wade through a load of crap to turn the idea into a reality. He drives in stony silence, steeling himself. He and Vin Palmer and Darius Aristides—partners and best friends—used to all be on the same page. For the longest time, Carson couldn't imagine a difference of opinion they couldn't work out over a couple of beers on Carson's showy back deck, or down at the Haven on Main Street, which had been called the Tap Room when they were all in high school peddling fake IDs to get shit-faced.

Lately, he's not so sure, and nothing comes as easily as it should. Especially consensus.

If I can put my finger on where we started heading off the rails, I can reel them back in.

He parks his Ford Super Duty pick-up truck on a patch of pea gravel alongside Vin's and Darius' trucks—all the same make and model, except Carson's is a couple of years newer, and looks it. It's a typical distinction. Vin and Darius each weigh about 20 pounds more than they did in high school, though all three have the muscled forearms and shoulders of men who routinely lift heavy objects. Vin's shoulder-length red rock-star hair is now a close-cropped reddish-gray fringe. Darius has kept his thick, black wavy hair, courtesy of Greek immigrant parents, but his face is already lined and pouched. Meanwhile, Carson is a tad leaner than he was at 20 and his hair is still blond and full, his blue eyes as piercing as ever. He wears his untucked denim shirt, Dickey khakis, and steel-toed work boots like a man who knows what he's about. What sets him apart even more, to anyone looking closely, is the Rolex he insists on wearing even to job sites like this one—a 20th anniversary gift from Sylvia, who'd had her best year ever and was eager to commemorate her (and their) good fortune. It isn't the watch as an ostentatious status symbol he cares about. It's more like a talisman, solid proof that he and Sylvia are checking off all the right boxes, making all the right choices. Progress is on their side. It's kind of their mantra.

Carson scans the site for his partners. Three houses have been partially framed up, but are still transparent as ghosts. Three additional sites have been excavated for foundations, but that's as far as they go. A small backhoe is parked askew on the side of the crescent-shaped private road of the "enclave," but the road is just flattened dirt, for now, ending abruptly at a threshold of torn grass, bent carpenter nails, and cigarette butts. Several caches of power tools are stacked neatly between houses. It's mid-morning, but there's no activity, no workers on site. Nothing is more ominous than a quiet construction site, Carson thinks.

When Carson finally tracks down Vin and Darius, they're standing behind house number two, discussing the placement of the air conditioning units.

"If we put a line of shrubs in, right here," Vin says.

"Ficus," Darius says.

"Yeah, exactly."

"Or maybe a lattice fence. Vinyl. Stained dark blue," Darius adds.

"Anyway, there's a million ways to do it, so the unit doesn't stick out like a sore thumb," Vin says.

Carson steps around a pile of lumber. "What's going on? Where's the crew?"

"Cap, we talked about this," Vin says.

"This is what austerity looks like," Darius says.

"Goddammit! This isn't austerity, this is a fucking ghost town. Why didn't you ask me first?" Carson scoops up construction rubble and chucks it hard out into the rubble-strewn yard, like he's hell-bent on striking out a guy on third base.

"Bruno and Jorge will be here at noon. We cut the shift to take pressure off payroll," Vin says. "We're still on schedule. More or less."

"We agreed last week, Cap, that Vin and I would handle the site, while you handle the suppliers." Darius steps closer to Carson. "So where are you on *that*?"

"Cutting Bruno and Jorge loose is a big mistake. You see that, right?" Carson grits his teeth. *Reel them in.*

"What about the suppliers, Cap?" Darius and Carson are squared off now, as if gearing up for a boxing match, while Vin, as usual, hangs back. "Are you negotiating, like we said?"

"Well, if you're gonna shut down the fucking work site," Carson says, "what's the point of re-negotiating terms with our suppliers? They're not delivering any more fucking lumber or plumbing or electrical any time soon, are they? And did it occur to you"—poking Darius in the chest—"that cutting shifts means the guys are gonna find work elsewhere, and leave us with a bigger hole than we're in now? Did you think of that?"

"We're not the fucking enemy, Cap!" Vin says.

"Brass tacks," Darius says, unphased. "Our raw material costs are skyrocketing, what with the copper shortage, the tariffs, and the rest of the bullshit. We gotta start with the guys we've done business with the longest, get them to come down."

"Like Tipper and Sons," Vin says. "You can start there. Talk to him, Cap. Sandy will listen to you. Maybe. You gotta try."

"We can't just stop work!" Carson chunks more rocks into left field.

"We're bleeding out," Darius says. "You can choose to ignore a fact, but that doesn't mean—"

"It isn't true," Vin adds.

"If we're serious about surviving, Cap," Darius says, "then we gotta pull back. Now. Not a week from now."

"There's not a Goddamn thing wrong with our business, our strategy, or this site. You're scared. And not thinking straight. Either of you."

Vin and Darius exchange a look, which Carson catches but ignores.

"I'll talk to Bruno and Jorge," Darius says.

"What are you gonna say?" Carson challenges.

"What do you *think* he's gonna say?" Vin says.

Carson kicks a cloud of gravelly dust in his friends' direction. "Don't you fucking fire them."

"I'm gonna do what's best for this company. For *all* of us." Darius uses the slow, measured voice he always uses when trying to talk Carson off a ledge—even literally, like the summer after senior year when Carson was obsessed with diving off the 60-foot ledge at the quarry known as Last Leap. Carson strains the leash, Vin and Darius pull it back.

But Carson never stops tugging.

"You cut them loose and you're waving a white flag to our competitors," Carson says. "Those idiots—Touchstone, as well as Ross, and those assholes at Whitney-Blanchard. Do you want them to think we're going down? Because that's what you're doing. And they'll poach our guys in a heartbeat. That what you want?" Vin and Darius let him play it out. "Austerity is one thing. But giving up? On us? No. No fucking way."

The three men, glued at the hip for nearly 30 years, stand and glower at one another. A lifetime of jokes, pranks, triumphs, scrapes, near-misses, insults, and trivial misunderstandings pass among them like jagged bolts of lightning. Add this one to the list.

This would have gone better at the Haven, Carson thinks.

"Cap, go see Tipper. That's the deal," Vin says, quietly.

Carson turns his back to his partners and heads toward his truck, pausing to survey Willing Enclave: a brand new neighborhood, top quality all the way, filled with prosperous homeowners and their scampering children. *I'll make them see what I see.*

Carson heads south on Route 12 toward Tipper & Sons' unassuming corporate office. He's eaten nothing today, just a few swallows of coffee, but his gut churns with anger and he has no interest in stopping for lunch. *Send a man to do a man's job.* Tipper's is in a nondescript office park filled with identical, one-story buildings that hide all kinds of semi-obscure companies—from portrait photographers to custom glass cutters. Several of the units bear "For Lease" signs on the front door. *Another fucking ghost town. Maybe Sandy Tipper is on the skids, too. Which works to our advantage.* Inside the small, beige reception area, Carson and Sandy Tipper shake hands as if they're old friends, which they are not. Sandy already knows why Carson King is here; it's no secret that Willing Prime Contractors is struggling. They sit in Sandy's dark, cluttered office, which is decorated only by stacks and stacks of price sheets, supply catalogues, and back issues of *Contractor Magazine*, *Construction Today*, and other obscure trade periodicals. A framed document, declaring Tipper & Sons a member in good standing of the Gypsum Association, hangs crookedly on the wall. Next to that is a grayish yellowing photo of Sandy Tipper, about 16, standing on a construction site with his dad, Sandy Sr. An ancient Apple computer sits on a corner of the desk, the keyboard buried under paper. Carson figures Sandy Tipper wouldn't recognize a *blog* or a *friend request* if it jumped up and bit him.

"Look, Carson, things are tough all around," Sandy says. "You guys have had an amazing run."

"An amazing run? Jesus, Sandy, I don't think you know who you're talking to. We're still going gangbusters."

"Yeah. Okay. So..."

"So," Carson says, nonchalantly, "this is pretty routine. My partners and I just want to review margins with you. We've done a lot of business together, as you know. We only want what every good customer wants: the best price. That's it. Really. No ulterior motives. No dark night of the soul." Carson waits, every muscle in check.

"Let me explain something to you," Sandy Tipper says. Carson grimaces. "Our health premiums went up 39 percent last year. They're going up another 15 percent this year. I'm sure you understand, we can't absorb all that, so we have to pass some of those costs on to our customers." Carson has little sympathy for this line of defense. Willing Prime Contractors doesn't cover health insurance for any of its work crew, only the three partners, which has helped their bottom line. And because Carson and his partners are equally capable of serving as supervisors and foremen on every job they take, they keep even more profit in-house.

"And?"

"And nothing," Sandy says. "In my father's time, this was a much simpler business. A lot more straightforward. And it was a lot easier to cut deals with our customers when times were rough. But let's not forget—"

"Sandy, let's cut the bullshit. I know that we're paying at least a point higher than Touchstone for your wallboard. We're not asking for favors, just parity. So what's the problem? Why are you feeding me this bullshit about health insurance?"

"You're not the only one with bills to pay," Sandy says, with an edge. "If you'd ever bothered to join the chamber—"

"A bullshit group that sits around bullshitting."

"—you'd know that small businesses in Willing, like yours, like mine—"

"—Speak for yourself—"

"—Anyway," Sandy continues, "we're getting it from all sides. Health insurance is driving everything up—rent, materials, heck, even the lease on our office copier is higher than it's ever been. And don't get me started on the fucking tariffs."

Carson stands up. "You gonna charge us the same as Touchstone, or not, Sandy?" Carson's boot nudges a stack of magazines piled near his chair. The pile tumbles sideways. Sandy steps around from behind his desk.

"I'm going to run my business best way I know how," Sandy says evenly. "I'll take it under advisement."

"'Under advisement.' That's a shitty answer."

"Well, I won't stand here and tell you I'm gonna cut your prices. I won't do it, Carson."

"What kind of deal did you cut with them? With Touchstone, huh? Because this doesn't seem on the up-and-up, to me, no matter how you look at it."

"Fact is, Carson, Touchstone's order sheet with us is damn near double yours."

"That's impossible. I think you're just looking for an easy way out."

Sandy takes a breath. "Are you calling me a liar?" Silence. "We're done here." He yanks open the door.

"You'll regret this." Carson slips out into the spring afternoon sunshine.

You just fucking lost, buddy.

Carson King is not a day drinker. His affection for the Haven is built on all the good times he's had there over the years. Carefree times. But today, he makes a rare exception. He does his best thinking at the Haven. As he eases down Main Street, he expects to cruise for several minutes before finding an open angled parking spot. But it seems most of the spots are empty. And something Sandy Tipper said pings him: small businesses in Willing are struggling. *He's grandstanding to make a point.* Still, Carson begins taking inventory, and realizes, for the first time in a long time, maybe ever, that every block on Main Street has at least two vacant storefronts, three on some blocks, or even four. The Ben Franklin is long gone, but so is the children's clothing store that took its place. The Sudsy is still going strong. *Maybe I should've invested in laundromats.* But the Willing Diner, Cutie-pie Hair, and the Raven Bar & Grill are all gone, creating an uneven patchwork of darkened storefronts and padlocked entrances, interspersed with businesses where the lights are still on, where proprietors sit waiting for customers, waiting for their cash registers to ring up sales, waiting for their impossibly thin margins to fatten up, even just a bit. When did Willing begin to resemble an Edward Hopper painting? And why? *Peddling that horseshit about health care. Sandy Tipper has his head up his ass. Something else must be going on.*

Carson parks directly in front of the Haven. By two o'clock, he's on his favorite bar stool, nursing a Dogfish Head brew, thinking about the town of Willing and the fortune he still plans to make off it. He looks around the bar and counts six losers, all guys who never had the guts or the hustle to make a go of it—a go of anything. He recognizes half of them from high school, but they're strictly on nodding terms. Carson lives on hustle. What else is there? At four, he remembers in the nick of time that he's got to head over to Willing High, his own alma mater, to pick up Jeannie, who will almost certainly talk his ear off about some political bullshit he has no time for. But she's passionate and that's a good thing. You don't get anywhere without a fire in your belly.

Chapter Three

Bruno Fernandez and Jorge Garcia are both originally from Sinaloa, Mexico, but they've been working their asses off in construction in the U.S. for 20 years. They met on a job site a few towns over from Willing, and then, almost in tandem, they met their mates, married, and started families. They are best friends, as close as brothers, and always tell one another when a crew foreman is hiring, and then try to convince the foreman to hire their friend as well. For several years now, the work in and around Willing has been steady, though the gaps have been growing more frequent, and longer in duration. When Vin reached out to the men for the Willing Enclave project, they jumped at it. The Willing Prime partners have treated them fairly well over the years, all things considered, so this was a welcome opportunity to make up for some rather lean months.

Darius pulls Bruno and Jorge aside, as promised, right about the time Carson is sliding off his bar stool at the Haven to go pick up Jeannie. The three men stand around awkwardly for several seconds, pulling on cigarettes, which they stomp out in the dirt. Darius forces himself to hide deep-seated irritation. Cap's ego is out of control and Vin is too fucking passive. Somebody has to step up and be the grown-up here. And it fucking stinks. Bruno and Jorge are the most reliable workers they've ever hired, showing up on time, never complaining. But the three of them are running a business, not a charity. And he's got family to think of. Bruno and Jorge will land on their feet; guys like them are always in demand. Hell, they can find work anywhere, any time. It's not like they'd been promised lifetime employment.

"Hey," Darius begins. The men nod, bill caps shading their eyes.

"We still got daylight," Bruno says. "We keep working."

"Yeah." Darius says, squinting into the afternoon sun as if to show he's in complete agreement. "Here's the thing, though."

Darius stammers out the bad news, using words like *temporary* and *over the hump*, but in fact he won't remember later exactly what he said. Still, by the time he finished saying it, he's about ready to quit the construction business for good. It wasn't supposed to be like this. It *wasn't* like this. Until now.

Bruno and Jorge frown, look at the ground, and take the bad news in silence. When Darius is done, the two men walk away, heads down, speaking anger-inflected Spanish, which they know Darius does not understand.

"This project is going to shit, anyway," Jorge says. "I don't think they have the money."

"How do you know?" Bruno asks.

"Look how they act. They argue all the time. They used to joke around on the site. Now they fight—about money, I'm guessing."

"You got any saved up?"

"A little. But I need new tires for my truck. You?"

"I'm broke. Whatever comes in, goes out."

"Vivir el momento y morir."

"Sí."

By the time Sylvia pulls up to the curb in front of the Walters "estate"—the sellers' term, not Sylvia's—she has the first stabs of another migraine. If she could just figure out what brings these on with increasing frequency, she would do something about it. Maybe. There doesn't seem to be time in the day to squeeze in a visit to the doctor's, and if this is menopause, or peri-menopause, then fuck it. She'll suck it up. Nothing gets in the way of holding onto her position as the second-highest closer in Greater Willing—the "Greater" territory encompassing Carson's latest enterprise, the shock-and-awe-inspiring perfection of Willing Enclave. Grabbing the top closer spot for the year is so tantalizingly close, she can taste it. Sylvia pops four Advil and heads up the long walkway. The brokers are due in less than half an hour. *Big girls don't cry.*

The Walters property, in Sylvia's private opinion, is a misbegotten McMansion composed of nearly 10,000 square feet of architectural schizophrenia and disastrous lighting choices in every room. The three modest bungalows that stood on this property for nearly a century were probably easier to live in than this monstrosity. Be that as it may, she fought hard for the listing, beating out not only several "friends" in her agency but also rival agents from two other franchises. These days, real estate listings are to Willing-area realtors what a dead gazelle is to a pack of hyenas: the feeding frenzy is ferocious. There are, after all, only so many commissions to go around. And while none of the area agents would admit it, making a decent full-time income off commissions, under current market conditions, is far from easy. Sylvia calculates she does better than most, grinding it out to reach the high-five-figure territory—year before last, anyway. The recent downturn in her numbers is just a blip on an upward curve. Contrary to popular wisdom, past performance often *is* an indicator of future performance. That's not just Sylvia's opinion; Carson wholeheartedly agrees.

And anyway, Sylvia knows the numbers don't tell the whole story. She's confident in her own brand of grit and imagination. For instance, she knew which tack to take within 30 seconds of meeting Selig and Seema Walters for the first time. The Walters, in their seventies, had built the place only 10 years earlier, but now, with their hopes for grandchildren unrealized, and their children flung to the far corners of the earth, they had to admit the house was just too much for the two of them, despite the housekeeper, the gardener, and an in-home chef. Sylvia suspected her rival agents would spin castles in the air for this couple—lay out plans for fancy open houses and upscale sales brochures and professional video splashed on a website. But Sylvia sensed the Walters wanted none of this. They wanted the house sold as quickly and quietly as possible. At a premium, of course.

"I'm guessing you'd like to move on, with a minimum of fuss, am

I right?" Sylvia perched on a turquoise settee, waiting for the right moment to close the deal.

"Thank you for understanding," said Selig Walters, as Seema nodded.

"I propose a handful of discrete open houses, for top brokers only. No cocktail parties, no fancy websites and so forth. I'll bring just one photographer through, and that's it. How does that sound?"

The Walters smiled. "Perfect," said Selig.

"Do you think you can sell it in 30 days?" asked Seema. "We're booked on a cruise, you see, and it would be nice not to worry."

"Well, I'm not sure I can guarantee that. I hope you appreciate I'm being perfectly honest with you." The Walters slumped with disappointment. "But I tell you what: Let's draw up an agreement for a 30-day contract, and I promise you, I will do everything I possibly can to get this done for you."

Sylvia called Carson from the car, moments later. "Bora-Bora or Oahu?" she asked.

"You bagged the Walters!"

"I did indeed, Cap. That's about forty-K coming our way."

The two of them felt the same warm rush: expectations met, hopes realized, money in the bank. This is the plan, *their* plan, and they both know how to execute. After a win like this one—which surely was a win, they didn't begin to question it—they didn't only discuss big vacation plans, but also whether they should form a new LLC together. Buying and flipping houses, maybe. They spent that night spinning each other up about the possibilities, the likely profit-taking, the manageable risks. They ended that evening having energetic sex on the living room couch while the kids did whatever in their bedrooms above.

But now, on this headachy April morning, Sylvia winces. *Such a stupid rookie mistake. You greedy cow.* This is Day 24 of the 30-day contract, and so far, Sylvia hasn't even had a nibble. The price is only part of the problem. At $3.2 million, the Walters property is far and away the most expensive house on the market in Greater Willing. But Sylvia distinctly remembers a time, not long ago, when a small cadre of elite buyers always swarmed around listings like this one. And Sylvia had pocket listings to spare for this A-list crowd. She figures she's on speed-dial for probably a billion-dollars' worth of past, present, and future clients. So where are these buyers now? Where did they go? And then a very unpleasant thought rises like bile in her throat: *What if I got this listing because the others didn't want it? Because they knew this was a white elephant that would never sell? Because they saw something I missed?*

Sylvia unlocks the agency's padlock on the hulking front doors of the Walters' white elephant and walks into the chilly front hall. She heads to the kitchen and scoops water from the faucet with her hand. She holds a cold, wet hand to her throbbing forehead. The doorbell rings. The brokers are arriving. Sylvia can barely look them in the eye, as she's convinced they are laughing at her even as they trip over themselves to offer air kisses. *The eager beaver who should know better.* The brokers fan out around the house, taking self-guided tours, spec sheets in hand. For several, this is their second time through. *To witness my humiliation?*

"I'm surprised you haven't already dropped the price," says Angela, a broker from across town. "Why is that?"

"The sellers want full-ask. They're adamant," Sylvia replies.

Angela smiles. "Well, you have your work cut out for you, don't you?"

And in that instant, Sylvia knows, she knows as surely as she knows her own children's names, that she is not going to sell this house in time. Or ever. Nobody wants it at $3 million. Nobody wants it at $1 million. Nobody wants it, period. It's going to stand empty, a monument to the Walters' disintegrating family ties and to Sylvia's blind allegiance to the almighty dollar. She dashes discreetly into the nearest powder room and vomits.

From that moment on, the brokers' open is merely an endurance contest. Sylvia stands in the huge, marbled kitchen, a smile pasted on her face. She answers questions mechanically, stealing frequent glances at the clock on her phone. Her phone, which hasn't buzzed in over an hour, fuels the fire raging in her head and her gut. Nothing terrifies a realtor more than a silent phone. Finally, the ordeal is over. Sylvia wipes the counters, locks up, and rushes down the walkway to her car. She knows she's going to have to face the Walters, who will call her from their next port of call. Lisbon. Dubrovnik. Who knows. Who cares. And she has to tell Carson something. Prep him. They're already counting on that hefty commission—some toward the twins' college fund, some toward a vacation for just the two of them, and whatever other hole seems to need or want plugging. So much for flipping houses: a dream deferred, hopefully only temporarily. But right now, a large hazelnut iced coffee at Cyn's Café, her favorite Willing way station, just off Main Street on Berkley, is all Sylvia can think about.

She heads into downtown, distracted, driving on sheer muscle memory because nothing looks the way it should. Sylvia has this weird feeling, as if some unseen power, or force, has lifted everything familiar up from its roots and foundations, and then settled it back down again—but not quite as it was before. She knows these roads in her sleep, yet there is something unsettlingly unfamiliar. Even the green and white Main St. sign looks different; darker, dingier, and vaguely tilted on its post. Because of the Walters fiasco, Sylvia is gripping the steering wheel tightly, as if the car itself might make an unexpected turn beyond her control, just as the Walters put her unexpectedly into the "loss" column. Not a place she wants to be, ever.

Finally, Sylvia turns onto Berkley. Her nerves are jangling, because here, too, something isn't right. Sylvia pulls into an angled parking space directly in front of Cyn's, which is wedged between a tiny dry cleaner's and an old head shop that's now a dingy used bookstore. The plate-glass storefront window says "Cyn's Café" in gold letters; the window is nicely set off by white woodwork. But the window itself is covered from the inside with taped-up brown butcher's paper. Sylvia tries the front door of the café. It's locked. *She's on vacation,* Sylvia thinks. *But I would have known that. And why would she cover up the window? To discourage burglars while she's away? Ah! Renovations! Cynthia always said she'd spruce the place up as soon as she saved up enough to do it right.* Sylvia peers into the window through a gap in the butcher paper. It's dark inside but she can just make out the familiar, long wooden counter and bar stools, neatly tucked under the counter's lip. The bones of this old pharmacy—when pharmacies doubled as lunch counters—are still apparent. The floor appears to be swept clean. *I can't wait to see what she does with the place.* Sylvia sighs, and heads, begrudgingly, to the nearest Dunkin' Donuts, five miles away. She nearly runs a red light because she's distracted by something she's never noticed before—or is it new? There are weeds poking up through the asphalt in the middle of Main Street in downtown Willing. Weeds! As if a median were growing there spontaneously, but there's never been a median on Main Street. She slows to a crawl, staring at the tufts of yellowish-greenish plant life that seems to have sprouted every couple of yards. And then she notices something else: irregular chunks of sand-colored stone, as well as fist-sized pieces of bricks striped with ivory mortar, seem to have dropped randomly onto the sidewalk. Some chunks have tumbled into the street, just off the curb. *But where…?* Sylvia looks up. The century-plus old buildings with their fussy turrets and crenellations suddenly look their age, like old men who seem to slip overnight from spry to ailing, as their bodies finally betray them on the slide toward death. *Migraines always disorient me.* Nonetheless, she pumps the gas and pulls away from Willing, as quickly as she can.

At 11:30 pm, Sylvia gratefully crawls into bed. Her head feels better but every bone in her body aches for the release that sleep should bring. Whether it does or not remains to be seen. She considers taking half a sleeping pill, but decides against it. Just knowing she *can,* if she really *needs* to, is relaxing in its own way. Carson sits up in bed next to her, cruising his laptop. The two have not had time for a real conversation all day. Both were silently grateful that the twins were fairly talkative (well, argumentative) at dinner, which consisted of leftover roast chicken and rice, followed by a cold-cereal chaser (the twins), another pour of white wine (Sylvia), and bourbon (Carson). Jeannie said she'd run around school all day collecting signatures to force the principal to create a safe space, or at least a safe *room*, where students could hang out if they felt threatened.

"Threatened by what?" asks Zeke. "That's bullshit."

"Zeke," Carson warns.

"What?" he replies. "It *is.* We go to school with a bunch of mainly white kids who cry when they crack their iPhones. Gimme a break."

"You don't get it, Zeke," Jeannie says. "You're incapable of putting yourself in somebody else's shoes. It's like you were born without the empathy gene."

"Oh, and you're Taylor Swift."

"Like, I know three sophomore girls who were almost raped this year."

"What do you mean, *almost?* You're either raped or you aren't. So, like, maybe these girls need *half* a room to hide out in?" Zeke laughs. Jeannie punches him on the shoulder and gets up to pour cereal.

"Fuck you, Zeke."

"Jeannie!" the parents chorus.

Sylvia and Carson gave up on the mythical notion a long time ago that twins, even fraternal twins, have a special understanding, an inseparable bond. Not *their* twins. The two have been at odds, one way or another, since they were toddlers. Sylvia has wondered, guiltily, from time to time, if she's done something wrong. If she missed out on a crucial lesson somewhere along the line. But she can't see how she'd raise them any differently. Besides, they're healthy, they're safe, and that's a strong foundation right there. Carson isn't especially bothered by the twins' mutual antagonism, as long as they don't actually inflict physical or lasting emotional harm on each other. Real life is all about conflict, so they may as well get in all the practice they can, he figures.

Sylvia, in bed, curls up and closes her eyes, desperate to quiet her mind, which is forcing her to walk through the Walters' house over and over, and to hear Angela saying over and over that she's got her work cut out for her, trying to sell that house.

"Did you know Cynthia was renovating the café? She didn't tell me."

"Uh-uh," Carson responds, eyes on his laptop. "Somebody reminded me today that if I joined the chamber of commerce, I'd know more about what's going on in this town."

"Waste of time."

"That's what I told him. They should all be coming to *me,* if they really wanna know what's going on around here."

"Anyway, Cyn's is closed. The window is, you know, papered over.

Don't you think she should've put up a sign letting people know? She could at least drum up some excitement about the makeover. It wouldn't kill her to increase foot traffic."

Carson looks up from his computer, frowning. He remembers all the empty storefronts dotting downtown Willing. If Main Street is hurting, it makes sense that a side street like Berkley might be hurting even more.

"Are you sure she's closed just for renovation?"

"I can't think why else. She wouldn't cover the window just to go on vacation. Besides, she would've told me all about it. She's not shy about sharing her plans."

"Huh."

"What?"

"I don't know. Nothing. How was the broker's open at the Walters' pile?"

"Good turnout."

"And?"

"And nothing. You know how this goes. Tomorrow, I follow up with everybody, figure out who's got a buyer to bring back. The usual." As she tells her husband this, she tries convincing herself this is what she will actually do. That the feeling of sick, bitter defeat that overtook her this afternoon was just a passing cloud, a spring shower bringing May flowers.

"But you're running out of time, aren't you?" Carson asks.

Sylvia sits bolt upright in bed. "No shit, Sherlock. I don't need you to remind me that the clock is ticking. I'm well aware of what the contract says and I'm handling it, ok?!"

"Hey," Carson says, leaning over to kiss her. "I'm not that old turd Selig Walter, am I?"

"And how's everything out at Willing Enclave," Sylvia asks, turning the tables because she can't help it. "You guys figuring a way to get out of the red any time soon? You know damn well we can't afford to take a loss like that, right now."

Carson slams his laptop shut and turns out the light.

"We know what we're doing, Syl," he says, testily. "Everything is under control."

That night, Sylvia has a nightmare that wakes her, gasping. She dreams she is walking down Main Street, heading toward Cyn's around the corner. Suddenly, the buildings on both sides begin to shake, and rumble, and tip, as if an earthquake has struck. Chunks of stone and brick and mortar come crashing down upon her.

Chapter Four

The next day, Jeannie's best friend Gina Martinez yanks her into one of the three girls' bathrooms out of commission at Remington High (bad plumbing plus not enough hand soap or toilet paper to go around thanks to radical budget cuts) for an urgent convo right as second period is about to start. Jeannie would actually rather not miss Biology, but then Gina begins sobbing and shaking and Jeannie hates herself for putting her own desires ahead of her friend's. The snake coiled inside her skull hisses at her: *Listen up, bitch!*

Gina grabs Jeannie's hand. "It's my dad."

"Is he sick?" Jeannie's eyes grow wide. She sees herself carrying casseroles and baked goods to an ailing Mr. Martinez, who always treats her with a kind word and a Spanish endearment.

"No. I don't think so. I don't know!" Tears roll down Gina's face. "He's…"

"What, Gina? Tell me."

"He's punching holes in the wall. In the kitchen. Last night, he almost broke his hand and my abuela—"

"I don't understand—"

Gina's tears stream down her cheeks in black mascara'd pathways. Gina has only recently begun wearing any makeup, on the grounds that being a feminist doesn't preclude styling yourself anyway you want to. Jeannie is still bare-faced, and prefers to remain so. But as a kindred feminist, she supports Gina's choice.

"That's super-intense," Jeannie says, giving Gina a chance to catch her breath. "If my dad started punching walls, I'd totally freak out. You actually saw him do this?"

"I just told you." Gina sniffs.

"Yeah, I know, but, like, I'm trying to picture it." Gina pulls her phone out of her pocket and shows Jeannie a collage of photos—spidery dents in a white wall, where Mr. Martinez's knuckles must've hit it really hard. Jeannie knows Gina's house as well as her own, so it's obviously the wall in the kitchen near the back door.

"That's serious shit," Jeannie says, her inner snake hissing at her not to be so *lame.* "Why is he so upset?" Gina shrugs and shakes her head. "If *my* dad…well, he probably wouldn't punch the walls. He'd just burn the whole house down."

Gina snort-laughs in spite of herself. "Yeah. Probably."

"And then start rebuilding from the ground up the next day."

Gina smiles wanly. "My abuela made him stick his hand in a bowl of ice water for like an hour. And it was weird, 'cause she didn't say anything the whole time. She just watches him pound the wall, then she gets the bowl and put it on the kitchen table. I just stand there, like I'm watching a movie. A movie that gets scarier each time."

"And you don't know—"

"We're not like that, Jeannie. You know. We don't talk about…a father doesn't tell his daughter stuff."

"What can I do?"

"Nothing." Gina smiles again. "You're already doing it."

Jeannie and Gina are known at Willing High School as "the Jeans" or sometimes "the Genes," depending on who's calling them this and whether it's just said casually, as in "Hey, Jeans," when they're passing by, or posted online, as in "The Genes marching for trans rights." Jeannie and Gina are fine with this. The nicknames confer just the right amount of status—not too cool for school, not too mean, not too dorky. As a first-generation Mexican-American, Gina posts a lot on Instagram calling out ICE raids and clamoring for protections for undocumented immigrants. Jeannie—whose own ancestry has always seemed rather murky, as she thinks maybe the Kings used to be Jewish but aren't anymore—totally admires and secretly envies Gina's legit claim to a legit cause. She wants one to call her own. She's always on the look-out for her authentic cause—the one that really counts. The snake always lets her know when she's faking it, which seems like almost all the time.

Jeannie squeezes Gina's hand and helps her up. Her sympathy, at least, is real. And so is her relief that she can still make most of second period. And if Mr. Kennedy calls her out for being late, she can honestly say that her best friend was in crisis and needed her full and undivided attention.

On her way to class, Jeannie tries to imagine things going haywire at home—enough to make somebody want to punch a wall. She can't think what that might be, or what it would look like. Surely her father would *not* burn down the house. A dire situation would probably have to involve Zeke. Her parents were too busy working to get into trouble. But if something *did* happen, would Jeannie tell Gina right away? Or even first? And Jeannie hears a quick *'No'* inside her head—followed by a realization: *I'll keep my own counsel. I'm here to give compassion, not receive it. It's neater that way.* The snake settles down.

At lunch, Jeannie sees Zeke on the far side of the cafeteria, and she knows he sees her too. Despite being at loggerheads most of the time, there is a weird kind of twin radar that operates continuously on its own low frequency, no matter what. As neither twin has ever known anything else, they don't pay it much attention. But they know it's there, like the faint "zzz" of a high-tension wire that's always just out of sight.

Zeke and his friends crowd around Zeke's phone, laughing. Due to budget cuts, there are no cafeteria monitors present, so the room is a free-for-all. The whole school has lately taken on a *Lord of the Flies* vibe. Zeke and his friends watch a *Common Side Effects* clip they've all seen a gazillion times before, though it seems to get funnier with each viewing. Like Jeannie, Zeke finds the sophomore-year academics pretty manageable. He gets B's across the board without trying very hard, and then once in a while, he pushes himself a little to land an A—but only when he wants to. The last time he wanted to was on the History midterm. The unit was on voting rights, with special attention paid to the suffragist movements in the late 19th and early 20th centuries in the

U.S. and England. The assignment was to write a paper arguing either *for* or *against* voting rights for women, and of course, students had to back up their arguments with historical sources *beyond* those found through Chat GPT. Zeke, being a natural-born contrarian, argued *against.* And he goaded Jeannie, at home, with his research.

"A woman's proper sphere is in the home," Zeke said in a high-pitched voice with a hammy English accent. "Else she ought to be made to bear arms alongside men, and that is unthinkable!"

"Yeah, but you're on the losing side, Loser," Jeannie retorted.

"Yeah, but those women were hypocrites, right? They were never gonna learn to fight, and crawl in the mud, and shoot Germans or whatever, were they? So why should they get to pick and choose to do only what they *wanted* to do, like vote?" Jeannie stuck out her tongue at her brother and returned to her own room. She knew it wasn't her finest moment, but it was excellent preparation for becoming a *compassionate person.*

Zeke actually took the assignment seriously and turned in a neatly typed, typo-free, eight-page paper—the longest he'd ever written up to that point. He got an A+ and the teacher, Mrs. Sandborne, read the whole thing aloud to the class, which, if Zeke had known she was going to do that, he would've gone for a C. It's one thing to work hard to prove a point; it's another thing to be held publicly accountable for it. He never asked for that. Zeke was pretty sure that after the reading of the paper, the girls who usually came by his locker between periods, the girls who stopped by his table at lunch to talk, began avoiding him. Not in a super-noticeable way, but enough to make a point. *Well, fuck these girls if they can't take a joke.*

But this unexpected turn of events had unintended consequences. It cleared the field for Farrah, who *did* stop by Zeke's locker to chat, and who hangs around the field now on days when her soccer practice ends before his. Farrah was named after a sexy, voluptuous superstar in the 1980s, who was most famous for her wild mane of blonde hair. Farrah spends every waking moment putting the lie to this legacy and cursing her parents for their weird sense of ironic fun. She is stick thin, wears her dark hair almost skinhead-short, and dresses in over-sized flannel shirts, baggy jeans, and cowboy boots. Zeke digs her—or at least, he finds out he does once she's the only girl in school who still seems willing to speak to him. And this leads him to another discovery: Zeke is attracted to girls who aren't girly-girly, but who look more like boys, or at least, could be mistaken for boys at a distance.

Chapter Five

Ten days after Darius gives Bruno and Jorge their walking papers, the three partners of Willing Prime Contractors, wearing business suits (work clothes thrown into the back seats of their trucks), are seated together at a walnut conference table in the office of Thomas Jergens, the chief lending officer of the Second National Bank, which is still a going concern on Main Street in downtown Willing. Second National is part of a rapidly vanishing breed—a locally owned institution that strives to build and maintain personal relationships with its commercial borrowers. The bank is out to make money like any other, but Jergens likes to boast that they do it with a "friendlier face" than the average banking conglomerate.

To say that Carson, Vin, and Darius would rather be anywhere but here is an understatement. All three had received an e-mail from Jergens with a personalized greeting ("Dear Carson…"), which they all saw through immediately. When Tom Jergens requests a meeting, it's not to hand out gold stars. The e-mail prompted a late-night strategy session by phone, after their respective households had quieted down for the night.

"He's going to cut us off," Vin says, speaking softly but intensely into his cell phone. "It's obvious."

"The question is, how drastic is the cut," adds Darius. "And how do we keep the work going?"

"I think it's pointless to speculate 'til we get there," Carson says. "You can spin all the doomsday scenarios you want, but there's no point in assuming the worst until we know more."

"We should go in with a game plan," Vin says. "So we're not caught off-guard."

"Agreed," Darius says.

"You just wanna hand him our heads on a platter, is that it?" asks Carson. Vin and Darius come at Carson together, yet again, telling him to get his elbow out of his ass and get real. "Have you totally forgotten what we signed up for?" Carson responds. "You know the construction business involves risk. And you know—or you should have known all along—that we'd have good times and bad times. Just because we're going through a rough patch—"

"This is more than a rough patch, Cap," Vin says. "We might be forced to borrow on disastrous terms, if—"

"If we're gonna keep the lights on," adds Darius.

"I told you that firing Bruno and Jorge wouldn't make a difference. It was penny-wise and pound-foolish, and now look where we are," Carson says, trying to keep his voice in check. "I don't want to game this out. Let's just get in there tomorrow and see what he says. We don't have to give him any answers on the spot."

Vin and Darius know there's no point in trying to convince the stubborn son-of-a-bitch otherwise, at least until they know where they really stand.

So now, as Jergens goes through the ritual of distributing bank-logo coasters and water glasses so that each man can slake his thirst from the water-beaded silver pitcher at the center of the table, they're about to find out where they really stand.

"Gentlemen," says Jergens, in his hearty banker's baritone. "How are things going?"

"Well, Tom, we figured you called us in here to tell *us,*" Darius says, seeking to lighten things up and send a signal that they're not overly concerned. Jergens laughs appreciatively.

"Let's start with what you already know." Jergens scans his laptop screen. "You're maxed out on your line of credit and six months behind on interest for the sum total of the loan. Does that square with your assessment?"

Vin clears his throat. "Yes. We're all fully apprised of the situation." Vin always was a brown-noser, Carson thinks, but once in a while, you need a brown-noser on your side. "We'd like to discuss our options."

"We assume we *have* options," Darius says, with a mild chuckle. Carson always lets Vin and Darius forge ahead in tricky situations, because he knows, from experience, that he'll take sweep on the back end of whatever's going on, and tidy things up in a way that puts him on top. Like that time shortly after they all moved back to Willing, right after college, eager to hatch a business they could all start together, be their own bosses, call the shots. They'd been drinking steadily all night, and Vin, usually the tame one, decided they should drive over to the Collinses, in Willing Heights, and take a dip in their pool. Vin seemed to know that the Collins family was away, traipsing through Europe, or something. Carson was on board immediately, and Darius could see he'd have to go along. So off they went, cannonballing into the Collins' big in-ground pool at their big German Drive estate. Vin jumped onto a fancy blown-up lounger floating in the pool; it sprang a leak and deflated into a vinyl heap. Darius broke a pool-side flowerpot; dark soil spilled out onto the tiled pool deck. They all laughed hysterically, and left abruptly. But it was Carson who called the family a week later to explain what had happened—and talked himself into a summer job doing pool maintenance and general handiwork, both to pay off the debt incurred by their damage and to make some extra money, which he desperately needed.

Carson's take-away from this escapade was that taking a risk isn't all that scary—and it usually pays off, one way or another, in the end, if you just keep both your cool and your wits about you. It also dawns on him now, here, in Jergens' buttoned-down office, that the Collins' spread on German Drive—the pool, the big house, the manicured lawn—is probably why he and the guys got so excited about building houses. Back then, it seemed entirely probable they'd all own houses like the Collinses one day—they'd work things out so that they not only built these babies, but lived in them, too.

"Yes, there are always options," Jergens says. "But you need to consider risk against reward." *Here it comes,* Carson thinks, *the stodgy banker talk. Buzz killer. Kill joy.* "We might begin, for instance, by requiring the business to secure the line of credit, which, as you know, has been unsecured up to this point."

"What might that look like?" asks Vin, almost wishing that Jergens wouldn't answer.

"Well, the most obvious mechanism is to place a lien on your houses—your personal property, I mean. As collateral."

And there it is: bombshell dropped, landed, exploded.

Nonstarter, Carson thinks. *What else you got?*

"That, uh," Darius says, after a brief lull, "that seems like a last resort, rather than a first resort."

"I think all options are on the table, at this point," says Jergens, with a very straight face. "We might consider a term loan—lump sum up front, repaid over time. Though of course, you'd have to make good on the outstanding credit line loan, as well. And we'd freeze all further borrowing for the foreseeable future."

"A term loan," Vin says, looking at Darius and Carson for a sign.

"I want to be very clear," says Jergens, "a term loan, in your situation, carries an interest rate that's well above prime."

"How far above prime?" Darius asks.

"We're probably talking..." Jergens clicks through a few screens. "North of 20 percent, for sure. Maybe considerably higher."

"Well, Tom," Carson says, as all eyes turn to him. "We appreciate your time and your candor. I think my partners and I need some time to discuss all this." Carson shoots them a look.

"Of course," says Jergens. "It's a lot to consider. Just be sure and let me hear from you in 48 hours—less, if possible—so we can keep everything on track." *Whatever that means. Is there a veiled threat in there?*

The men shake hands, murmur good-byes. Jergens feels it's incumbent on him to have the last word. "Look, if it's any consolation, you're not the only small business in this position. This economy—it's, well, forcing a lot of shake-outs." *What the fuck does that mean?* "What doesn't kill you, makes you stronger, eh?"

Carson realizes there wasn't much opportunity for a sweep maneuver today, but there is still tomorrow. *Tomorrow, everything is possible.*

Out on the sidewalk, the three partners look at one another, sucking teeth, taking advantage of the telepathy that aids very long friendships. Then, without a word, they head to their trucks, each heading in a different direction because they all know they're not yet ready to face whatever comes next.

Chapter Six

Jeannie is astonished when she sees her mother's car pull up front as school lets out, on a rare day when Jeannie does not have lacrosse practice. This is a first—and not in a good way. Usually, she bums a ride home from a friend, or rides her bike, or her dad picks her up. But Mother? She's always showing houses, or meeting with prospective sellers, at this time of day. As Jeannie well knows, her mother literally equates time with money and gets antsy if she's not doing something that leads to a commission check. Picking up Jeannie at school certainly isn't part of that equation.

Something's up.

Sylvia rolls down the passenger side window. "Get in."

"Why?" Jeannie asks. "What's wrong?" Maybe Dad has started punching walls, after all. Or Zeke did a bone-headed thing and landed himself in jail and they're going to bail him out.

"Just get in. Please. Nothing's wrong."

Nothing's wrong.

Sylvia knows Carson and his partners are at the bank today. She told him she was confident that, given Willing Prime Contractors' many quarters of financial success, the bank would be more than willing to play ball, as they weather a bit of a downturn. Carson agreed. Their mutual aid society was back up and running after their recent tiff. But Sylvia had no way of knowing, this morning, that she'd be walking on coals herself before lunch. With just two days left on the Walters contract, Sylvia had exhausted every avenue for selling the place, and she's drawn a complete blank—just as she feared. Today, she had to let Betty and Barnaby Bachman, who own the powerhouse real estate agency she works for (and who lived in tony Linton Crossing, several price points above Willing Heights), know where things stand. She'd been counseling herself on how best to handle this since 4:30 a.m., when she lay awake reviewing strategies. Despite her status as a senior broker and a stellar track record, in real estate, you're really only as good as your last quarter. And Sylvia's last quarter, due in part to the deal with the Walters heading south, has not been good. *Be honest and straightforward... Be matter-of-fact... Stick to facts, keep emotion out of it... Be confident; this is a rare miscalculation...Or tell them anything can happen in two days. No. Don't do that.*

But the come-to-Jesus meeting with the Bachmans that morning would have to wait, it turned out, as the Bachmans called an unexpected staff meeting with all the brokers, agents, and associate agents, shortly after the staff had checked in for the morning before heading out to appointments. Barnaby played good cop, as usual, thanking everyone for working hard, prospecting hard, and selling hard. He led the team in a round of self-congratulatory clapping. A born salesman. This act paved the way for Betty to play bad cop. The Bachmans were the kind of power couple who had their public act down. They were a perfect *yin* and *yang.* Barnaby never seemed out-of-sorts, always had a kind word, and never failed to ask after an agent's children or grandchildren. Betty occupied the role of Grand Inquisitor and seemed to maintain a deep and complex list of property data all in her head. No one who worked for the Bachmans had ever had a truly personal conversation with either of them, or been invited to their spectacular, sprawling contemporary home in the woods. Sylvia wasn't exactly afraid of them—she felt that would be beneath her—but she reluctantly had to admit she was somewhat in awe. They made success appear so easy. Of course, as far as she could tell, they didn't have children.

"If you love the real estate business, I mean really love it," Betty said, parading slowly across the room in spiky four-inch Louboutins, "then you have to love it not just when times are good, when our commissions are rolling in, when we're setting new records for property prices...," Betty paused to face the room and jangle gold bracelets, "... but you have to love it in hard times, too." She paused again, scanning the room for reactions, but the room was pin-drop silent and every face was a practiced blank. "Now, our numbers over the last 12 months are not where they were the prior year, or the year before that—or even the year before *that.* Sales volume is down 22 percent this quarter alone over the same period last year. Moreover, I regret to say we see this downward trend continuing. While I doubt any of this comes as a real surprise to any of you, Barnaby and I feel it's important to let everyone know where we stand now, so that you'll understand why some changes may be necessary in the near future."

Everyone knew what came next. The dreaded "L" word: layoffs. Up to 30 percent of the staff. Seniority would be taken into consideration (Sylvia exhaled), but would not be the only deciding factor.

Damn the Walters! How much could this hurt me?

When Betty was finished, Barnaby stepped back in to deliver a string of heartfelt clichés: Chin up. This isn't personal. You are all outstanding realtors and don't let anybody tell you otherwise. The staff shuffled off silently, to pick up the pieces of their day. Sylvia huddled briefly with Ben Wang and Ann Likert, both senior brokers like Sylvia, and fairly straight shooters who avoid double-crossing colleagues as much as any competitive broker can. The three agreed, fatalistically, that there was nothing they could do at this point, except wait for the chips to fall where they may. Ben Wang called it a bloody massacre. Sylvia decided to hold off on the Walters conversation; enough was enough.

And now, on the other side of three dismal, unpromising prospecting appointments, she's freaking out her daughter by showing up out of the blue for...for what? A one-off mother-daughter outing? Or would she rather dive into a bottle of Zinfandel?

"I thought we might, you know, hang out," Sylvia tells her daughter.

"Dad's ok?" Jeannie gets into the bright red Audi a bit cautiously, as if it were rigged to explode.

"Of course, why wouldn't he be?" *And I'm fine too. Thanks for asking.* "How about a mani-pedi?"

"Oh my God, that's so bougie, Mom! Why on earth would I want to force exploited, underpaid women from Vietnam to paint my fingernails and scrub my feet? It's disgusting. I don't even think it should be allowed. Those women deserve so much better."

"Well, if everyone felt that way, those women would be out of a job, wouldn't they? And then where would they be?" Sylvia wills herself to engage in a normal quarrel with her 16-year-old crusader.

"That's the point. If everybody did the right thing, those women wouldn't have to work there, breathing all those chemicals. They could get much better jobs somewhere else."

"Like what? If those women went to work at Cyn's, for example, pouring coffee and making avocado toast, they'd probably earn even less. Sometimes, Jeannie, the obvious solution isn't the best solution."

"Cyn's is closed," Jeannie replies.

"She's just closed for renovations."

"No, Mom. She's closed for good. Her niece, Alison, is in my English class. She told me and Gina that her aunt totally ran out of money and probably has to move in with them. Alison was complaining because she's gonna have to move out of her bedroom, and give it to Cynthia. I wanted to tell Alison that's a first-world problem, and she should get over it, but I didn't."

Sylvia absorbs this news quietly. She isn't completely certain that Jeannie has her facts right, because how could this have gotten by her?

"Anyway," Jeannie continues, "I'm *never* getting a mani-pedi. I can't *believe* you thought that was a good idea."

"What should we do, then?" Sylvia asks, recognizing that she's completely out of ideas. She can't think where to point the car next.

"Let's go out to Dad's new project."

Sylvia is surprised. "You mean Willing Enclave?"

"Yeah. I wanna see it."

"I don't even know if your dad's out there now."

"So? Does that matter? I just wanna see what it looks like. Have you seen it?"

"No," says Sylvia.

"Aren't you curious? Don't you always visit Dad's sites?"

"I haven't in a long time, actually. But okay."

It occurs to Sylvia that her daughter has reached the age when she is beginning to have her own secrets, her own ideas and misconceptions about the world and how it works, and, in fact, her own hidden agendas. But Sylvia is warming to the idea of visiting Willing Enclave. It wouldn't hurt to get a sense of just how far along the somewhat hobbled project actually is, at this point. Because Willing Prime Contractors is operating as the developer on this project, Sylvia assumes that Bachman Realty will eventually get the listing, meaning, *she* would. It wouldn't be the first time deals lined up just this way—giving the Kings a perfectly legal way to win twice—first, by selling the properties built by Willing Prime Contractors at a profit, and second, by reaping commissions on the sales themselves. There was a time—a while ago now, wasn't it?—when these tandem deals were a regular thing. It couldn't hurt to take a peek at Willing Enclave in the flesh.

As Sylvia and Jeannie pull up to the partially framed houses and the new foundations, the afternoon sun is casting long shadows through the wooden ghost-houses and across the foundation pits. The site stands on a gentle rise, with undeveloped acres and small stands of trees providing a picturesque backdrop for the properties—or at least, it's picturesque with a bit of imagination. Sylvia understands why Cap and the guys were eager to buy up this parcel; it's one of the last great undeveloped sites in the region, and just the right distance from the interstate to afford a sense of exclusivity without being so far out in the boonies it's merely inconvenient. Yes, it was a gamble, but that's not a reason to shy away. The site is empty and silent, and rather forlorn in its quasi-naked state. Of course, it's late in the day. She and Jeannie probably just missed everyone—and all the pounding and sawing—by minutes. The pair get out of the car and walk along the partially built road that parallels the houses to get a better look.

"How long does it take? To finish them, I mean," Jeannie asks.

"It depends."

"On what?"

"Oh, on things like materials. Sometimes they're not available when you want them. And sometimes, you have to wait for other people to do some of the work, like plumbers and electricians."

"These houses are for rich people, aren't they?" Jeannie scrutinizes the columns of lumber, trying to imagine whole rooms filled with furniture and fancy appliances.

"We hope so."

"But why can't Dad build houses for ordinary people? For people like the women who work in the nail salon? They need a nice place to live, too." Sylvia laughs. "I don't think it's funny, Mom. You should care more, y'know?" Jeannie tromps off, her Beane boots kicking the pea gravel.

"Oh, Jeannie," Sylvia calls after her. "Someday you'll understand that nothing is possible without money. It's money that makes you who you are, whether you realize it or not." Jeannie heads back to the car and slams the door, waiting for her mother to make her way back. *Compassionate people don't need money and stupid new houses to make a difference*, Jeannie thinks.

We didn't need to come all the way out here just for you to get on your adolescent high horse, Sylvia thinks. Still, it's not a wasted trip. For one thing, Sylvia recognizes that she and Jeannie probably said more to one another this afternoon—even if there was antagonism on one side of the exchange—than they have in weeks, if not longer. That's something, at least. And the visit to the construction site helps Sylvia pull herself back from the precipice of dread and anxiety that has overwhelmed her since the meeting at the office. *Those houses should be easy to sell, especially if they're careful about the finishes. I can still make shit happen around here.*

Sylvia and Jeannie arrive home to find Zeke and somebody Sylvia doesn't know sitting in the den watching TV and eating string cheese.

"Mom, this is Farrah."

"As in Farrah Fawcett?" Farrah mumbles yes, eyes averted. Zeke and Farrah both appear sweaty and red-faced, which Sylvia chalks up to all those hours on the soccer field, or whatever sport Farrah probably plays. Jeannie stares at the two of them like they've both just returned from a trip to the moon. There's a sharp tang in the air. *Something's different.*

An hour later, Farrah is gone, Carson slips in quietly with a couple of large pizzas, and the four Kings retreat to their private corners of the house to take stock of the day and figure out what on earth they're each expected to do next to keep fear, doubt, insecurity, and injustice at bay for as long as possible. On top of that, Zeke is also privately replaying his revelatory afternoon with Farrah.

At around 3:30 a.m., Sylvia's phone rings. She fumbles to answer. It's Selig Walters, calling from several continents away. He either doesn't understand, or doesn't care, about the time difference. It's a short conversation, anyway. He's calling to say they've decided to look for another broker, with a different firm, and wish Sylvia all the best. Even though the decision isn't unexpected, her stomach flips again and again.

Three hours later, Carson's phone rings. It's Vin. He's been up all night, worrying. So has Dizz, apparently. What's the plan?

THE FIRST SUMMER

Chapter Seven

Hero_Foreclosures.com

JUST LISTED!

27A Berkley St., Downtown Willing. 1100 sq. ft. Retail café/restaurant. Lease or buy. / 2456 Hunter Ave., North Willing. 2 BR condo. As-is. Visit our website for more great listings!

Javier Miguel Morales Martinez thought long and hard about what to name his new business. He made a list of Spanish proverbs and names of girls he'd known and loved as a teenager back in Guerrero. He considered borrowing his wife's name, Eugenia (impossible!), and tried out his own initials. But nothing felt right. So eventually he settled on *Vida*. Life. Vida, Inc., owned and operated by Javier Martinez, President and Chief Executive Officer. Vida was the perfect name for a business bringing oxygen and other life-supporting medical gases to hospitals and homes. By 2005, Javier had finally saved enough, and burnished his credit sufficiently, to rent and equip a small, cinderblock building located on an ugly, no-man's-land stretch of frontage road on the outskirts of Willing; sign a lease on his first truck; and purchase gas cylinders along with a host of other supplies and equipment he needed. He'd attended the industry's national conventions, read all the literature, and consulted a small business consultant who offered free advice at the Willing Public Library. He registered his company with all the local authorities, obtained the proper certifications, and opened a business bank account at Second National, where he was complimented on his thorough business plan.

All this preparation was just the background to Javier's all-consuming dedication to pursuing contracts, without which there could be no business. He began by approaching the smallest nursing homes within a 150-mile radius, the ones not yet swallowed up by corporate medical conglomerates; the ones that still housed elderly residents in old houses with peeling paint and rotting rattan rockers on the front porch, or in small, modest brick buildings that resembled old boarding houses. These places still existed, if you knew where to look for them, and Javier made it his business to find them and to call on them—over and over, until he'd won the right to supply all their patients who needed oxygen therapy, sleep therapy, and other ventilation services covered by Medicaid, Medicare, and private insurance for the lucky few. Javier had thought of everything. He likes dotting the "i's" and crossing the "t's"—his favorite American expression in the country he has called home, and his lifeline, since 1978.

As to why he chose to chance everything on this particular business, one of Javier's first steady jobs after coming to the United States was as a van driver for a mom-and-pop medical equipment supply company that delivered, among other things, medical gases to local hospitals in southern California. He earned little, but learned a lot. He silently vowed to himself, in those early months, that he would someday be his own boss, and since there would always be sick people everywhere who needed things like oxygen, he guessed the opportunity would wait until he was good and ready. And he was right, at the time.

On a crisp fall day in 2006, Javier drove to Vida, Inc. for the first official day of business. He blasted a vintage Red Hot Chili Peppers CD all the way. His thick brown hair was neatly trimmed and pomaded; his mustache clipped to a shape he considered appropriate for business. Javier did not wish to appear too ethnic to his clientele. He thought a CEO should look masculine, confident, and generically corporate—and *political correctness*, a phrase he'd recently heard for the first time, be damned. Of course, for the time being, this CEO was also the office manager, the receptionist, the loading dock guy, and the delivery driver. But that suited him fine. He pulled up in front of the cinderblock building, freshly painted all in white, with a red and turquoise sign on the wall above and to the left of the front door that said VIDA, with the "i" in the name replaced by an upright metal oxygen canister. He'd sketched the design himself, for the sign company to fabricate. He stood in front of the building for several minutes, taking it all in. He pulled a few wilting leaves off of a nearby shrub. He pictured exactly what awaited him inside: White-washed cinderblock walls and a gray cement floor. A no-nonsense sort of a place, a place that means business and hard work, and no fooling around or frou-frou adornment. Metal shelves are neatly organized with all the important tools of the trade: analyzers, purge alarms, medical gas pipe markers, valve tags, leak detectors, thread sealants, copper fittings, and all kinds of colored tape. He'd ordered minimum quantities, at first, and assumed he'd stock up as business grew. He'd set up a separate, small, no-frills office at the back of the building, which would soon become his home away from home. It didn't occur to him to bring any personal touches from home into his place of business. So the office didn't have a single family photo, or piece of art, or memento of his life's journey from the poor, dusty roads of Guerrero to the comparatively prosperous, bustling town of Willing. He stood a moment longer before entering his new domain. He didn't think "American Dream," not in so many words, but deep down in his gut, he felt it.

Two other things happened to Javier around the time he launched the company. In 2006, his daughter, Gina Rosa, was born. And six months later, Gina's mother—Javier's wife and soul mate—Eugenia Rosa Martinez Cruz, was diagnosed with Stage IV metastatic breast cancer. She died after a brief, agonizing battle, leaving behind a deeply grieving husband, a fussy baby, and Javier's 62-year-old mother, Carmen Guadalupe Martinez Flores. Javier had not, up to then, taken a full day off since starting Vida. The only time he truly allowed himself to relax, and give himself over entirely to his family, was at Sunday dinner, when his mother made fried shredded beef empanadas and corn tamales, just as she had done in Guerrero for her own father, before times grew so lean, and jobs so scarce, that she emigrated with Javier to the United States, leaving her husband and other relatives behind to fend for themselves, as thousands before and since had felt compelled to do when that was both possible and desirable. Both Eugenia and Carmen were immensely proud of Javier's American-style success. Eugenia had toyed with going to nursing school, but once Javier started his own business, and she became pregnant, they both counted on his success to support the family. Carmen worked part-time for years as a receptionist in a local dentist's office that served a largely Latinx population, many of whom worked in and around Willing but did not live there, preferring instead, for economic reasons, the smattering of small, semi-rural, barely commercial towns that dotted the map around Willing (and light years, economically, from Linton Crossing or even the budding Willing Enclave), where rents were lower, gas was cheaper, and the local grocery stores stocked foods they knew and needed. Carmen spent much of her modest salary on groceries and then household supplies for baby Gina. She also managed to save enough to purchase a white lace layette for Gina, as well as a christening gown, which made the new parents very happy.

After Eugenia died, Javier began spending every day, including Sundays, at Vida itself, stocking shelves and doing accounts, meeting with hospital procurement managers, nursing home operators, and other customers and prospects. He came home to eat dinner out of a container (a practice Carmen despised but tolerated because she picked her battles), hug Gina briefly or kiss her sleeping in her crib (and then her little-girl bed), and read business papers and trade journals before falling asleep on his side of the marital bed. Carmen was not surprised to see Javier double-down on his workaholic tendencies, but she wasn't happy about it, either. And while there was no upside whatsoever to losing Eugenia, the truth is that Javier's business, under his relentless attention, began thriving. He hired a delivery driver and leased a second truck. He hired a part-time office manager who also kept the accounts, as well as a sales rep, Fran Hauser, who could service current accounts while Javier continued cultivating new business. His territory expanded to almost the entire 150-mile radius he envisioned early on. He was able to draw a comfortable salary—not a fortune, but more money than anyone in his family had ever enjoyed on a steady basis. Mother and son also took pride in the monthly ritual of wiring money back to Guerrero to support family members who continued to struggle but had no immediate plans to chance the trek to the U.S., as borders tightened and, in time, the economy cooled. Carmen quit her job at the dentist's, both because her income wasn't a necessity any longer and because both her knees and her right hip were hurting, which made the daily walk to and from the bus stop and the dentist's office increasingly *dolorosa*. Besides, Gina needed her.

The last time Javier punches a hole in the kitchen wall, he lets out a loud, guttural, anguished string of Mexican-flavored curses as he transferred the kinetic energy stored in his entire body into his right arm, and then into his coiled right fist, until it connects with the wall with a sickening bang-crunch. Gina bears witness, bewildered and horrified. Hard to believe this is the father who, when Gina informed him she didn't want a *quinceanera*, took her side against his own mother railing about the breakdown of tradition. Gina knows, intellectually, that her father's violent behavior isn't directed at her, but still, she feels guilty by association. She wonders, briefly, if her father is possessed by demons—then dismisses the idea as the kind of old-world garbage her grandmother would latch onto, to explain the unexplainable.

The day after the most recent episode, after Javier leaves for work with red, swollen, scraped knuckles, Carmen pulls a handful of dried flowers from a vase in the living room and burns them in a dish, to rid the house of *malo*—evil. On her next shopping trip, she purchases fresh flowers and pins them to the outside of the front door. She discusses none of this with Gina, who doesn't care all that much what her grandmother does, as long as it doesn't involve nagging. Gina begins listening for her father to come home at night, which is never before 9 or 10, now. Each time she hears his key in the door, all the muscles in her body begin to unclench.

As summer vacation unfolds, Gina is at loose ends, restless and jittery. She wants to work, but cannot drive, so there is no easy way to get around and her father has not offered to transport her. Gina asks her father quietly, tentatively, if he could use her in the office, which she has scarcely ever set foot in. He glowers and offered a terse no, which clearly shuts down further discussion. She scans online classifieds for low-end retail jobs, but there are none listed in downtown Willing. She tries finding baby-sitting jobs, but as she really does not like being around small children, she doesn't try very hard.

Tonight, a very warm Thursday in June, Gina cannot sleep. Lying in bed is torture. Her mind races. Her father and grandmother have virtually abandoned her, she concludes. Sure, they feed her and house her, but that seems to be where the care ends. Her grandmother has always alternated between petting and scolding, and lately, the scolding has been winning out. At 2:00 a.m., Gina is posting indignantly about the mistreatment of undocumented immigrants, especially the tragic miscarriage of justice when parents are deported, torn from their U.S.-born children. It feels good to take a stand, to call out immoral behavior and, as she sees it, corrupt government policies. It feels a lot better, and a lot more comfortable, to vent in the public sphere than dwell on her own private frustrations. There's a whole community out there, she thinks, and *they* care what happens to all sorts of people. And still, she cannot sleep. She goes downstairs for a cold caffeine-free Coke and is startled to see her father sitting at the kitchen table. There's a half-empty bottle of tequila next to him.

"Papá," Gina says. Javier slowly lifts old photographs and letters out of an old, battered shoebox. He rips them into small pieces, one at a time, piling the little bits of paper onto the table. "Papá," Gina says again, softly. Javier continues ripping; he does not look at her. She thinks she sees an old photo of her mother, taken when she must have been around Gina's age. "What are you doing?" Javier takes a swig of tequila. Slowly, he turns to Gina, but she feels his unfocused eyes look past her.

"My life. Our life," Javier says. He returns to his task. He holds out the bottle of tequila to his daughter. "This too is life. Are you ready?" Gina does not understand what he is saying, or what he is perhaps asking. She shakes her head and backs away from her father. She turns around and runs back upstairs and closes her bedroom door. She is shaking, breathing hard, the desire for a cold Coke now forgotten. Her stomach heaves. She thinks about waking her grandmother, but decides that would only make things worse and besides, what could Carmen do? Gina spends the rest of the night perched on the edge of her bed, listening, listening intently, for her father to come upstairs. The summer morning light is just coming through her windows before she hears his slow, heavy tread, and the sound of the light switch going on in the bathroom they all share. That sound is like a signal to sleep. Gina tips over onto her bed and closes her eyes. When she wakes up, four hours later, she jumps up and rushes downstairs. The kitchen table is clean; there's no sign of the tequila or the shoebox or the pile of minutely ripped photos. Carmen is there, wearing the flowered apron she's worn Gina's whole life.

"You want eggs?" Carmen asks her in Spanish.

"Where's Dad?" Gina asks in English.

"At work. Where else would he be? It's Friday, sleepy head. He's busy earning our bread, your father."

Gina stands in the kitchen, still wearing yesterday's clothes. Her short jet-dark hair is sticking up. She looks around the room as if she's never seen it before. She forces herself to look at the spidery dent in the wall, where Javier's fist did its damage.

"Why isn't that fixed?" Gina asks angrily, pointing to the dent. Carmen shrugs. Then Gina sees it: a tiny, torn corner of a black-and-white photograph—the old-fashioned kind with a white, scalloped border—caught under the leg of a kitchen chair. She claps her hand to her mouth to keep from screaming. Gina goes to her room, throws clothes into her mother's old striped canvas overnight bag, and walks out the front door while Carmen is in the kitchen. She walks two miles in the morning sunshine to Jeannie King's house, where the houses (and of course, that lawn) are bigger than hers, and where she hopes, and needs to believe, that they will cheerfully take her in, no questions asked.

Chapter Eight

Zeke's favorite thing to do at the Willing Enclave construction site is to walk across one of the second-story I-beams that run the width of the house. He likes the controlled danger of it. He's just high enough off the ground that a fall could seriously injury him. But the smooth beam is wide enough to walk across, one boot in front of the other, without any real risk of losing his balance. Of course, Zeke isn't supposed to do this. Ever. It's as far from Construction Site Safety 101 as you can get. But he does it anyway, when everybody's attention is elsewhere, which it often is. Technically, Zeke shouldn't be on the site at all. He's 16, under age, and reasonably unskilled. This doesn't bother Zeke a bit. He figures, his dad's the boss, so if it's okay with him, who is Zeke to argue? And besides, he's pocketing $50 a week this summer. It's not much, but it's not nothing, either.

The whole thing fell into his lap, anyway, so it would be stupid to complain. As the school year ended, Zeke was thinking mostly about when and where he and Farrah could find a private space to have sex. Summer, in his mind, opened up new geographic possibilities, as it was warm enough to do it outside, if an inside space wasn't easily available. They'd already found a nice soft patch of grass at the far back end of his vast backyard, just a few yards from where the grass petered out into roots and trees. It was easy to spread a towel, enjoy a few beers swiped from the fridge, and just chill. Nobody was back there; nobody could see a thing; and nobody was keeping tabs, anyway. Finding a job wasn't really on the radar, until Carson said out of the blue one night after dinner, in the last week of school, "Zeke, how'd you'd like to swing a hammer with me out at Willing Enclave this summer?"

Zeke immediately wondered how much this would encroach on his free time. "I dunno. Why?"

"Well, you'll build some muscles. Pick up a few skills. It'll be good for you."

"Huh," Zeke said.

"And I'll pay you. I don't expect you to work for free."

"How much?" Zeke asked.

"We'll figure that out later. You hop in the truck with me in the morning. We'll be back in time for dinner. Keep you busy. Out of trouble." *Ahh, too busy,* Zeke thought, *but the money….*

"Yeah, ok, I guess."

Jeannie wasn't around for this conversation, and it was just as well, as she might well have asked her father point blank why he didn't make *her* the same offer. It never occurred to Carson to invite his daughter to work construction over the summer. Subconsciously, he'd already rejected the idea, not just because he doubted she'd have the physical strength to work with heavy tools, but because he didn't want to subject her to the wandering eyes of the crew. He decided this without even thinking there was something to decide. Let Jeannie trail around with her mother, if she wants professional exposure. *A building site is no place for a teenaged girl.*

Zeke now has $150 in cash shoved into a drawer in the little table next to his bed, where he also keeps condoms and a baggie holding a couple of joints.

Zeke is sneaking in a well-practiced walk across the I-beam installed in the middle house. Technically, he's on a lunch break. The other guys on the skeleton crew that Willing Prime Contractors keeps at the site these days are also on lunch break, and they've all wandered off to smoke and eat lunch they either brought from home or picked up at the 7-Eleven on the way in. Zeke doesn't know, and wouldn't care, that his dad and his partners are paying shitty wages to a couple of guys not half as experienced as Bruno and Jorge, for the sake of keeping the job site active. Zeke walks slowly, arms stretched out like airplane wings, enjoying the sense of suspended-animation that requires him to concentrate on his feet while tuning out everything else. It feels like free-floating. *I could buy a better bike,* he thinks, as he makes his way across the structure. *Or better weed.* Zeke is realizing he likes the sensation of having money, but he isn't much of a consumer. He doesn't care about clothes or brand-name athletic shoes. He thinks video games are lame. As he prepares to step off the beam, he makes a list in his head of stuff he likes to do. It's pretty short. *Sex. Walking on I-beams.* Neither of those requires money. The thought strikes him: *I'm into experiences, not things.* This idea makes him ridiculously happy, though he doesn't know why. But it feels as though he's figured out something important, something he'll need to know about himself for the future.

Carson pulls up in his pick-up after lunch. He's hardly ever at the site, so father and son haven't done much hammer-swinging together so far this summer. Zeke is a little disappointed about this, but also a little ashamed. His dad sold him a line, it seems, and he fell for it. Sweaty afternoons with the two of them hammering and sawing and whatever, and trash-talking about sports and so forth...well, in hindsight, it's pretty corny. Pretty lame. But it's okay. This way, he's got plenty of space—all the space he needs to walk where he shouldn't and figure out shit about his life.

"How's it going?" Carson asks. He's looking up at the houses, then across to the empty foundations. Zach can tell immediately that his dad is not happy. Despite the sunglasses and the WPC bill cap shading his face, Zeke can see his dad is frowning. There are deepening lines around the corners of his mouth. His dad remains something of a mystery: never where you expect him to be; often brooding, a million miles away in his eyes, yet perpetually ready to talk a good game, take a chance, claim a win. He can't figure him out, and doesn't know what to ask. Zeke removes his own WPC bill cap—one of the only souvenirs he's determined to hold onto for the foreseeable future.

"What is it, Dad?" Zeke asks.

"What's what? Nothing. What did you do this morning?"

"Vin taught me how to use the power nail driver. We got two boards up pretty quickly."

"Did he?" Carson says. "Did he make you wear the work gloves? And the plastic glasses?"

"Well, duh. He's not stupid, Dad. *I'm* not stupid."

"I know. Just one less thing to worry about, Zeke."

"What *are* you worried about?"

"Oh, just the usual. Business. It's complicated." *Great non-answer, Dad,* Zeke thinks. *Guess I'm sorta sneaky, too, just like you. Hah.*

The afternoon is growing hotter and Zeke is sleepy and bored, the thrill of walking I-beams now worn off. Maybe not bored, exactly, but lulled. He didn't realize that construction work is like this. You often perform the same set of actions over and over. And though everybody keeps reminding him to be careful, and stay alert, it's pretty hard when it's 88 degrees out and nobody's talking about anything interesting. In the beginning, Zeke gets a kick out of eavesdropping on Bud—one of the new guys on the site for a few hours a day, barely a few years older than Zeke himself—complaining about how his wife (*this guy's married??*) has been cheating on him since before they were married. But since Bud won't shut up about it, and keeps asking everybody (except Zeke) what he should do about it, Zeke is bored stiff by the conversation. If Bud *did* ask Zeke, Zeke would tell him to kick her out. But, Zeke thinks, *if Farrah were sleeping around with other guys, would I even care?* The idea raises a whole host of images, even possibilities, in his mind. For now, Zeke decides to push it away. Bud's on his own.

"You're pretty good with the nail gun, Z. Clean, straight lines. Nice. Guess I'll have to pay you this week, won't I?" Carson doesn't ruffle Zeke's hair; they don't do things like that. But they're both pretty satisfied. "I'll be back in time to pick you up later, ok?"

Vin is supposed to be Zeke's on-site supervisor, because Carson doesn't really trust any of the other guys to do it, or to care. Of course Vin cares; he's known Zeke since birth, and he and Darius are as good as uncles to the twins. *The 'uncs.'* Darius hasn't been around today, either. He's at the lumber yard. It's a mystery to Zeke what these guys actually do for a living. The whole thing seems like a lot of running around, and bossing people around. And in the end, you have a brand new home to show off to people. Not bad, really. *Maybe I'll be a partner someday, when Dad and the 'uncs' get old. If I decide to stick around.*

Vin is around. He took time, after all, to show Zeke all about the nail gun. But he's spent most of the day wandering around the site, taking pictures of the work, and talking on his cell phone. In the hottest, quietest stretch of afternoon, Zeke is continuing to drive nails into long wooden slats that he's attaching to the studs of the house. He feels his right deltoids getting sore, holding the hefty nail driver, and worries briefly about whether he's developing lopsided muscles. What will Farrah think of that? Half Superman, half Clark Kent weakling. She'll probably laugh, not with him, but at him. But it doesn't really bother him. *She's sexy when she's laughing…those crooked teeth.* One of the rules at the site is that cell phones are supposed to be off while you're actually working. Zeke notices the guys pretty much follow this rule, but he doesn't really think it applies to him. He's not official, after all, just the boss's son helping out for a few weeks over the summer. So he takes plenty of work breaks to text with Farrah, or sneak a few minutes to watch comedy clips, if and when he gets a good enough cell signal. He's holding the nail gun in his right hand when he feels his phone buzzing in his right rear pocket. He goes to put the gun down quickly so he doesn't miss the call, as the phone keeps buzzing, but his muscles from his shoulder to his hand are tired and twitchy. As he bends to set the gun down, he reaches across with his left hand to grip it. But his right index finger is still on the trigger and in a split second, he accidentally shoots it, driving a two-and-a-half-inch sinker nail right through the palm of his left hand. The nail actually pokes out on the other side of his hand, just below the space between the third and fourth knuckle. There really isn't a lot of blood.

Shit.

Chapter Nine

Sylvia whips her car into the ambulance bay entrance at Sturgis Memorial Hospital about 30 minutes after Vin arrives with Zeke, his hand wrapped in clean white gauze yanked, by Vin, from an emergency medical supply kit kept in a large white plastic bucket on the site. Vin is now in the waiting room, well aware that an ugly conversation is waiting too. The unbridled wrath of Carson. He guesses—he hopes—that Sylvia will take out her wrath on Carson, rather than on him. Carson is swinging by the day camp where Jeannie is volunteering, and they'll come to the hospital together. Sylvia enters the curtained medical bay where they've taken Zeke just as the young medical resident on call is gently, and expertly, rewrapping the injury with fresh gauze, after debriding the wound and slathering antibiotic ointment on both sides of the hand. She lets the tip end of the nail poke through the gauze, so there isn't extra pressure. Sylvia winces, swallows the bile she feels rising in her throat, and sits down in a plastic chair. Zeke is white as a sheet, and so is Sylvia.

"Pretty cool, huh?" says Zeke, weakly. His teeth are beginning to chatter.

"Okay, young man," says the resident. "I'm going to have you lie back, and—" she pokes her head out of the curtain and summons a nurse. "Let's get a heated blanket on him."

"Oh, jeez," says Zeke.

"What's happening?" Sylvia asks. She stands, shakily, and takes Zeke's right hand. The resident, small with frizzy hair, calmly explains that Zeke is experiencing mild shock, which is entirely normal. The good thing about this type of injury, she says, is that there isn't a lot of blood loss. But time is of the essence, which is why, she explains, she's already called the hand surgeon. He is expected within the hour. Sylvia has trouble taking in everything the doctor is saying. Something about neuromuscular function. Tendon damage. X-rays.

Sylvia wants to ask so many questions that she can't actually think of a single one to ask. *First things first.* "But he'll be ok, right? I mean, he'll make a full recovery?" The young doctor does not answer. Sylvia can't tell if she's avoiding the question or just trying to do her job. The nurse returns and asks Zeke to swallow two pills.

"Just a mild sedative," the doctor explains. "It will take the edge off the pain and help him relax a bit." Zeke is not displeased about the drugs. *All legal and controlled. Heck, I've even got permission.* The "trip" he's about to take, whatever it's like, gives him the sensation of being on an adventure, *having an experience*, rather than just being a stupid-assed kid who screwed up big time. Zeke re-lives the split second when his left hand reached for the nail gun to steady his right hand, the phone buzzing in his pocket. *You asshole. And where's my phone?*

Carson and Jeannie rush in, joining Sylvia at Zeke's bedside. For a rare moment, all the interior messiness, the doubts, fears, and difficult questions that each member of the family wrestles with individually—as if they're a set of individual pillars upholding a single large structure—all of this is submerged, invisible, in the heat of the crisis.

"I'm sorry, son," Carson says. "I'm so sorry." Carson clenches his jaw, withholding all the questions he wants answered and the decisions he wants to take back. *Were you alone? Where was Vin? I should never. You should not be. This is not what. Fucking bean counters.*

Jeannie stays behind, while her parents confer with the medical resident and the hand surgeon, who has just arrived. She has spent the last few weeks biking back and forth to volunteer as a counselor-in-training at Camp Waymore, serving children with disabilities, including kids with cerebral palsy, missing limbs, brittle bones, and paraplegia. *Compassion in action.* She has seen it all, she thinks, and she's ready to face whatever else anybody wants to throw her way. *Action hero.*

By now, Zeke's hand is completely cocooned, so she doesn't have much opportunity yet to test her fortitude. Or her super-powers.

"Zeke Eel," she says, using her secret twin name.

"Jeel," he slurs in reply, "Jeel" being her twin name, which they coined when they were seven to rhyme with Zeke Eel, which in turn came about when they were introduced to a dog named Ezekiel. They thought it was hysterically funny.

"Idiot," Jeannie says, though she's not exactly sure what happened, since her dad was only able to give her a hasty second-hand version of the story. But she assumes her brother did something stupid and entirely avoidable. She sits in the plastic chair vacated by their mother and reads funny stuff out loud from her phone, as Zeke lies on the hospital bed, his wrapped hand resting uncomfortably by his side, palm up, on a white hospital pillow.

"Yeah," Zeke replies, laughing.

"You're drooling." Jeannie wipes a speck of saliva from the corner of Zeke's mouth.

Vin jumps up when Carson, Sylvia, and Jeannie finally arrive in the family waiting area, now that Zeke is in surgery. Vin pounds them with questions: What's the prognosis. How long in surgery. Is he in a lot of pain. "You know I'd shoot a nail into my own hand right now, if it would undo it," Vin says, his eyes filling with tears. "You know I'd do anything for that kid."

"Except watch him," Carson says quietly. "What the fuck, Vin."

"He may never be able to make a fist with his left hand," Sylvia says, looking Vin straight in the eye. "He may have trouble gripping things." Vin sits down, shaking his head.

"What can I do?" he asks. "Is there a single thing I can do—for you? For him? Just tell me. Anything." Vin will never know if Sylvia acts on instinct, or by pre-arranged signal. But she turns around and walks out of the waiting area, without another word to him.

Vin is the one who introduced them 25 years ago. Back then, Willing's population was at its peak, and the town supported two high schools—one on the south side, one on the north. The schools have long since been consolidated, but back then, it was possible to grow up in Willing and still never lay eyes on all your peers. Carson and Vin lived on the north side, Sylvia on the south side. Vin met Sylvia at a party at his cousin's house. He liked her immediately—her brashness, her clear desire to go out and get what she wanted. But her dark, tightly curled hair and rounded features didn't turn him on. He always goes for skinny, talkative blondes—a choice that has not worked out well for him, not because there's any inherent flaw in these women, but because Vin actually prefers to live in a quiet, conflict-free world. His ongoing failure to acknowledge his deepest needs, or make a life for himself that thrums to his inner rhythms, has kept him walking a razor's edge his whole adult life. When he met Sylvia, he thought immediately of Carson. He felt the two of them were kindred spirits, though he couldn't exactly say why. Maybe it was because they both seemed to want so many things so badly, far more badly than he did.

"He was doing fine all morning. I watched him working long enough, I thought I could trust him. Build his confidence." Vin says to Carson.

"He's sixteen. He's green. He's so easily distracted that a mosquito could buzz in his ear and he'd forget where he is."

"I'm not a father, Cap. I don't know shit like that. But I know Zeke, and he was doing okay."

"Except he wasn't."

"If you'd been there, it still might've happened!"

"Never," Carson says.

"If we weren't falling down a fucking rabbit hole, then a shitload of crap wouldn't be happening right now! And this is just one more fucking thing!"

"My son practically blowing his hand off is not one more fucking thing!" Carson shouts.

"If you hadn't pushed us so hard to take on all this debt then I wouldn't have had to spend the day on the phone trying to convince Sandy Tipper and three other guys like him to deliver us the supplies we need to build these fucking houses and get them sold! 'Cause if we can't get that done, then I don't give a shit how many nails you, or Zeke, or anybody else pounds into those studs!"

"Fuck you," Carson says. "You signed your name next to mine, next to Dizz's. You're not a fucking victim here. My *son* is the fucking victim. And that's on you." Carson turns his back, then comes back around. "And *I'm* the one handling that lying shit Sandy Tipper. So stay out of it!"

Both men recognize there's no more to be said that can't be unsaid. Carson walks out of the hospital family room and goes to find Sylvia. Jeannie has put in earbuds to save her sanity, though the peals of rage still get through. Vin leaves the hospital, worrying much more about the state of his finances—and the future of their company—than about Zeke. And he's disgusted with himself, disgusted with his own cowardice, for not telling Carson on the spot that all the suppliers, every single one, said 'No.' He dreads the call to Dizz. He dreads even more whatever is going to happen next.

It's their first date night in forever. And it's not much of a date. It's only the Haven, which serves the same burgers and fried-everything—potatoes, pickles, onions—as it has for 40 years. But Carson and Sylvia are sitting face-to-face on worn bar stools with drinks in front of them, and that's enough to make this feel like a date. A married date, anyway. They are both exhausted and unsure where to steer the conversation. Sylvia notices, as Zeke has, the deepening grooves around Carson's mouth. His blond hair is flopping into his eyes; he's overdue for a haircut. He, in turn, sees the puffy bags that have developed under her eyes and the silver strands threading through her dark hair. They both think it: *We're not young anymore.*

It's been three days since Gina Martinez showed up at their front door early one morning, just as Sylvia, still in a bathrobe, was making coffee. Jeannie and Zeke were both sleeping. Carson sat in his little office cubby, off the living room, staring at his laptop, which he does a lot lately. Sylvia saw immediately that Gina planned to stay, though for how long, she couldn't guess. Gina is practically a second daughter in the King household. Sylvia and Carson know that the girls spend so much time together, they share a nickname. They are practically a brand. And they believe the girls are mutually good influences, as they're always embarking on new schemes to help poor kids, or immigrant kids, or whatever cause seems to ignite their indignation over all the injustice in the world. It beats sneaking out to get tattoos. Sylvia admires their shared seriousness of purpose. Carson is struck by how different girl friendships are from boy friendships, although maybe it's just that times have changed. He and Vin and Dizz bonded over, what? Scoring beer. Getting into trouble. Chasing girls. But what else? They all wanted to get rich quick, or as soon as possible. Which isn't working out quite as planned, *but there's still time,* Carson tells himself. He has wondered, more than once, how long it will be before Jeannie and Gina lose their idealistic passion, and wake up one day to realize that getting from *here* to *there* isn't a straight line, or any line at all. You just grind it out. That's all there is. Part of him wishes they would hurry up and reach the stage of disillusionment. Get it over with.

The Kings stare down into their drinks at the Haven, lost in thought.

"Are you okay?" Sylvia had asked Gina, when she turned up on their doorstep.

"Yeah. I guess." Sylvia waited for more, but Gina just stood there.

"Do you want to go up to Jeannie's room?"

"Yeah, if it's okay." Sylvia nodded. She was about to ask Gina if her dad knows she's here, but she just could not bring herself to open up this can of worms at 7:10 in the morning. *This will sort itself out. Like everything else.* Sylvia suddenly realized that Javier has never been to her house. She didn't know him when Eugenia was alive, and they were both pregnant. She never runs into him at the supermarket, or the Haven, or anywhere around Willing, and neither does Carson, as far as she knows. She's spoken to him just once or twice at PTA meetings, when the girls were younger. And the grandmother is even more of a mystery—and doesn't speak much English, Sylvia gathers. Sylvia realized she has no idea what goes on in that household. It's as if Gina is an orphan, living alone two miles down the road.

Now that Gina appears to have settled in, the teens have taken over most of the living space in the house. Zeke, in recovery, does little with his days besides one-handed texting and binge-watching Netflix with Farrah, who has taken on the responsibility of changing his wound dressing every other day. She's not gentle about it. She's not especially nurse-like. She practically yanks off the old dressing, rips white surgical tape with her teeth, and briskly winds his hand in clean gauze. Zeke takes a new picture of his wound—for the brief time it's exposed to air—every few days. He's making an album. He's toying with the idea of turning it into some kind of stop-motion video, so you can watch the healing progress in quick spurts, like those videos that show a flower growing from a seed to a full blossom in 10 seconds. Or maybe not.

Gina (using Zeke's bike) now bikes with Jeannie to Camp Waymore from Monday to Friday, where the two of them are immersing themselves in the care and comfort of severely disabled kids, while learning how to casually socialize with the older ones without making it seem like it's a big deal. *Everybody is somebody,* Jeannie thinks.

This evening, as Sylvia and Carson sit drinking quietly at the Haven, wondering where to begin with one another, the kids are at the house, streaming God knows what. Farrah has brought beer, and nobody asks how she got it. Jeannie and Gina sip one beer together. It doesn't do much for either of them, but then, they don't realize that their giggling grows louder and more frequent, as do their take-downs of every sexist, colorist, or racist line uttered in whatever movie or show flickers by. Zeke and Farrah drink like adults, meaning, casually, without fanfare. Farrah will make sure all the evidence is gone, out of the house, before Sylvia and Carson return. Farrah and Zeke also slip away for a while, to Zeke's room, during an especially boring stretch of movie exposition. Jeannie doesn't let herself think about this.

"I don't know, Cap," Sylvia says at the bar, as if continuing a conversation out loud that's already going on in her head. "I just don't know."

"We'll get there. We always do. We will again. Remember when we bought the house? How we panicked after we sank everything we'd saved, everything we had left over from our parents, into the down payment? We took a risk. Turned out pretty well, didn't it?" Neither of them has looked on Zillow recently, to see where their property value stands. Sylvia knows full well the market is down, quite a lot, in all of Willing. Yet she believes—or she very much wants to believe—that their house and its magnificent, unique, backyard remains a crown jewel and more to the point, a nest egg. She doesn't want to tell Cap that she doesn't have the same appetite for risk that she once did. She doesn't want to come across like a tired wife, a defeated No. 2 in the Willing real estate market. She doesn't want to feel any of that, period. "And there's still Willing Enclave," he adds, leaving it to her imagination to fill in all the blanks, which he is scrambling to fill in himself, both with, and without, his partners' cooperation and knowledge. He doesn't know Sylvia went out to the site, to see for herself.

"We haven't had Vin and Dizz over in ages," Sylvia says. "Let's have a cook-out, just like the old days. We haven't done one all summer." Sylvia hasn't exactly forgiven Vin, but he is her husband's business partner and one of their oldest friends, and she accepts that he's in their life and will remain so, as far as she can tell. And Zeke is doing okay, though it's too soon to tell if he'll regain the full use of all the muscles in his left hand.

"Sure," Carson says. "Maybe after the Fourth of July." He hasn't spoken to Vin since the hospital. They've traded only business e-mails—and short grunts at the work site. And Dizz just told Carson this morning he's taking a two-week vacation, heading off to hike the Grand Canyon with his wife Elena and his 10-year-old stepson, Greg. Needs to clear his head, he told Carson. Carson took this as Dizz's own way of saying "Fuck you." As if Carson is solely responsible for keeping Willing Prime Contractors afloat. Carson is evolving a strategy to deal with all of this. Sort of. *Containment. Keep the lid on. Keep the gears turning. Do whatever it takes. Just don't stand still. I'd fucking buy them out if I could.*

"Another round?" Sylvia asks.

"Sure. Why not."

The July picnic never materializes. Neither Sylvia nor Carson feels like entertaining, although this goes unmentioned. It's just a time crunch, they believe. And they don't have anything like a straightforward conversation about finances for the rest of the summer, either. That time crunch again.

The First Fall

Chapter Ten

LEGAL NOTICE

Notice hereby filed of the proposed acquisition of Second National Bank of Willing by Contrails Capital, LLC. Public comment period extends through Dec 20.

Cynthia Hart, proprietor of the beloved Cyn's Café, did indeed move in with Jeannie's classmate, Alison, who was Cynthia's niece. That move came at the end of a long, slow, slippery slide—a slide Cynthia didn't see coming until its inevitability was overwhelming. When Cynthia opened her café in 1989, downtown Willing was still a living, breathing organism. And this was Cynthia's dream, right out of high school: to be her own boss, and run the kind of friendly place where people want to go and hang out. In her high school yearbook, she was voted Most Likely to Succeed in Business, her photo revealing a smiling brunette with large green eyes, ready to light out into a world that surely welcomed her. Her sister and other family members each coughed up a modest stake to get her going. It didn't take much, back then. And it all seemed to come so easily, at first. Workers like Bruno and Jorge could pop into Cyn's for a cheap, fast plate of eggs and beans on toast or a decent tuna on rye. They came in droves—small droves, but steady.

Sylvia loved settling into a wooden booth at Cyn's for coffee and a fragrant cinnamon scone—a reward after a string of client meetings, when the promise of fat commissions gave her a glowing sense of satisfaction. If the place wasn't too busy—which come to think of it, was pretty often—Cyn would join Sylvia in the booth to share town gossip.

Sylvia never once asked her how the business was doing; it seemed like an intrusive question. Plus, this seemed like the kind of place that would go on forever, because why wouldn't it? And Cynthia never seemed to have a care in the world; she wiped counters, rang up orders, talked affectionate trash with her short-order cook in the kitchen (just the one cook), with breezy, cheerful efficiency. She made the baked goods herself, beginning at four o'clock every morning.

But anybody looking at Cynthia's books would clearly see that customer traffic had been declining fairly steadily for as long as 10 years. Downtown Willing, the living, breathing organism, was gasping for air. By the time Cyn's closed, the café, like much of Main Street, had been on life support for months. She had to let her cook go; they both cried when she told him. And soon Cynthia lost everything: her business, her own modest home, and most of all, her purpose. Cynthia was married to the café; it was the love of her life. She was forced to declare bankruptcy, and still, some creditors were hounding her. She moved in with her brother, and felt ashamed when her brother insisted that she take Alison's room, while Alison moved into a tiny spare room that had to be cleared of junk.

It was Alison who found her in the morning, a week ago. She needed something from her old room, and was surprised to see Cynthia still in bed. Cynthia had taken every pill she could find in the medicine cabinet. Alison saw Cynthia's gray face, and a trail of white foam dribbling from the corner of her mouth. She screamed and ran from the room. There was a short note on the nightstand: *Sorry I let everybody down.*

Sylvia holds a massive black umbrella, her other hand gripping the neck of her beloved lavender coat against the wet chill.

Why does it always rain at funerals?

She scours her memory for signs that Cyn's—and Cynthia—were in trouble. But all she comes up with is the fragrance of her favorite scone. Carson, getting soaked without an umbrella, his black trench beaded with rain, is wondering when another tenant will fill Cyn's space, or whether the building will be sold. Come to think of it, he should see who owns that property. It's probably ripe for a fire sale.

When downtown recovers, there'll be a neat profit to take.

Afterwards, Sylvia and Carson walk back up the hill from the gravesite toward the parking lot, sharing the umbrella.

"There are so many places where real estate and construction are booming right now," Carson says. "Like Dallas. And Phoenix. And North Dakota, for God's sake. I'm just saying." He doesn't tell her he's itching to buy something, even if the capital to make that happen isn't immediately available.

"Did I tell you? I have two new listing appointments this week. I think it's a sign that things are turning around. I think this slow-down has really run its course." Sylvia doesn't tell her husband that the market value of these two properties is less than half of what she is used to handling, which translates into miniscule commissions when she gets these sold—and she will get them sold. Betty Bachman had dumped the listings paperwork on her desk, with no discussion, treating her like a junior associate being thrown a bone, rather than the senior broker she actually is. Perhaps most humiliating of all is where these properties are located: in the 1970s tract-home belt not far from the office, where Sylvia never imagined handling properties, even when she was just starting out.

"Yeah, I think so too—the turn-around is in sight," Carson says, willing this mutual optimism to radiate out into the universe and become true, just as all their success up to this point has come true because they worked for it, earned it, made it happen. *Nothing is beyond your control if you take control.*

After the funeral, Carson disappears into his study, but not before pouring a generous tumbler of bourbon. The twins, now in their junior year, are off doing Saturday things. Gina has moved back to her own house, secretly relieved to do so. Sylvia, listless, goes out to the back deck, which is finally devoid of teenagers. She looks out over the yard and sees a family of rabbits hopping near the shadows. She leans back on a damp recliner and closes her eyes, her face tilted toward the last of the summer-strength sunshine that has popped out after the morning's rain…

Now, suddenly, all the grass, the entire acreage, has been trampled into dirt. Nylon tents cover the yard. Cooking fires send up columns of white and black smoke. She can smell the smoke…

The vision is horrifyingly familiar, as if it's been lying in wait for months, coiled and ready to spring when she least expects it. Sylvia opens her eyes and sits up. The rabbits are still in the yard. The yard smells earthy, giving off the first scent of autumn leaf decay. She inhales. There is no smoke.

I should have known Cynthia was in trouble. I should know more than I do. I must get better at seeing the signs. Listening for alarms. Sensing trouble before it begins. I need to be alert.

Sylvia rises slowly. Her whole body feels heavy and sleepy, the antithesis of alert, as though she's been drinking, but she has not. She considers going upstairs to lie down. Perhaps the funeral took more out of her than she realizes. But no. The refrigerator is nearly empty, again, and many staples are missing from the pantry. The teen locusts have taken their toll. A major grocery trip is unavoidable. Sylvia takes her keys and her purse, and slowly walks out to her car, without a word to Carson. She pulls into the ShopFine parking lot and heads towards the row of shopping carts lined up parallel to the automatic sliding front doors. She cannot shake the feeling that she is sleepwalking; a tent flap whipping back and forth in a stiff wind keeps crossing her vision. She pulls a cart away from the pack, but before she crosses the threshold, she sees something else, something real to her left: a woman who looks familiar sits a few feet away from the doors, leaning against the wall of the market, her knees awkwardly drawn up against a large belly, her legs splayed open, a thin dress stretched tightly across them and barely reaching to her calves. On any other day, Sylvia would almost certainly not notice this woman. She would speed right in to the market to get the shopping over with, her mind on a big to-do list: phone calls to be returned, home inspections to follow up on, open houses and home stagers to schedule. And oh, yes, commission checks to deposit. But not today. Not on the day that Cynthia Hart is buried, her cheerful café curdling into sorrowful nostalgia. And not today because the truth is, Sylvia does not have a big to-do list at the moment.

Sylvia releases her cart and walks over to the woman on the ground. "Are you okay? Do you need some help? Do you want me to call someone?"

The woman tugs on a stretched-out sweater, and folds her arms across her chest. She appears to be in her sixties, though it's hard to tell. Her face appears drawn, though her body is large. Her silver hair is wiry, uncombed. "Mrs. King?" Sylvia is startled. She cannot place this woman, yet she is certain she has seen her, more than once. "Winnie Suggs." Sylvia stands there, looking down, embarrassed by the one-sided recognition. She wonders if she should offer to help the woman get up. "I guess you never really noticed my name tag. Customers usually don't. Just part of the furniture, ain't we?"

"I'm so sorry, I…"

"I suppose you been through my check-out line—" Winnie points to the supermarket— "hundreds of times. Maybe thousands. I don't know. It sure feels like thousands."

Sylvia puts it together. Winnie Suggs has worked at ShopFine, forever. Sylvia calculates rapidly that she and Carson have been shopping here since they moved in. The store has changed hands a few times, as big chains swallowed up smaller chains, but Winnie Suggs has been working the register the entire time. To be fair, Sylvia really only sees her from the waist up, and certainly never on the ground, all curled up. She sees, now, that Winnie wears the store uniform under her ragged sweater.

"Ms. Suggs," says Sylvia, using her name for the first time in 16 years. She suddenly realizes she's never said more to this woman in all that time beyond 'Hello,' or 'I sure am ready for spring,' or 'Yes, I found everything I needed.' "I didn't—I should have known. Of course. Um, how are you?" *Stupid.*

"Just fine, Mrs. King. Just taking a moment to sort things out, get things straight in my own mind."

"Are you sure I can't"—Sylvia pulls out her cell phone and waves it. Now that she and Winnie are talking, Sylvia figures she's somehow complicit in the *problem*, whatever it is, and that she is now morally obligated to help solve it. Calling somebody, even a cab, to take Winnie away where she'll be someone else's problem, is what Sylvia hopes to accomplish. Someone else has wheeled her cart into the market.

"No, I got my own phone, Mrs. King. I'm just, like I said, taking a moment here."

"Oh…Well, if you're sure you're all right, and there's nothing I can do..." Sylvia takes a small step back.

"Sometimes," Winnie says, "when you get real bad news, you just gotta stop in your tracks, turn things over in your mind. You can't do nothin' else, for a bit. You know what I mean?"

Sylvia purses her lips. She doesn't know what to say. She's afraid Winnie is about to tell her that her child was murdered, or died in combat in an overseas skirmish, or that she's just learned she has terminal cancer, which looks possible.

"Mr. Bill, he fired me, just like that," Winnie continues. *Oh, is that all,* Sylvia thinks. *There are at least two other grocery stores in Willing. Surely these types of jobs are always available. It's not like putting everything you have into a café, making a success of it, and then losing it all. Oh, God, maybe she's thinking about killing herself.* "Says I been clocking in late. Says I can't remember the look-up codes as good as everybody else. So I spend too much time looking them up. Holdin' up the line, he says. I think Mr. Bill just plain don't like me, and that's all the reason he needs to fire me. And there ain't a thing I can do about it."

"I *am* sorry," Sylvia says, wondering now how to end the conversation. "Maybe you can take a little vacation now, you know, rest up, before you look for another job."

Winnie laughs, then shrugs, then coughs. Then she lights a cigarette. "I never been on vacation. No money, is all. It's that simple. But it's a nice idea."

"Well...I wish you all the best. I mean, I wish you luck finding a new job quickly."

"Thanks for stopping by, Mrs. King," Winnie says, as if they were old friends. "Go on now. Get your shopping done."

Sylvia turns away and feels her cheeks burning, but what can she do? What's to be done? She wheels a cart into the store and gets through the shopping as quickly as possible. When she comes out, Winnie is gone, and Sylvia wonders if she moved to another spot, just to save Sylvia the embarrassment of figuring out how to say goodbye and still save face. And then she wonders if she, Sylvia, were in Winnie's shoes, would she be capable of thinking of someone other than herself?

Chapter Eleven

Darius is sitting at their regular table near the far side of the bar at the Haven. He's always the first of the three to arrive and he likes it that way. Gives him time to think about what they need to accomplish—and how to plot his own arguments. Carson has always been the fast talker of the group, the first to score points or float an idea, which he and Vin fall in with, often as not, if only because it's easier than arguing. Darius often thinks the reason the partnership has lasted as long as it has is not because they know each other so well, or even because they were making money for a good stretch of years, but because he and Vin habitually defer to Carson without fully realizing that's what they're doing. Darius really did spend part of his Grand Canyon vacation thinking about this—thinking about what he really wants at this stage of his life, and how to get it. He and Elena sat up late one night on the porch of their cabin, admiring the sunset and the outstanding views of the north rim of the canyon, talking about the fact that Greg would be starting college in just eight years. And they had saved only a fraction of what they'd need. They admitted that this trip, which cost a fortune, would probably be the last of its kind for a long, long time.

What does a midlife crisis feel like? Darius wonders. Does it feel like you want to quit everything and just start over? Does it mean you question everything you've done up to this point? Darius is feeling rudderless. His dad, born in Athens, was only five years away from retiring when he was Darius' age now, 48. His small self-funded pension from running two dry cleaning businesses for nearly 30 years, coupled with a few good blue-chip stock investments, sustained a quiet, uneventful retirement. But by the time he died, at 97, every penny of his modest savings was gone. The reverse mortgage on his small house proved a disaster, and Darius inherited nothing but some faded family photos and his dad's rusted out Chevrolet. Darius cannot imagine ever retiring, yet he doesn't know if he wants to stay in construction, either. He also can't imagine bringing this up to his friends and partners. He doesn't want to look like a quitter. And he assumes they're not feeling as demoralized as he is. Carson is a relentless optimist and plotter. Vin is, well, pretty placid, a go-along-get-along kind of guy. Vin lives alone; he doesn't need a lot, Darius thinks. It takes a lot to rile Vin, he thinks, but then, he wasn't at the hospital when Vin had the blow-up with Carson.

Sitting at the sticky wooden table at the Haven, drinking a beer, Darius is especially glum because of the *Wall Street Journal* article that's up on his phone screen. It's a front-page story about the perfect storm confronting much of the U.S. residential construction industry: rising labor costs (brought on, ironically, by *demand* for housing), rising material costs (tariffs are fucking everybody sideways), rising interest rates, and a new wave of bank mergers that make lending tighter and more expensive (for borrowers) than ever. The article goes on to document other economic trends affecting new-home construction, ranging from the impact of crushing student debt on young adults' ability to buy any home, let alone a new home, all the way to the decline of aging suburbs, as malls collapse and retirees hang onto their homes while squeezing out cash by way of reverse mortgages and other things designed to shore up an aging population with declining incomes and reduced spending power.

Darius isn't sure he quite understands how all these different trends fit together, but one thing is clear: Willing Prime Contractors is in deep shit, and if he and his partners don't find a way out soon, then the end is in sight. And even though Darius is feeling restive, feeling ready to switch up his life, maybe even leave Willing entirely, and move with Elena and Greg to the desert beauty of Arizona, the prospect of his business crashing and burning is terrifying and depressing. He really can't picture what would come next.

He stares at the article and circles back. If labor rates are going up, why did they fire Bruno and Jorge, who were under-paid to begin with? What did that accomplish? Whose idea was it—and why did he just go along with it? What are they doing now? Darius wonders. Did they find other work? Maybe they're happily employed at Touchstone, or Whitney-Blanchard, drilling away, sawdust flying…while Willing Enclave sits nearly still, progress slowing to a barely perceptible crawl. But surely the conditions so brutally described in the *Journal* article will catch up with these companies, too, if they haven't already. And then where will they all be?

Carson and Vin arrive within a few minutes of each other. They need only wave to the bar, and their drinks will appear. "You see this?" Darius asks, holding up his phone in front of their eyes. "We're fucked," he says. He doesn't mean for this to slip out, but it actually feels good just putting it out there. Carson and Vin don't seem interested. Or aware. Darius thinks maybe *he's* the big-picture guy here, not Carson.

"You know what's fucked?" Vin says. "Main Street. Looks like everybody's folding up their tent. Not just Cyn's. The old head shop is closed now, too. And that crappy Chinese take-out place that's been there forever. Space for lease, it says." Vin shakes his head.

"Let's buy up the whole block," Carson says. The guys snort. That's Cap. "This is real estate 101. Buy when the market's down. Hold on. And when it comes back—"

"It's not coming back, Cap," Darius says. "Get serious."

"I *am* serious." Carson swigs a beer. "Everything is cyclical. You don't make a killing when the market is booming."

"Even if I *wanted* to do that, where's the money coming from?" Darius asks, knowing full well there is no rational answer, no matter what Carson says.

"Look," Vin says, pulling out a piece of paper from his wallet, on which he's scribbled a numbered list written in thick contractor's pencil. "Let's focus on our own bottom line. We're about to run through our entire reserve account just to meet our loan obligations."

"We know, Vin," Carson says testily. "We need revenue, obviously.

I have an idea about that." Here it comes, Darius thinks. Carson will talk fast and get them to agree to something before they've really thought it through. Not this time, Darius thinks. Not anymore. "We pre-sell the Enclave properties. All of them. Now because they're not finished, we have to lower our prices. But if we make some really great renderings, and we set them up on easels, at the property, and hold a kind of rough-and-tumble outdoor open house for brokers and buyers. A website too, of course..." Carson pauses to see how he's being received. *This is a fucking brilliant idea. And now I'll sit here while they hem and haw. I'm sick of this shit.* Darius and Vin raise their beer bottles to their lips, exchanging a split-second glance. Carson is used to these silent little sidebars. He already knows what they think, about nearly everything, so he's not missing anything, in his view.

"Sell all six before they're built? With half of them just foundation holes?" Vin asks.

"That's what I just said, Vin," Carson says, tapping his fingers on the table. "Do you have a better idea?"

"Even if we do that, all the revenue will go to service our debt," Darius says. "So it's not really an answer." The partners had, after surprisingly little discussion, agreed to ask Second National for a high-interest term loan—one of the unpalatable options put on the table by Tom Jergens a few months ago. But they'd all reached the same conclusion then, which was that they had to keep going; pulling the plug on the business they'd worked so hard to build from scratch was not yet an imaginable, or honorable, option. They were now in the difficult position of needing to pay back this high interest loan (Jergens had warned them) as well as pay down their maxed-out line of credit. They're well aware that, from the bank's perspective, the onus is on them to figure out how to do this. The bank is no babysitter. The "F" word—foreclosure—is not in their vocabulary. Not yet.

Vin shakes his head. "What happened to us? Where'd this shit-storm come from? Three years ago, we had spec projects going flat-out all over Willing and we made a profit every quarter for, how many years? A lot of years." He looks down, shakes his head again. "What did I miss?"

"Everything runs its course," Darius says.

"Maybe…" Vin hesitates. "Maybe we should talk to Nick French." Nick French owns Touchstone, the contracting firm that's getting better terms on bulk gypsum wallboards from Sandy Tipper.

"Nick's a complete asshole!" Carson says. "He doesn't pull permits, half the time! OSHA has fined him at least twice! I'll never get in bed with French! He'll only drag us down. And he's arrogant as shit. You wanna get into bed with that motherfucker? Go right ahead, but you'll do it without me. No, we gotta double-down."

"What's that mean?" Darius asks.

"Cash out our retirement funds. Pre-sell the houses. Restructure the loans with Second National," Carson says. Darius and Vin are silent.

Darius leans forward. "Ain't happening, Cap."

Vin sighs, wishing, pointlessly (he knows), that they could just turn the clock back and build nice homes that sold quickly for a tidy profit. He also wishes he could find a woman to love, who wouldn't drive him up a tree after three months. That's how it's supposed to work. How it's *all* supposed to work. Anything but this drip, drip, drip… He looks around the Haven while Carson and Darius try to one-up each other (they don't even know they're doing it, Vin observes). The Haven isn't living up to its name, either, any more. It's just another low-rent, sticky bar. And not much fun, for anybody, judging by the glum, hunched looks of the other patrons. Probably mice in the back room, Vin thinks, his mind wandering off the painful present.

"Well, then," Carson says with a bitter edge, "maybe we should all take up gambling." They all laugh, ruefully, breaking the tension a little. Carson doesn't tell them, he's already doing exactly that.

Chapter Twelve

At first, it's just an experiment. Just for fun. Just to see if he can. He'll learn what's out there, where the action is. Pick up a few tips, maybe. And if he keeps the stakes small enough, then it's a good investment in his business education—with a potential upside in the form of much needed cash, none of which he intends to declare on his taxes. *All business is a gamble, anyway; this is just a more direct approach.* It's Thursday night and Carson, back from the unproductive meeting at the Haven earlier, is at his small desk in the alcove, peering at his laptop. A desk lamp shines down on his blond head and is answered by the glow of the computer screen. He is otherwise shrouded in darkness. Family dinners seem to be a thing of the past; perhaps it's another sign the kids are growing up, Carson thinks. They are off doing homework, he assumes, or at least, homework is getting done alongside other online activities. He also assumes that Sylvia, glued to her own computer, is catching up on real estate paperwork, analyzing listings, perhaps even reading the online obituaries to identify properties that might be ripe for listing. *Willing Enclave will be on that list—soon.*

When Carson thinks about his family these days, heck, when he *listens* to them, it's through a haze of distraction. Zeke let it drop the other day, when he and Carson were surfing channels together in the living room, that he's joining the debate team at school. It's a license to mouth off, he thinks, and besides, getting credit for arguing? What could be better? Carson thinks he must've said something complimentary, something encouraging to Zeke. But the whole time the TV was on, Carson was thinking of many other things at once—his new online poker strategy; the pre-sales scheme at Enclave; whether he and Dizz and Vin could literally build those houses themselves, and not take any paychecks while doing it; whether there's another hand to play with Tom Jergens at the bank. And: What does "tapped out" really look like?

Carson dislikes the word "gambling" because it sounds irresponsible, as well as hapless. He believes he is taking calculated risks—risks that involve intelligence, cunning, strategy, and yes, some luck, but doesn't everything in life require some luck? Weren't he and Dizz and Vin lucky they started their business when they did, at the beginning of a long boom cycle in home construction? They didn't realize they were getting in on that, at the time. But in hindsight it's clear that they had the wind at their backs for a long time. Of course, it wasn't merely luck that enabled them to build, at its peak, a $250 million business—depending on how you counted assets and liquidity. They were smart about picking projects—where, when, at what price point. They were smart about the parcels they bought to develop. They took calculated risks. *And that's what I'm doing now, just in a different arena. You have to move forward or die. No standing still.* He isn't sentimental about poker, even though he had a good run in college, doing this sort of thing, in a modest sort of way, playing real-time games. Why not take it up again, now that he's older, wiser, steadier, and try to capitalize on the quiet anonymity that online gaming affords? He plays 7-card stud, Omaha rules, Texas Hold'em, and whatever game looks promising. Now, after a cautious start, Carson is up by $50,000. All on the down-low, for now. Maybe use the cash to make a low-ball offer for the Baker block on the south end of Main Street, in downtown Willing.

The Baker block is a series of four attached commercial buildings, all built in the 1880s from the same handsome, dark sand-colored stone. The Baker name is etched into the stone, just under the roof lintel in the center of the group. Baker's identity is long forgotten, but his entrepreneurial spirit endures. These buildings are solidly made, to Carson's professional eye. They just need some sprucing up, new plate glass, maybe fresh paint on the front doors and trim. They're just waiting for their turn in the limelight—for their turn to step back on stage and play a starring role in the next act in the commercial life of a town that could really benefit from some calculated risks and, yes, a little luck, too.

Carson can see it, he can almost taste it: A modest investment in the downtown core that's ripe for all kinds of invigorating reinvestments to bring people back into Willing. New restaurants a lot hipper than Cyn's. Maybe an art gallery or two. Why not a hookah bar? A wine bar, too. A virtual gaming spot, for the kids? It's time to give the sodden Haven a run for its money. Done right, the monied crowd from Linton Crossing and places like that will make a point of patronizing Willing's Main Street. A sort of 'refreshed quaint.' *Maybe I should write that down.* A decade from now, Carson imagines he will be recognized and celebrated as the visionary who got the ball rolling again, who put the step back into Main Street. It's not impossible. In fact, it's distinctly possible. Why let somebody else get the credit for his vision? Why can't *he* be the next Baker? *No guts, no glory.*

Sylvia is on her laptop. Carson is right about that. She's sitting on top of the covers, on their rumpled king-sized bed. *A king for the Kings.* That had been the joke, back in the day. But she isn't cruising obituaries. Not right now, anyway. She's reading an e-mail from a guy who came with his wife to see one of the nondescript split-level homes she's taken on not by choice, but because Betty Bachman "asked" her to. They've seen it twice, now. And the second time through, Sylvia was hoping they'd fish or cut bait. She wasn't going to walk them through it again. There wasn't that much to see, in the first place. White vinyl-clad siding. Black shutters. Two small, ugly bathrooms. Outdated fixtures. Too much carpeting. A tiny yard (especially by Sylvia's standards) that peered openly into three other surrounding yards. The e-mail says:

Dear Mrs. King:

Thank you for showing us 35 Kelsey Drive. We've thought about it alot, and we think we need to hold off. We really like it, but the truth is, and we should have told you, we haven't been able to sell our condo so we can't put a down payment on anything. And it might be more than we can aford anyway. So, thanks for showing us the house. Maybe one day, right? We hope so!

Sylvia is incensed. Disgusted. Ashamed. These are not the kind of people she is used to dealing with. *They can't even spell. They don't deserve to waste my time.* This is not the caliber of property that the No. 2 listing agent in Greater Willing is accustomed to handling. Perhaps *any* sale, or potential sale, is a good sale, but Sylvia can't quite see it this way. This is not the level of commission—*potential* commission—that she should have to work for, at this stage of her career—or life, for that matter. In fact, this is exactly the point in her life when she should be at the top of her game, working only with the cream of the crop in properties and clients. This is what she's worked toward, since the early days of married life. And what's the point, really, if you put in the work and the time, you make progress, you do better, you get better, you get your hands on the lever of market forces—and then something shifts, the lever slips from your hands. Time seems to be moving sideways, rather than forward.

A sacrilegious thought creeps in: Progress is no longer something you count on, it's something you bargain for.

There was a day, a golden day, about 18 years ago. Sylvia and Carson had been married less than two years, not quite ready to start their family, but basking in the certainty that becoming parents was one in a series of gifts they knew they could claim at any point. On this particular day, both rushed home to their apartment—the second floor in an old boarding house about a five minutes' walk from Main Street—glowing with news. Sylvia, newly armed with a license to sell real estate, had been hired by Bachman Realty. She was to start as an associate on Monday. Carson and his partners had secured their first loan with Second National, which meant they could buy the old Howard mansion on the outskirts of Willing Heights, raze it, and build the row of modest two-bedroom houses they had excitedly sketched on napkins at the Haven. There was no way they'd lose money on this deal. They were right. And Sylvia earned her first commission within 30 days. She held the commission check up in the air. She and Carson poured whiskey into shot glasses and toasted that commission check, before depositing it into the bank.

Sylvia forces herself now to open the spreadsheet she uses to track her commissions. The spreadsheet goes back over a decade. The line goes up continuously for most of that time, keeping her securely in the No. 2 spot. Then it begins to dip. She stares at an inverted "V." It resembles a bumpy mountain with a treacherous downslope. Like the family vacation they took when the kids were little, hiking Mt. Chocorua in New Hampshire. The climb up was fun. They sang songs. Ate lunch at the top. But the climb down was agony—her knees screamed, her back ached, and she had blisters on two toes. *Nothing good comes of going down.* Sylvia opens a new browser. She clicks to the site of a favorite retailer. There's the lavender coat with the pretty buttons she wears. And there are new skirts, and blouses, and trousers with a flattering cut, all of which call out to Sylvia, the proverbial mountain-climber. None of these clothes can be purchased in Willing. As a commercial town, she thinks, Willing is almost more of an idea now, than a reality. It is a town that *was,* now partially extinct.

I am not a dying town.

She puts several items into her online basket and checks out.

Chapter Thirteen

Javier Martinez stands with arms crossed on the gravel parking pad outside his company, Vida. The only remaining delivery van is parked at an angle, the back doors flung open. The white truck needs washing, and the red and turquoise lettering on the side of the van is chipping; the dot over the "i" in Vida is nearly gone. These imperfections are like a fresh spout of lava emanating from Javier's constantly erupting inner volcano. He is holding off on getting the van freshly detailed, however, as cash flow must go toward serving what is left of his customer base and his route structure. Javier watches Bruno Fernandez and Jorge Garcia load canisters and supplies into the back of the van. He needs to be sure they secure the hazardous equipment properly, just as he has taught them. Javier pays them one delivery run at a time. They take it; they do not grumble. Construction work is so sporadic these days, every odd job is welcome. While all three men were raised as children in Mexico, the two construction workers have little in common with Javier. Bruno and Jorge are reasonably satisfied with cash in hand, so long as there is enough to feed their families, repair their own cars, and watch soccer on the weekend. Neither of them wants or expects much beyond basic creature comforts. Having achieved that, more or less, they both feel so far ahead of where they started—the grinding poverty and violence of Sinaloa decades ago—this is a big enough step forward. And besides, these days, around Willing, at least, dreaming about more, or wanting more, seems pointless. It just isn't there for the taking.

Javier will not revert to being a one-man operation. There is only so much turning back one man can stand. By throwing a little money at Jorge and Bruno, Javier can still be the CEO of Vida. He can hide out in his little, undecorated office and continue looking for ways out of the squeeze play that's killing his business. Most days, he feels like a mouse that's been swallowed by a python, and he wonders if the mouse, in those final moments, as it begins drowning in the digestive juices of the python, as its tiny bones are squeezed until they break inside the python's dark gullet, if the mouse still thinks about finding a way to escape its fate.

"Pull those straps tighter," Javier tells Bruno. The three men converse in Spanish, but the shared language does not mean there is a shared bond. "Like this." Javier climbs into the back of the van to show Bruno how tightly to cinch the strap holding each oxygen canister in place. Bruno nodes. Jorge emerges from the building wheeling a hand truck stacked with more canisters and equipment. The men continue to load the van, as Javier watches. Once the loading is finished—and it goes relatively quickly, as the payload is small—Javier goes over the delivery route loaded on a tablet. "Get in, get out, and don't get in anybody's way," he tells them. "Be sure to get a signature on every delivery. Put gas in the van before you bring it back. The cheapest gas is on Caliber Road. Go there. Here." He hands Jorge a gas credit card. "For gas only," he says. "Nothing else goes on this card." Both men nod. They are wearing grimy caps and dark blue Vida coveralls, which Javier insists they wear for deliveries. This is still a business and there is a tone that must be maintained. The men climb into the cab of the van. "If anyone has any questions, tell them to call me. Got it?" The men nod again. They drive off. Bruno turns on the FM radio in the van, and finds the Spanish station he likes, playing upbeat music. He turns the volume up. They roll the windows down. Jorge gnaws on a giant Slim Jim. *Podría ser peor*, both think. It could be worse.

Javier watches the van disappear around the bend, the lava roiling in his gut. Javier has never been to Canada, and had never thought much about the northern portion of North America until Canada's largest medical equipment supply company, known as MedCan, decided a few years ago that, in the wake of a sudden diplomatic thaw between the U.S. and its northern neighbor, it was time to expand into the states. Now, if Javier could wield a powerful chainsaw that would enable him to cut Canada loose from the lower 48 states, he would do so and spit on them, and call on all his ancestors to curse them, as they float away toward the Arctic Circle. MedCan's expert consultants devised an expansion plan that happened to include Willing and the surrounding area as part of a large, complex, multi-faceted campaign to penetrate large swaths of territory across much of the country. MedCan's method of accomplishing this is as old as business itself: They under-price rivals, reduce order and delivery times, and reward loyal customers with even deeper discounts and 24/7 technical assistance. Plus, they are able to offer aggressively low prices on a variety of other medical products apart from the gas business—everything from hospital gowns to surgical beds and back-up generators. Javier never saw them coming. How could he? For years, now, he had been expanding his routes, and his customers, turning on all the charm he could muster, to ensure he had their confidence and their business. The last new customer to sign an agreement with Javier 15 months ago was a small, community hospital nearly 100 miles southwest of Willing. The week he signed that deal, when he sat down to Sunday dinner with his mother and Gina, he was as close to happy as he'd been since Eugenia had gotten sick. His family could hardly tell, as he remained his usual taciturn self, but he allowed himself a Cerveza in the evening, and watched Gina clear dishes, with tears of love in his eyes. Just two months later, the hospital CEO called Javier to tell him they were switching suppliers for medical gases. Javier, taking in the news on his cellphone, began pacing his tiny office.

"May I ask why?" Javier said.

"MedCan," the hospital executive replied.

"Who?"

"You know. MedCan. They're offering us better terms, and access to some things you can't supply. We don't get a lot of choices, out here in the sticks, so this is going to help our bottom line, tremendously. I'm sure you understand."

Javier did not understand, at first. It never occurred to him that MedCan, which he knows by reputation, of course, from trade journals and conferences, could want anything to do with Willing, or anything near Willing. But he was wrong, and he hates himself, still, for leaving a flank exposed, even if there is nothing he could actually do about it. In a matter of months, Javier could see he was the mouse, MedCan was the python, and he tried everything he could think of to break away from the death grip. He visited every single account, barely getting home at night for a few hours of sleep, before getting back on the road to travel his 150-mile radius of business. He tried to impress upon his customers the advantage of working with a local vendor, a vendor who feels responsible to the community, and who is able to provide personal service. What if a canister valve should fail in the middle of the night? (Not that this was likely to happen, he explained, but it could.) Javier could personally drive out a replacement—or ensure that one of his sales reps could.

But nothing he did stopped the python from tightening its grip. And one by one, all but his smallest accounts fell away from him. His agreements with his customers were just that—agreements, not iron-clad contracts. He cursed himself for his courtly ways, for operating on a handshake, which has always seemed an honorable way to do business, rather than a written contract filled with all kinds of restrictive clauses and implied threats. He berated himself for not spending the extra money on a lawyer to help him lock in these customers, for years on end. If he'd done that, if he'd been more cut-throat, he wouldn't be in this position, he thinks, bitterly. Instead, he trusted his instinct, he trusted the people who trusted him. And where did that get him? Vida's revenues plunged down to where they'd been a decade ago, when he was just building up the business. First, he sold off two of his vans. Then, he let his office manager go. Then the part-time sales rep who had been brought on to begin scouting business opportunities outside Vida's current territory. Finally, Javier had to fire Fran Hauser, the first sales rep he had hired. He called her into his office and sat her down. He was so angry at the situation, Fran thought he was angry with her.

"No, no," he told her. "This is all my fault. But I cannot...," he faltered. "Soon, I cannot pay you."

"Javier, if this is just a temporary setback, I can last without one paycheck," Fran said. She is a widow, over 60 now, and out of work a long time before Javier hired her for a position so unglamorous, he found it hard to fill. Who wanted to provide customer service and support to mid-level administrators in small nursing homes and hospitals, with a focus on therapeutic medical gases? It involved a lot of driving, a lot of dull paperwork, and a product line that doesn't set hearts racing. But Fran wanted it, and she was good at it. And Javier respected her work ethic and her status as a widow.

Javier shook his head. He looked grim. "No, no," he said again. "This big company, this python from Canada, it's killing me." Fran turned pale. She cannot imagine landing a new job in Willing—not at her age, not in this line of work, not given the economy. She knew, in a flash, she might have to reach out to MedCan herself, and she assumed that Javier already knew this too. She gave Javier a brief, stiff hug that left them both even more uncomfortable. He took out his wallet and held out several bills, unable to look her in the eye. She shook her head, put her office keys on his desk, and walked out. Javier locked the front door as soon as her car pulled away. He returned to his office, picked up his coffee mug, and hurled it against the wall as hard as he could, leaving milky, brown streaks trickling down toward the floor, now littered with shattered crockery.

Jorge and Bruno return the van on time. They tell Javier all the deliveries were made without incident. Nobody asked any questions. Jorge and Bruno are not fools; they have seen the shabby nursing homes that do the minimum for indigent, aging residents whose lives depend on Medicaid and a paltry Social Security check, if that. They see there are no respectable hospitals on the route. They see a fellow Mexican suffering, but there is nothing they can do. No help they can render. No words of wisdom or consolation that will make any difference, or change any reality. It is what it is. Javier pays them from his own pocket. The two workers nod, strip off their coveralls, and stuff the money in their jeans before heading to their own pickups. None of the three men has earned enough today to count toward necessities, let alone dreams about the future. Javier walks back inside and stares at the metal shelves that occupy most of the floor space. For years, these shelves were so fully stocked, top to bottom, Javier had begun thinking about where else he could put inventory. Now, they stand three-quarters empty, mocking him with their metallic, gleaming uselessness. He can't imagine what he will tell Gina—or if he will tell her anything at all.

THE FIRST WINTER

Chapter Fourteen

FOR SALE BY OWNER

Willing Tobacco. 354-B Main St. 400 sq. ft. Furnishings also available. Seller motivated.

SHORT SALE

Dean's Bric-a-Brac. 267 Berkley St. Willing. Property damaged by water. Contact Second National Bank, Willing Branch.

Inside the empty store that used to be Cyn's Café, Jeannie King is explaining to a gaggle of volunteers how the winter coat drive works. Spread out along the long wooden counter that was a coffee bar, and long before that, an old-fashioned soda fountain, are bags and boxes filled with donated coats in every size, shape, and color. Jeannie assigns one group to empty and sort the coats, based on whether they seem to be men's, women's, or children's. There are a couple of racks with plenty of hangers, so as the sorting progresses, other volunteers will hang them up and tape labels to the racks, using Post-its and markers Jeannie has provided. Jeannie is not entirely sure this is the best system, but it's what she's come up with, and she's discovering that people generally don't mind being told what to do, as long as you ask them politely. Some of the volunteers are Jeannie's high school classmates, but many are adults. Fran Hauser, Javier Martinez's former sales rep, is there, but Jeannie doesn't know her, and wouldn't know that Fran knows exactly what it feels like to teeter on the edge of insolvency, to feel as though you'll never be able to buy a warm coat again.

MedCan, it turns out, brought in its own people and they weren't interested in hiring anyone from a two-bit competitor.

Sylvia has promised to stop by to lend a hand, but Jeannie isn't counting on it, and therefore does not expect to be disappointed when Sylvia doesn't show up. Her dad and her brother showed no interest when she casually mentioned at home one evening that she had organized this whole thing. Actually, what Carson said was, "That's great, Jeannie. Good for you," and then he disappeared into his office. Zeke simply grunted and kept his eyes on his phone.

The idea came to Jeannie in a flash, in the middle of history class. The class was looking at projections from a website about the Great Depression. There were photographs of men and women in long lines, waiting for food. They looked cold and their coats appeared thin and torn. *Is this happening now, right here in Willing?* Jeannie wondered. *The man at the bus stop. The woman near Gina's house. Maybe there are people like this all over. You just have to see them. Why isn't anybody talking about this?* At home, Jeannie went online and started reading the local newspaper, the *Willing Courier News.* She doesn't read the newspaper, as a rule. Her information about the issues and causes she cares about are splashed all over social media, and it's hard enough to keep up. *But maybe I've just been stupid, or blind,* she thought. So she searched the *Courier News* for articles about people who were desperate, people who were hungry, or homeless. There was nothing. Not one article. The paper was filled with stories about the local Eagle Scouts going on a winter wilderness camping trip, a home economics teacher who had just died at the age of 101, and recipes for healthy winter soups. *What a load of shit*, Jeannie thought. *You can't see it, but it's there. And they're too embarrassed to write about it. Or maybe they just don't care.* And she knew she'd found a mission—or the mission had found her.

She asked Alison Hart if anyone in her family still had a key to Cyn's Café, since she knew it was empty and a convenient space. Even though it had been closed for months, not even the bank that had foreclosed on the storefront had bothered changing the locks. The store had no heat or electricity, but during the day, with even a thin winter light streaming in through the large plate glass windows, this wouldn't be much of an issue—and the volunteers could keep their own coats on. Then she made posters soliciting coat donations, and road her bike around town, in the cold, putting them up on street lamps and telephone poles and anywhere she could. She made a Facebook event and shared it. She didn't ask for or expect a lot of help. This was *her* mission, *her* job.

And now, on the day of the drive itself, Jeannie is astonished to see people begin to line up outside the café. The doors are still locked, as the drive—the actual give-away—doesn't start for another half-hour. But here they are. Mostly women, but some men and some children with parents, too. Jeannie walks over to the plate glass window and looks out at the line of people, which is stretching down the block, a few blocks away from the Baker block that her father has his eyes on, unbeknownst to her. She tries not to stare, but the sight sends real shivers through her. *Just like the photograph. The Great Depression. Tired eyes. People hugging their arms because they're cold.* Jeannie turns back toward the room. Peers she's known since kindergarten have stopped sorting, or hanging, and are laughing at something on somebody's phone. This doesn't bother Jeannie a bit, because she knows, she's known for a long time, that she takes stuff like this way more seriously than other people, and it makes sense to her that she'd believe more strongly in *her* mission than anybody else ever would or could. You either get it or you don't.

"Are we ready?" Jeannie asks in a loud voice. All but the last few coats are on racks now.

"Let's do it!" says Fran Hauser. She sprints to the door, and stops. "Jeannie?"

Jeannie is suddenly nervous; she has butterflies in her stomach. *This is about real people. I'm helping real people.* She unlocks the door and people walk in. Within five minutes, Cyn's Café is more crowded than it was even on Cynthia's busiest day. Some of the smaller kids who'd been waiting in line have been set by their mothers onto the old red leather-topped swiveling bar stools that line the counter. The kids spin around on the stools, kicking out their legs, laughing. The adults browsing the racks work quickly and quietly. They are here because they need to be, not because they want to be. In fact, a hush has fallen over the room, except among the kids. The volunteers have all sidelined themselves, watching, but not knowing whether they should, whether it's impolite, and whether they should just sneak out now and feel good about putting in the time. Fran is not the only one who is longing for something hot to drink, maybe hot coffee with a shot of whiskey. The Haven is only steps away.

Jeannie watches a woman in her sixties, with a huge belly and wiry, silver hair that's practically sticking straight up. The woman looks uncomfortably familiar, like someone Jeannie knows, has always known, yet Jeannie cannot place her. She sees that the woman's hands and forearms are streaked with dirt, and so are her legs, which are bare and chapped. The woman finds a full-length brown wool coat with a faux-fur collar. She puts it on and closes her eyes, and she pulls the soft collar up around her face, relishing the heavy material against her skin.

The quiet business of taking off and putting on continues. People drop their own used-up coats on the floor where they stand, as they try on something that's only gently used, as good as new. A soiled down jacket with huge holes ripped in the arms, with the shiny lining buckling out, is exchanged for a fresher down jacket with a designer label, which looks barely warn. A mother yanks her young daughter's arms into a bright pink wool coat that looks like something she'd wear on a cold Easter Sunday. The girl twirls around in the coat, her thick, long hair flying out around her. She wears white sneakers with holes in the toes. *A shoe drive,* Jeannie thinks. *A food drive. An everything drive.* A thin man, nearly bald, who looks to be in his seventies, Jeannie guesses, puts on a lined baseball jacket. He looks jaunty. He used to work as a teller at the Second National Bank, but nobody here knows that, or at least, nobody seems to recognize him. Or maybe nobody cares who he was, or is, or will become. Jeannie worries whether the coat he's chosen will keep him warm enough.

Another man slips in so quietly, no one notices him amid the swirling piles and clicking hangers. He wears a rumpled plaid shirt, jeans, and scuffled work boots. He pauses, looks around, then lifts up the hinged counter panel that separates the serving side of the long lunch counter from the customer side. He stands on the serving side, slowly shaking his head, his eyes filling with tears that no one notices. This is Joe Finnegan, Cynthia Hart's former cook. He lost everything the moment she did. A widower living alone in a studio apartment on the far south side of Willing, Joe paid a call on every commercial kitchen and greasy spoon within 70 miles of home, his old Dodge Daytona leaking oil all the way. Everywhere he went, it was the same: Not right now. We'll call you when things pick up. Leave your number. Joe doesn't really need a coat; he's here to remember there was once a purpose and rhythm to his days, which he took for granted, and now he wishes he'd known how it would end. Maybe he would've saved a few more bucks, he thinks. Giving up cigars a few years ago might've made a difference in his cash situation, now. Maybe, he thinks, he can crash here at Cyn's, in the back; he knows every nook and cranny of the old place.

And then the quiet is shattered. Two women put their hands on the same coat at the same time. "No! Let go!" The woman who shouts is shouldering an enormous cotton tote bag that is bulging with things that strain the bag's fabric. All Jeannie can see, poking out of the top of the bag, is a box of Ritz crackers and a hair brush. "Carlina!" the woman shouts, and one of the girls who's been twirling on a bar stool hops down. She is so dizzy, she cannot walk straight, but she makes her way over to the woman whose hands are now gripping the coat, still on the rack. Jeannie guesses they are mother and daughter. Or maybe the mother is actually the grandmother. She can't tell. "We're going. Now!" The woman tugs on the coat, but the second woman, who is bigger and taller, reaches across and yanks it even harder from the hanger. "I need this!" the mother (or grandmother) says. "I got it first!" The second woman bunches the coat to her chest, out of reach of Carlina's mother. "You got kids? I got kids. They're cold. So'm I. Give it here. Go take yourself somethin' else." By now, everyone in Cyn's Café has paused to watch this exchange. The volunteers have their backs up against the walls, frozen, or texting on their phones as a way to absent themselves from the present reality. Those seeking coats form a ragged semi-circle around the two women, waiting to see what happens. Jeannie is terrified, embarrassed, she has no idea what to do—or if she is expected to do anything. She doesn't understand unbridled anger; she's never personally witnessed a shouting match between two adults. She suddenly feels totally inadequate, like she's built a Frankenstein and now has no idea whether, or how, to let it out into the world. She's put off by her own creation. *The coat drive is supposed to be a good thing. Just one thing. Not this thing.*

The thin, older man in the newly acquired baseball jacket steps forward. "All right, ladies. You take this outside and settle it. You take this coat and work it out between you." He can't pull the coat—a short, ivory-colored fake Persian lamb, barely soiled, with shiny glass buttons—he cannot pull it away from the woman who is clutching it. But he puts a firm hand on each of them and gently pushes them toward the door. Carlina follows her mother.

"Goddammit, that's my coat!" says Carlina's mother.

"Fuck you, bitch," says the larger woman, clutching the coat. Jeannie does not think it would even fit the larger woman, which confuses her more. *What are they fighting about? What's going on?* But the women respond to the man's gentle pressure, like a reflex, and they walk out of the café, onto the sidewalk, where they argue, loudly, for several minutes. Carlina, shivering in her old coat, which her mother did not replace, blows steam onto the plate glass, drawing smiley faces on the smeared-up window, the window that used to be filled with posters advertising specialty coffee drinks and the morning muffin...corn, blueberry, chocolate chip. The girl waits patiently for the argument to end. Jeannie stares out the window, wondering if the police will need to get involved, and how that even works. She suddenly feels way out of her depth, totally inadequate, and *What do I think I'm doing? Who do I think I am?* And then, quickly, the woman holding the ivory coat hands it to Carlina's mother and walks away—but not before spitting on the mother's shoes. Carlina's mother appears calm. She takes Carlina's hands, and they walk away. She doesn't bother wiping the spittle off her shoe.

Moments later, the coat drive is over. Every single coat has been claimed. Some people claimed more than one, but why not? Maybe someone at home needs one too—especially if home is the back seat of a car. The mothers take their children down from the stools and put the new coats on them—coats that most of the kids will need to grow into, and thus get more than a year's use. Jeannie remembers coat-shopping with her mother when she was in sixth grade, and going through a growth spurt. Jeannie insisted the only coat she'd wear was a short Navy blue puffy down coat from either Land's End or Patagonia. And it had to have a particular kind of sheen. Nothing else would do. She's ashamed, now, at how shallow and materialistic she used to be, and thankful she outgrew that phase. The children in the store today don't seem to care what they put on. They zip, and button, pop up their hoods, and hug their arms as they walk out the door, enjoying the newfound warmth. The mothers and fathers say thank you, and God bless you, as they leave, and many ask their children to do the same. The volunteers who are left—those who did not slip out earlier, before the altercation—smile and say you're welcome. They bag up the dirty and ragged old coats left behind and tie them up in trash bags—and pass around hand sanitizer immediately afterwards. Everyone tells Jeannie she did a great job. Fran Hauser mentions something about the mayor issuing her a proclamation. Jeannie smiles. But instead of feeling that she has accomplished something worthwhile, that her *mission* is fulfilled, for now, she is depressed and deflated. The snake hisses and stirs. There's a heaviness in the air, on Main Street, all around her, in fact. *I have done nothing. Fixed nothing. Solved nothing.* She begins to understand that being *useful,* really useful, means going deeper, doing more, being more.

That night, as Jeannie is trying to fall sleep, she replays the argument between the two women, over the coat, and cannot help feeling that this was all code for something...something way bigger than she is...but she doesn't know what it is. *Fuck you, bitch.* What's this about, really? Is it really just about a coat they both want? Or is something else going on? *Fuck you, bitch.* And then something else clicks, hard. Jeannie suddenly realizes who the heavy-set woman is from the coat drive, the one with wiry, silver hair, and the chapped skin. It's the checkout lady from the ShopFine. What's happened to her? Jeannie doesn't know her name. She tries to picture the nametag that's always pinned to her smock, but she can't. And she hates herself for this. *I'm so fake. I need to figure out how to be real.*

Chapter Fifteen

On the following Saturday, the passage Jeannie is supposed to be analyzing is about methods for comparing poverty rates among developing nations. But the words don't hang together, don't seem to mean anything. Jeannie hasn't been sleeping well. She replays the argument at last week's coat drive over and over. Sometimes, she sees herself as the one who steps forward to settle the matter with Solomonic perfection. But every time she pictures this, she can't think what to say to the women, what to tell them, or how to persuade them that it's okay, that everything will be okay, that their lives are going to be better than this because these women, and their children, deserve more. They shouldn't be spending an afternoon picking used coats off a rack. They should be buying pretty lavender coats, brand new, like the one her mother wears.

Jeannie feels a stinging, pricking behind her eyes. She also feels panic rising in her throat, like bile. This is the SAT. There's no time for daydreaming. But she's this close to putting her head down on the desk and giving up. The bubble sheet is nearly empty. Jeannie looks over at Gina and Zeke, who are here as well. Their heads are bent in concentration. Maybe they already figured out the best answers in response to questions about international rates of poverty. Maybe they've figured out the answers to the big questions, period. Maybe *she's* the only stupid one here. *Why don't they ask any real questions on this test?* Jeannie thinks. *Why don't they ask why there are people right here in Willing walking around without decent coats, or shoes?* But then, other questions pour in: *What if I get such a bad score I can't get into college? How will I get a decent job without a college degree? What if I end up with nothing, and my parents can't help me, or refuse to? What if I can't afford my own winter coat, some day?*

Suddenly, Jeannie is standing up, flush with panic. She forgets she's supposed to be filling in little black bubbles on paper. *Nothing is real,* she thinks. *Things don't last. I could be erased tomorrow. Hit by a bus. Struck by the plague. Nothing, nothing, nothing is guaranteed.* She is shaking all over now, her breathing is shallow.

"Jeannie King?" Who is calling her name? Jeannie looks up, her eyes wide. It's the exam proctor, a teacher she barely knows. "Are you all right? If so, please sit back down immediately and keep your eyes on your own paper." Jeannie does not move; the teacher takes a step toward her. "Are you ill?"

"No," Jeannie says softly, sinking back into her chair. "I'm fine. Really."

When it's all over, hours later, Jeannie knows she'll have to take the SAT all over again in the spring, for sure. But she doesn't care. She is exhausted, rung out, waiting numbly for her father to pick her up, along with Gina and Zeke. Farrah boycotted the whole thing. The plan is to go out for pizza to offset the morning's long ordeal. The three of them are standing outside their old elementary school, where the testing took place because the high school is filled with pre-holiday activities—band practice, the regional robotics club championship. Zeke puts in his earbuds and gets on his phone, laughing over something or other. For once, Jeannie doesn't begrudge him the anti-social activity. She envies his easy ability to not take everything so seriously, to find comic relief so satisfying. She also despises him for it. She doesn't want to believe that her twin is as shallow, or as callow, as he seems to be. She looks at Gina, who has tears in her eyes. Things have been strained between them, ever since they became roommates over the summer. It's gotten complicated. Gina couldn't help out with the coat drive because she was doing her own thing—volunteering at a hole-in-the-wall outreach center for troubled and homeless Latinx youth. Gina does their social media and helps them figure out how to let the population they serve know that they're here to help. The

"Jeans" still support each other, still value each other, but each has come to feel, privately, that the other's "stuff" is just a bit too much to handle, right now. They're like a pair of magnets with reversed polarity; they used to be drawn together, and now, they repel, in the sense that they just aren't comfortable spending prolonged periods of time alone together. Still, Jeannie smiles when Gina puts a hand on her arm.

"When we were in fifth grade, my dad and my grandma both came to hear us perform our monologues," Gina says. "Remember? It's the only time my dad came to anything, at school. The only time. And he hugged me afterwards, and we all went out for ice cream, *mi papá y mi abuela.*" Jeannie is the only person to whom Gina speaks Spanish, outside of the house. "I didn't know that was as good as it was gonna get. It's probably better that you don't know things like that, in fifth grade, right?"

"There's a lot of things I wish I didn't know," Jeannie says.

"Oh, that's just fucking brilliant!" Zeke says to nobody—to his phone. Zeke pulls out his earbuds and turns up the volume. "You should see this. It'll crack you up." When Carson pulls up to the curb, he sees the three teens huddled around Zeke's phone, laughing. Jeannie is willing herself back to what feels like normal. *They don't understand—this is as good as it's gonna get,* Carson thinks.

The whole time Zeke is staring at the SAT score sheet, he's thinking about Farrah's small, pointy breasts. They're not really much bigger than his own boy breasts, but that little difference matters—her two soft little powder puffs, the red aureoles that swell under his tongue… *'For questions 1-15, solve each problem, choose the best answer from the choices provided, and fill in the corresponding circle on your answer sheet.' …Why does life come with so much bullshit? Why can't I just skip to the good shit?…* Zeke flexes his left hand, a new reflex since the accident, testing for today's degree of stiffness. He has assigned his own private ratings scale to the degree of flexibility he feels in the damaged hand. It's not the same every day, though he can't figure out why. Today is only a 2 on his 5-point scale. That means he's pretty stiff; he can't get his four fingers to touch the skin of his scarred palm. His unwilling fingers are a waxy yellow-white color. They're ugly. He wishes they weren't his, but what the hell. Maybe tomorrow will be better. *I wonder if stress has anything to do with this?* He makes a mental note to check and see if his left hand scores a 5 during sex. That would explain a lot.

Zeke asks his dad to drop him at Farrah's after the pizza run. He's bringing an extra pizza in a box—veggie, extra cheese. Farrah's breasts weren't the only thing ruining his concentration during the SAT. The two of them have cooked up an experiment, and today's the day to try it out. Something they discussed quietly, calmly, at length over the last several weeks. Zeke can't actually remember who brought it up first, and he thinks maybe that's because they've each had the same idea, and so it tumbled out fairly naturally—one speaking what the other was already thinking. So who can say whose idea it really was? The point is, Zeke and Farrah both want to explore a threesome. The real question was: Who should the third person be? Who is worthy of their shared awesomeness? And then the question after that: Male or female? Or should they invite the only trans student they know of at school, who tends to keep a really low profile? This is where the debate kicked in.

"I'm totally bi-," says Farrah. "So I'm really okay, either way. I think it'll be cool. But are you?"

"Am I bisexual?" says Zeke. "I don't know. Maybe. No. I don't know. I don't."

"So that'll be cool—to explore that, I mean. You won't know unless you try. You should find out. So we should ask a guy."

"What about Carol?" Zeke asks. Carol's dead name was Carl. "She's pretty cool, right?"

"I tried. She says she's not ready. Later, gater, on Carol."

"Bummer."

"I'm gonna name three guys," Farrah says. "And you gotta say which one you find the hottest. And that's who we'll ask."

"How do you know any of them will say yes?" Zeke asks.

"I've already done the homework. Trust me," Farrah says, grinning.

Well, this is something different, Zeke thinks. One of the things Zeke likes best about Farrah is that she's always about a half-step ahead of him. He's never bored when he's with her. The girls he messed around with a little in middle school just bored the shit out of him. He was beginning to think, back then, that maybe he didn't like girls at all. That changed when he got to know Farrah.

"Okay, cool," says Zeke. *I'm Mr. Experience. Up for anything—at least once.*

So now, this very minute, Geronimo Crawford is about to show up at Farrah's house, a stone's throw from Gina Martinez's. Geronimo is tall and skinny, with really narrow hips. He's got sandy brown hair that's cut super-short on the sides, with a long, floppy thatch on top that falls into his eyes. Zeke isn't really friends with Geronimo, but he's given him sidelong glances, almost without realizing it, from time to time. Zeke thinks Geronimo is...*coy.* That's the word that comes to mind. Maybe because Geronimo hardly ever seems to speak, and yet every room he enters he dominates with his tall presence. And his name—Geronimo—is like a secret, somehow, even though it's what everybody calls him. Zeke is secretly thrilled he's going to have a chance to get to know Geronimo—and that Geronimo thought coming over tonight was worth his time. Which must mean he thinks spending time with Zeke isn't such a bad idea. So maybe the curiosity is, actually, mutual? Zeke would never say out loud, to anybody, that Geronimo isn't just *coy,* he's a flat-out *cool dude.*

Farrah lives alone with her mother, who works nights as a nurse at Sturgis Memorial Hospital, where Zeke had his hand surgery. Zeke has never actually met her, since he and Farrah take advantage of her absence on many evenings to spend quality time together. The night shift pays considerably better than the day shift, and so Farrah's mother made a decision, years ago, to develop Farrah's self-sufficient qualities so that she could reasonably fend for herself after school. She taught Farrah to cook, so she could make dinner for both of them, leaving her mother packed-up leftovers in the fridge each night. Farrah can't remember any other arrangement, really, as her dad split shortly after settling on the famous name for the infant daughter he didn't stick around to get to know. Maybe he left to go find the real Farrah, or whatever. It is what it is, she figures.

The doorbell rings. Geronimo is right on time. "Hey," he says, cool and casual. He's got a sixpack with him. "We vibin' or what?" Zeke and Farrah look at each other, grinning ear to ear. Zeke is all upside-down inside, and there's a roaring in his ears, and he thinks, for a split second, that perhaps he should excuse himself and go home. But no. *Mr. Experience, that's me. Besides, he's smokin' hot.*

At some point, after a period of mutual exploration both on top of the sheets and under the sheets of Farrah's childhood twin bed, punctuated by noisy outbursts of laughter and arousal, Farrah decides to watch Zeke and Geronimo get it on together. She rolls off the bed and sits on the rug, next to the white wicker chest that still holds her American Girl doll knock-off (the original was too expensive), an Etch-a-Sketch, and a GI Joe action figure, among other things. This feels good, this feels peaceful, and no one can convince her it's wrong, or kinky, or weird. Actually, it's nice, and loving. And they really trust one another, and that's also a good thing. Farrah's already decided that next time—and there will be a next time, she's sure—they'll invite a girl. She's already making a list in her head of girls who won't recoil in shock and horror, should they be lucky enough to be asked to the party.

Around 10 p.m., Zeke walks the two miles or so back home. He doesn't feel the cold. He doesn't even zip up his jacket. He feels powerful. Invincible. He feels like he's joined an exclusive club that will change his life forever. He feels sexy, and sexually potent. He's happy with himself for following through with his new mantra: *living is experiencing.* He loves Geronimo—how he tastes, how he feels. He loves Farrah too. He loves everybody tonight, and that's a brand new sensation. If Jeannie were standing here in front of him, he'd even give her a big squeeze. *Please, let this be just the beginning of something—of my real life.* Zeke slips quietly into his house, passing the light that suggests his father is still at his computer. He tiptoes upstairs, takes a long, hot shower, and then lies on his back, in bed, naked, glowing, tingling in every nerve of his body. And his left hand? He gives it the test. It's a 5.

Chapter Sixteen

By the time Carson drops Gina off in front of her house hours after the SAT, she has a stomachache and maybe the beginnings of a winter cold, too. Too much greasy pizza. And the SAT was a bear. She is well aware that she must do well on the test to attract any scholarships, especially those catering to entering freshmen of Hispanic or Latinx descent as well as first-generation college students. Years ago, when she was in seventh grade, Javier told Gina that he was setting aside money for her to go to college, to become the first in his family, and as far as he knew, in Eugenia's immediate family, to continue past high school. He stroked her silky black hair and told her she was a good girl. He didn't say he was proud of her, but Gina knew that's what he meant. She was so happy she almost cried. Her grandmother smiled and patted her hand.

But Javier hasn't said anything about college in a long time. Her grandmother doesn't understand the American educational system, especially the post-secondary world, so she does her best to offer general reassurances. "You're a smart girl," she tells her. "You work hard, you do good, so everything will work out. You'll find your place, *chica.* And you're beautiful, and that never hurts." Gina has heard variations of this so many times, she just smiles and discounts whatever her grandmother says, which Gina does not consider a reflection of the real world, not *her* real world. Javier has barely said a word to her, period, since junior year began. Gina suspects the college fund is gone, and he doesn't want to tell her. She doesn't know this for sure, and has no way to confirm it without asking him. But she can't bring herself to do it. She's taking a wait-and-see approach, which is nerve-wracking, but she feels locked in to a situation so far out of her control, it makes her dizzy. She has concluded that his business isn't doing well, but she is forced to live in a kind of news black-out with respect to this particular topic. So she is reduced to guesswork, and on some level, she's ashamed that, at 16, she's brave enough to help an organization craft effective outreach strategies for homeless youth, but a complete coward, a pathetic little scaredy-cat, where her own family—and probably her own future—are concerned.

She looks for signs. There was a night, just last week, when Javier came home very late, after Gina was in bed and asleep. He came into her room and gently kissed her head. She thought, at first, she might have dreamed this, but she decided it was real. She cannot remember the last time Javier actually came into her room; it had probably been five years. She thinks about this tender gesture a lot, at odd moments throughout the following days. Does this mean everything is going to be okay, and her father is going to be home more, and able to relax? Or does it mean that everything is turning to shit, and he feels sorry for her—even though he doesn't confide in her? If he is the walking wounded, Gina thinks, then I'm the walking innocent—and also wounded.

The house appears dark when Gina walks inside on this late Saturday afternoon, which is often the case, these days. Gina takes a Coke from the fridge and begins to head upstairs, when she sees her grandmother sitting in their small living room, with just a small table lamp casting a meager glow. Carmen is almost never still—always cooking, or cleaning, or clipping coupons from the newspaper circulars, watching a *telenova* on the small kitchen TV when there is time to spare, always doing something. So to see her sitting still, in the dark, is upsetting. Gina pauses at the threshold. "Abuela, qué pasa?" Carmen asks her to sit down. She offers a plate of cookies, which Gina refuses, instead taking a swig of Coke to try and settle her stomach.

"I am going back to work on Monday," Carmen says.

"What? Why?" Gina asks. She immediately feels immensely stupid. There's only one reason why her grandmother, with bad joints, would go back to work. "I mean, what will you do? How will you manage?"

"It's not difficult. Easy money." Carmen explains she will mind the counter at a laundromat that caters to the Spanish-speaking families living on the outskirts Willing proper. She can spend most of the day sitting. It's not far from the dentist's office where she worked for so many years. "Same bus route, so I know what to do."

"If you have a job, then I will get a job too," Gina says.

"No! Your job is to stay in school, and go to college," Carmen says. "And besides, you're a young woman now. You don't need me so much, here. What am I going to do all day with myself?"

"But I—"

"Do not argue. Your father does not want you working." Gina doesn't know what else to say. And her father isn't there to be confronted—if she even dared. She hugs her grandmother and goes up to her bedroom. She kicks off her shoes and crawls under the covers, fully dressed. Gina guesses Carmen will earn minimum wage for this job, if she's lucky. It can't even make much difference, if the family is really in financial trouble. She can't stand thinking about how much pain her grandmother will have to endure, walking to and from the bus stop, to and from the laundromat, in all kinds of weather. This is just unacceptable, though her grandmother tries to make it sound like it's nothing. Carmen decides that if her father won't confide in her, and treat her like an adult, then she won't confide in him, either. She's going to find a job, anyway, and help her family survive.

It's bitter cold on Christmas Eve in Willing. There's a hard freeze, with slivers of ice glinting in the streetlights, like mica. Main Street is the quietest it's ever been. Even in 1902, horse-drawn wagons still clopped along a cobblestoned Main Street on a night like this. Hot chestnut vendors stood by their carts on the corners. And shopkeepers and families who lived above their stores had reasons to be in the street, or running to their neighbor's, at all hours, to borrow coal or sugar or cooking oil. Now, the apartments above the stores are used for storage, or not at all. Many of those doors are locked tight, and whatever is behind them is long forgotten. Tonight, the handful of stores that still operate during the day along Main Street, like the tiny sliver of a tobacco shop and the Sudsy laundromat, are closed. Loose trash blows along the street, catching on sewer grates half-clogged with older trash and lace-thin leaves.

In Willing Heights, the large, brick-front mansions are lit from within, sending out twinkles, through curtains and blinds, of colored Christmas lights and the shadows of families like the Collinses moving about and mingling. Up the hill at Willing Enclave, a few miles away, the wind blows through the wooden skeletons and the soil in the empty foundation sites is frozen solid. The site appears in the moonless night like the faint outlines of an archaeological ruin, an ancient city excavated from beneath a millennium of earth, or perhaps just the whittled remains of a once bustling village.

A few miles from all that is the ShopFine supermarket where most Willing residents buy groceries. It's closed for Christmas Eve. But Winnie Suggs made a point of catching the last bus from the women's shelter where she's stayed the past few nights. She was evicted from her tiny apartment a month after being fired, as she couldn't make the rent. She knows, from her long years as a cashier here, that nights like this—major holidays—are the best times to find edible food in the market's dumpsters. Winnie wears the long brown coat she got at the coat drive, along with a thick pair of ski gloves she found in a bin at the shelter. She's wearing boots, too, and a woolen hat, all of which are her own. Winnie is well aware that people toss around the phrase, 'living paycheck to paycheck,' as if it's a hypothetical warning—something that could happen, if the worst came to the worst. People often use this phrase, she's noticed, like they're recalling a wicked fairytale, where magical and mystical forces tip the scales between good and evil, in ways that normal people never experience. But for Winnie, living paycheck-to-paycheck means exactly what it says. She's put in decades working at the market, and received very small raises along the way. But by the time she was fired, she was still earning just a dollar above minimum wage, with such bare-bones medical insurance coverage that the high deductible made it feel like no coverage at all. Of course that ran out months ago. She's worried that Social Security can't find her, because she doesn't have a forwarding address since leaving her apartment. But even once she catches up to that money—if she ever does, as she's not quite sure how it all works—it won't be enough to cover rent anywhere in or even reasonably near Willing. She thought about trying to rent a room in somebody's house, to perch in some small place where she could practically disappear, and be no bother to anyone. But she couldn't figure out where to look, and didn't know if this kind of arrangement even existed. And she suspects she has begun to smell.

Winnie supposes she could stop eating and smoke herself to death, and that would solve all problems. But she isn't morose, by nature, and she doesn't view being poor as a crime or anything to be ashamed of. It is what it is. It's a damn shame that idiot fired her, but it is what it is. He had his reasons. Winnie thinks he's wrong, but he has power on his side, and there's not a damn thing she can actually do about that. Not at this stage of the game.

Winnie planned out her approach before she even got on the bus. She wheels a grocery cart around to the first green dumpster behind the store. With both hands, and using all her strength, she tips the cart on its side and pushes it right up to the base of the dumpster. Slowly, carefully, she climbs onto the broad side of the cart, testing to be sure it can hold her weight. This gives her just enough height to lean into the dumpster and see whatever is within reach. And her calculations are correct. Within reach is a white cake box, with a beautiful, whole chocolate cake inside. Even the icing inscription is intact: *Happy Holidays, Love, Sarah.* Winnie tries to imagine how or why Sarah didn't pick up this cake she had already paid for. Is it true that money means so little to some people? Or did something terrible happen, like a sudden death in the family, or a serious car accident on the way to the market itself? Shit happens to everybody, Winnie thinks. It's just a matter of degree. After less than an hour of browsing this dumpster and another one, as far as her arms can reach, she retrieves a portion of a deli platter still in good shape, boxes of expired cereal, a canister of prunes, and two loaves of bread with no signs of mold. Winnie climbs down, stuffing her food into a plastic shopping bag she brought with her. She doesn't bother to return the cart. Serves him right, she thinks. Mr. Bill. But she doesn't wish he'd drop dead of a heart attack. She just wishes she had managed a little better, for herself, all along the way. Maybe she could've gotten a little more of what everyone else seems to have, if she'd been taught better, how to manage—or if she'd been more clever to begin with, and figured out more about navigating life way back when she was young and limber. Or if she'd paid attention in school, instead of dropping out after 10th grade. Though, judging from the kids Winnie's seen in the ShopFine over the years, it's not clear what an education really gets you. So much of life is just a mystery that cannot be solved; Winnie decided long ago that she, for one, is stumped for life, maybe stumped *by* life. The answers are always just out of reach. Maybe she's used up her brain memorizing how to key in fruits and vegetables. Who knows? It's just one more tiny piece of the mystery she figures she's never going to solve.

Anyway, Winnie knows there's no way to get back to the shelter tonight. She finds a sheltered area in the exterior alcove of the store, so that, between the overhang above the doors and the rows of carts lined up in the dark, there's virtually no wind. She's not worried about being seen. And she doesn't much care, either. With her back against a cold wall, she opens the cake box, removes the glove on her right hand, and digs out a big, fairly moist chunk of chocolate cake, covered in vanilla buttercream frosting. She wonders how many customers have ordered this cake over the years. Hundreds? Thousands? This cake, which she's tasting for the very first time, after all these years. She imagines Mrs. King buying this very cake for her…daughter? Son? Or is she the one with twins?… A birthday party when she, or he, or they are little. Winnie is sure this happened, probably more than once. She eats the cake until her fingers are numb and she can't stand the taste anymore. She wipes her hand on the shopping bag, puts her glove back on, and closes her eyes. She uses her old trick to help her fall asleep: matching as many three- and four-digit codes to the corresponding grocery items as she can, until she is unconscious. Mr. Bill doesn't know what he's talking about, saying she can't remember the codes. It's just about the only thing in the entire world that she's pretty sure she actually *does* know. Deli-bakery-special-order rings in at 4027.

Part II

The Second Spring

Chapter Seventeen

REMINGTON COUNTY POLICE DEPARTMENT
QUARTERLY CRIME REPORT—HIGHLIGHTS

County-wide incidents of petty larceny and felony class offenses, including carjackings, are up 17% over same quarter a year ago. In Willing, B&Es involving vacant buildings rose 24%, and domestic disturbances involving arrest rose 11%. Due to cutbacks on the force, the average response time to a 911 call has nearly doubled.

Bachman Realty is pulling out of Willing. So Sylvia suspects, though the Bachmans have not confirmed it, directly. But the signs are there: rows of empty office cubicles. Phones that don't ring. A supply cabinet once neatly stacked with coffee paraphernalia and toilet paper, nearly barren now. Ben Wang must've picked up on the signals sooner, Sylvia thinks, or maybe he just isn't the bitter-end type, like she is. Ben decided to move his family a few months ago to Dallas, where his cousin is a partner in a mid-sized brokerage firm, handling both commercial and residential property. He had no active listings when he left, so he didn't do Sylvia and Ann Likert, the only two senior brokers left, any favors. And now Betty is asking Sylvia to come into her office. Betty is wearing a Chanel suit that Sylvia has never seen before, so maybe the retrenchment is more of a precaution than a death warrant. Maybe things aren't as bad as they look, and the Bachmans are just canny business people—cautious, in order to remain profitable. Sylvia pours herself a fresh cup of coffee on her way into

Betty's office. If the office is closing, she assumes she will be invited to join the Bachmans in their original home office, in Linton Crossing, where they live, and where they started the business 35 years ago. It means a hell of a commute, but it also means getting a crack at all that remains of the luxury end of the market within about a 600-mile radius. So not a terrible outcome, really. If she gets busy enough, perhaps she can rent a small apartment up there and stay over one or two nights a week. That would be a nice write-off, in any case. She allows herself to dwell on this scenario for a moment, not at all displeased with the prospect. *Lemonade from lemons.*

"So how are you?" Betty asks, with a cold, crinkly smile. Her gold bracelets jangle.

"I'm great," says Sylvia. "Of course, my numbers are down, but we're all getting clobbered, aren't we? I never thought I'd have to live through another 2008, did you? But we got through it then, and we'll get through it now. I'm sure you and Barnaby have seen worse, right?"

"Yes and no," says Betty, the smile gone. She looks at her computer screen. "What's going on with those two-bedroom ranchers?"

"I had offers on both. Neither could get financing approved. Times are tough, as you know."

"What steps are you taking to find more qualified buyers?" Betty asks, shifting her gaze from the screen to Sylvia, who is startled by the question. It's not the kind of thing you ask a senior broker with nearly two decades of experience. It's a question for a rookie, and even a good rookie might be insulted. Sylvia feels her face flush hot.

"What are you asking, Betty?"

"Exactly what I said."

"Look, I've performed extremely well for this company for many years. As you know. I really don't think that a run of bad luck, in the worst market in years, maybe ever, is a reason to question my competence."

"I'm not questioning your competence, Sylvia," Betty says with an edge. "I'm questioning your tactics in a down market."

"Let me ask you something, if I may," Sylvia says. "If I had landed the Walters, would we be having a different conversation?"

"Possibly. But there are other variables involved."

"Variables?"

"It's taken me a long time to learn the biggest secret in our profession. And I'll tell you what it is, so maybe you'll understand where I'm coming from." Sylvia sits very still, her coffee untouched. "Some brokers have the drive and personality to do their best work in a really competitive market—even an overheated market. And some do their best at the other end of the scale, when everything's going to hell in a hand basket, and there's scarcely a property or a buyer on the prowl." Betty turns back to her computer screen, and her long, blood-red nails click on the keyboard.

"And?" Sylvia asks, her breathing shallow. *When's the last time you sold a house, Betty? When's the last time you had to make cold calls, talk irrational buyers down off the ceiling, smile while a seller turns down an offer you worked your ass off for...And when's the last time—*

"Which type of broker do you think you are, Sylvia?" Betty asks, breaking Sylvia's angry reverie.

"Betty, with all due respect, I don't think I agree with you. A good broker is a good broker, period. I didn't get to number two sitting on my hands—as you know."

"Ann Likert has sold six units this month. Did you know that?" Betty asks, watching Sylvia closely. Sylvia's flush drains away; she turns pale. "You have sold none."

If I walk out of here right now, and come back tomorrow with a qualified buyer for one of those ranch houses, it'll be like this conversation never happened. I won't be tripped up by one thing, one small thing, one blip on a big radar screen.

"Betty, I like Ann, I respect her, but she's moving small houses and condos at the very low end of the market. You and I both know that's not the market I've been cultivating all these years, and it's not the way to generate a meaningful book of business."

Betty swivels in her chair and leans forward. "You're making my point, Sylvia. You need to chase the market. You can't wait for the market to come to you. I've been waiting and waiting for you to recognize that the streets are no longer paved with gold. I've given you a very long rope on this, I really have. And the Walters were the canaries in the coal mine. Do you understand?"

No. No, I don't understand at all. People like me don't fail. Carson and I—we only go forward, never backward. Nothing about this makes sense.

"Sylvia? I'm sorry. We're bringing Ann with us to Linton Crossing. I'm sad to say, our relationship has come to an end. I have no doubt you'll land on your feet." Sylvia stands, and does not even realize she's doing so. "Please leave your keys and your building access card on your desk."

Sylvia does not remember driving home and pulling her red Audi into the driveway. But suddenly, here she is, in the middle of the afternoon. The dogwood in the front yard and all the hydrangeas are nothing but barren brown twigs stoically withstanding the cold March wind, waiting with dumb, endless patience for spring to revive them. Sylvia notices that someone left the front porch light on all night. *These kids are too cavalier, wasteful, selfish. Don't they know we're not made of money. What was it the ShopFine cashier said, sitting on the ground…Winnie Suggs…she said, 'Just taking a moment to sort things out, get things straight in my own mind.' Yes, I need to get things straight.* Sylvia gets out of the car and pulls the fur collar on her winter coat around her neck. She sits on the front stoop of her house. *Just like Winnie. Sometimes, Winnie says, when you get real bad news, you just gotta stop in your tracks, turn things over in your mind. You can't do nothin' else, for a bit.*

Sylvia shivers and goes inside, bringing the mail with her. She picks up the monthly bank statement from Second National and rips it open. *At a certain point, pain is just pain. There's no such thing as 'more' pain.* She looks at the statement, then walks it into Carson's little office, where she drops the open papers onto his keyboard. *Later.* She opens a bottle of red wine, picks up her favorite wine glass—one of only two of the very large balloon glasses they received as a wedding gift, which hasn't yet broken. She carries the bottle and glass upstairs and runs a very hot bath. She climbs in, the wine glass perched on the porcelain ledge of the tub. Sylvia closes her eyes and stares at the blackness riddled with electric pinpricks of light, making room, making space, for something big and loud that's coming toward her. If only she could make out what it is. She feels the familiar ice pick, the stabbing in her left eye, that signals the onset of a migraine boring its way into her new life.

Chapter Eighteen

Carson doesn't think it's possible to be any more pissed off than he is right now. His feet are going numb in his work boots. His fingers are long gone. It's hard to hold a hammer, let alone a nail. He's up on a crossbeam in the second of the six planned houses at Willing Enclave, very near the spot where Zeke impaled himself last summer. He and Darius and Vin are all that's left of what was once a construction crew of 12. All three men are wearing WPC caps pulled down over the hoods of their sweatshirts. *It's fucking freezing* is the only thought all three have subconsciously agreed on in the last hour, hell, in the last month or three. The work is agonizingly slow, not just because they're all numb with cold, but because Willing Prime Contractors LLC is running on fumes. The partners haven't completed a projected since finishing a row of new condos in South Willing nearly two years ago. Those sold reasonably quickly, and the partners "made bank" on the project. They pivoted quickly to snatch up the Willing Enclave project—such a sure thing at the time, so much juice to be squeezed. Now, there's no new profit-taking in sight, only debt.

"Where is the fucking wrench set?" Carson asks, breaking a long silence. "It was right here." Vin walks the metal box over to him without a word and dumps it with a loud clatter. Carson swore it wouldn't come to this, but it has. Darius puts down his drill and picks his way over to his partners.

"We're out of long boards," Darius says. "There's not a lot more we can do without the lumber."

"So I'll buy some more fucking lumber," Carson says, picking out a quarter-inch wrench socket.

"How, Cap?" Vin asks. "How you gonna buy lumber? At retail? At Home Depot? You gonna walk in like any regular jerk and just toss it in your truck at twice the price? And then, what, we pay you back out of our own pockets? This isn't how we run our fucking business."

"That isn't even the issue," Darius says.

"The issue," Carson says, screwing in a bolt, "is why the fuck did we let Bruno and Jorge go? We'd be twice as far along by now."

"I'm not having that conversation again, Cap," Darius says.

"Me, neither," Vin says.

"I told you then—" Carson says.

"I'm done with you fucking telling us," Darius says. "I'm not having *that* conversation again, either."

Carson tightens his grip on the wrench; he can feel the icy metal through his work glove. "I'm telling you, anyway," he says. "If we want to get this debt monkey off our backs, we have to sell these fucking houses—and we have to do it now."

"We've been through all this," Vin says, his eyes watering in the cold.

"Don't be such fucking pussies," Carson says. "We're here. We got no choice. Let's do as much as we can, with what we have, or what we can get, and then see where we are."

"We know where we are," Darius says. "Up shit's creek without a paddle."

"I'm gonna do you both a favor," Carson says.

"Don't do *me* any fucking favors, Cap," Darius says.

"I'm going to make the sales signs," Carson continues. "I'm gonna advertise the shit out of it. We'll get brokers and buyers out here in the spring, let them use their imaginations. Like I said before."

"And if it doesn't work?" Vin asks.

"It'll work. Sylvia's got all the contacts, she knows all the best people," Carson says. Vin and Darius are silent. They're well aware that Carson is always the one who pushes hardest, who pushes them past any comfort zones. And financially, Vin and Darius are way past feeling comfortable. Vin is thinking hard about selling his own modest rancher—if he can—and renting a cheaper apartment closer to town. Or maybe he'll buy a condo; they're going for a song, now. Then again, condo fees are probably too expensive, Vin thinks, distractedly. If I'm downsizing, he thinks, I should do it right. Meanwhile, Darius and Elena are pretty far along in discussing a move to Arizona, to make a fresh start. It's cheaper, living in the Sun Belt. That would mean asking Vin and Carson to buy him out, which Darius doesn't see a way to bring up, any time soon. But he's working on it—working up to it, actually. If it were up to Elena, he'd lay his cards on the table, right here, right now. But she doesn't know Cap. And Carson is still sitting on his gambling windfall, now hovering around $75,000. He's keeping the money in a separate online banking account. The Baker Block is still on the market.

At this point, nobody's putting their cards on the table. The three men pick up their tools and begin working again.

"You know," Vin says, "it's not anybody's fault. It's just the market. There's no point in us pounding each other."

"So let's power through it," Carson says. Darius shakes his head. "What, Dizz? What?"

"I just think we're fucked," Darius says, putting a hand on his aching lower back.

"I don't know," Vin says. "Maybe Cap's right. We just wait out the market. Tighten our belts. Pay down the debt."

"And come back stronger than ever," Carson adds.

"That's a pipe dream," Darius says. "You and your fucking pipe dreams."

Carson squints into the cold, windy, March sun from his second-story perch within the framed-up house. *I still see it. I can still touch it. The family backyard barbecues. The kids riding their tricycles out front. The flower gardens and vegetable plots. The rakes and wheelbarrows. The couples sitting on their back decks—there will be decks—sipping gin and tonics on a summer afternoon. And they say, 'Look where we are. We made it to fucking Willing Enclave. Aren't we lucky. Life is good.'*

"Yeah," Carson says, turning back to his tools. "Me and my fucking pipe dreams."

Chapter Nineteen

By the time Carson arrives home that night, the skin on his cold-dry fingers is splitting, his cheeks are wind-burned, and he's tired as shit. He looks like one of those guys who fails to summit on Kilimanjaro, yet nevertheless they're back home to share deeds of bravery and near-death experiences. Carson has a way of looking like he's on top even if he's not. Maybe it's the curly blond hair. He moves wearily into the dark kitchen and pulls a tub of something from the fridge—Meatloaf? Chicken parm?—and stands at the counter eating. He takes a deep breath between bites, and tries to account for his family.

"Syl?" he calls.

"Upstairs!"

He pictures her on their bed, her favorite place to work, her round face frowning with concentration as she flips through images of houses, interior designers, sales spreadsheets, whatever she gets into. Jeannie, he thinks. Right. Out tonight. Presumably safe and warm. He doesn't know the details, and doesn't want to know.

In fact, Jeannie is with Gina, who's been acting weird and distant lately. Jeannie feels guilty that they aren't spending as much time together as they used to; she guesses things are tough at home, but she doesn't know how to help. So the least she could do when Gina invited her to a talk at Fox Community College about the travesty of ICE raids and the immigrant child's burden, was to say yes. They took a taxi to get there because Jeannie isn't allowed to drive at night and Gina doesn't have her license. Jeannie nearly cleaned out her little stash of cash, which she keeps in an old jewelry box in her dresser, to pay for the evening. But she's relieved to be running out of money; currency is an unnecessary evil, she's concluded, and the less she has of it, the better off she'll be.

Carson enters his little office, carrying the tub of food with him, a fork sticking out of his mouth. He turns on his stingy desk lamp and sees the bank statement, right where Sylvia left it. *Damn.* He feels the returning scourge of irritation that's needled him all day. It's not the bank statement per se, it's that he knows Sylvia left it here because she wants to discuss it. *Damn.* Carson has some serious online gaming to tend to—but now he has to choose between nursing his gambling stake and talking about finances with his wife. He stands there for a moment, processing the numbers on the statement. Primary Checking: way down. Savings: nearly drained. College savings fund: woefully inadequate. Overdrafts: two in the last four weeks. Overdraft fees: a rip-off. *Well, what the fuck am I supposed to do?* He thinks. *I can't fix it right this minute. She's gonna have to wait it out with me, like it or not. For better or worse. Richer or poorer. And time heals all wounds and I, we, will be whole again. Goddammit.* He pauses, eating absently, staring into space, face cards and betting strategies flickering in his mind's eye. He puts down the food and trudges upstairs. He pauses at the door to Zeke's room. Zeke sits at his childhood desk—his knees bumping hard up against the underside of the desk itself, Carson notices. He's bathed in a puddle of light like Carson himself, when he's at his own desk. Zeke's blond hair is identical to his own, though longer and fuller. Zeke has earbuds in and he's staring intently, closely, at his laptop; he doesn't even see his dad standing there. Carson waits a beat, then decides it's best not to break his son's concentration on…whatever it is he's concentrating on. Carson doesn't really want to know, or need to know. He can no longer put off the inevitable, so he heads to the bedroom.

"Hey," Carson says. He sees an empty wine glass on her night stand. And her laptop is closed, for once. She's staring, glassy-eyed, at the TV suspended on the wall above a dresser.

Sylvia shifts her unfocused gaze to her husband. "You look bushed."

"It's good for me. All the manual labor. Keeps me in shape." Carson pats his flat stomach. "So…" He sits on the bed and places a hand on her ankle. He admires her neatly trimmed feet and the cheerful red toenail polish. It reminds him how together she is; how together they both are, despite the recent headwinds.

"So," Sylvia echoes.

"You know what really bothers me? It's the fucking overdraft fees. We've banked with them how long? What a rip-off." *And hopefully, that is that. The rest is a given.* Carson peels off his filthy shirt and work pants. He sniffs an armpit. "I'm gonna jump in the shower." Sylvia watches him strip unselfconsciously. She feels a stirring, as she admires his lean body, the golden hairs on his chest. But she lets it pass. He pads into the bathroom and turns on the shower.

Sylvia calls out to him. "I think I can do better by going independent. As a broker, I mean. Play by my own rules, go after the clients I really want…Cap?"

"Yeah," he calls from the shower. "That's a great idea. Go for it." Carson emerges a few minutes later, draped in a towel.

"Aren't you coming to bed?" Sylvia asks.

"This is really great, Syl. Because your first new listing is Willing Enclave. This way, we keep it all in the family."

"And no Bachman bullshit."

"Yeah," he says. "Kick those stuck-up, blood-sucking snobs to the curb."

Sylvia hesitates for a moment, then she says, "I did. Done and dusted." Carson looks at her, a bit startled.

"Well, that was pretty ballsy, Syl," he says, "what with everything that's going on. Good for you." Carson leans over to kiss her. "You still got it, babe."

"We both do," she replies.

He tells her all about his plan to pre-sell the unfinished houses, and the outdoor open house he wants her to manage. She asks him pointed questions about timelines, price points, and whether new owners can select their own finishes. She feels her dark mood draining away like bath water. She's excited, because now, finally, after a long drought, they're both excited, sharing this vision, shaping it together, focusing on a really positive project that reminds them both why they do the kind of work they do—and why they take the risks. Neither Sylvia nor Carson doubts for a moment that this will be a successful joint venture. All the debt, the collapsing market, the fact that there's not enough cash on hand to actually finish the houses any time soon—these are all solvable challenges, under conditions that can be managed, one way or another. When the going gets tough, the tough get creative.

Sylvia turns off the TV. She's wide awake now. She pivots to the side of the bed and yanks the towel off her husband. They pause, take stock of one another, let the moment declare itself. And then they make love, quickly and intensely, for the first time in weeks. Afterwards, Sylvia reaches for her laptop, while Carson throws on sweatpants and a T-shirt and heads for the door.

"I still have some stuff I gotta take care of, in the office," he says, smiling. "Don't stay up too late."

Sylvia is already organizing a search to find the latest comps, so she can begin thinking about how to price Willing Enclave. "No," she says absently. "I won't."

By the time Jeannie gets home, Carson is so deeply absorbed in an online poker game, in which he's down by 10 grand, that he doesn't hear her step behind him.

"What are you doing?" Jeannie asks, startling Carson so violently he knocks over his whiskey glass and whips around to her.

"What the hell are *you* doing?" he yells at her, his eyes red-rimmed. Jeannie takes a step back. *He isn't going to start punching walls, is he? Is this what it's like?*

"God, Dad," Jeannie says, still backing away. "I'm sorry. I didn't mean—"

"I'm sorry, Jean Bean," Carson says, quickly shutting the laptop. "But, look, I'm right in the middle of something, and it's late, so, I'm glad you're home safe. Now, why don't you go up to bed." Jeannie begins to pick up the glass on the carpet. "Leave it," he says. She does not wait to be asked twice. Just as her father had done earlier in the evening, she stops by Zeke's room, deciding on the way whether he'll be remotely interested in hearing what she learned this evening about illegal ICE raids taking place at universities, poultry farms, everywhere! Or to find out whether her brother knows that their father seems to play card games online, late at night. *How weird is that? And what's that about, anyway?* But Zeke is in bed, lying flat on his back. He's traded in his earbuds for a pair of earphones and he appears, to Jeannie, to be blissed out on music. Or else he's asleep. *At least he's not, well, playing his one-man band,* Jeannie thinks. She's caught him out on that before, when his door wasn't fully closed. Jeannie then sees her mother, nodded off in front of her laptop. She gets ready for bed herself, feeling deflated, or maybe defeated, as it seems nobody in her household cares about the things that matter most to her—and that they're criminally blind to all the injustice going on around them. *Maybe I should make them care. But how?*

Carson crawls up to bed when the first ray of morning light is hitting the east-facing back deck and his winnings have been cut in half. He is dizzy with fatigue and his eyes feel as though they're full of cut glass. But the Baker Block is still on the market—probably getting cheaper by the day—and Willing Enclave will dazzle future buyers, so at some point, you just gotta believe.

Chapter Twenty

Around 7:30 in the morning, Sylvia, after a restless night from too much wine, is bundled in a bathrobe and a wool blanket, seated on the back deck, drinking coffee. It's cold, but sunny. The early grass is coated with silvery dew, the droplets not quite frost. Steam rises off of Sylvia's mug. The yard looks different this morning. The vast spread of ground appears, well, pointless, instead of purposeful. Drained of its potential—a void, rather than a map upon which future progress will be charted. She forces herself to think in practical terms: what's the land worth, now? Is there a buyer out there? Would somebody still want to build here, to make a home and a fresh start, just as nearby Willing literally begins crumbling? She makes a mental note to brave Zillow online, later. Sylvia hears noise in the kitchen, then the opening click of the sliding door to the deck. Jeannie and Zeke are both wrapped in puffy coats, and each carries a bowl of cold cereal. They settle deep into deck chairs.

"Aren't you running late?" Sylvia asks.

"It's Senior skip day," Zeke says. "But I couldn't sleep."

"Is that really a thing?" Sylvia asks.

"Really, Mom," Zeke says. "Get a clue."

"It's legit," says Jeannie. "Dad isn't up yet, is he?"

"I haven't seen him in, like, a week," Zeke says.

"I think he came to bed really late," Sylvia says, "so I guess he'll sleep in."

"Yeah, I figured," Jeannie says. "He was doing stuff on his computer really late last night, I think." Jeannie pauses and looks at her mother, waiting to see if she picks up the thread. She doesn't. Jeannie continues watching her mother, who is sending a thousand-yard stare across the lawn. *Does she know something we don't know?* Jeannie wonders. *Do I want to know what she knows?* She decides to push on, while Zeke slumps in a chair, his coat tucked up around his chin, slurping cereal. "Dad's a gamer, I think," she says, immediately realizing this doesn't make much sense, out of the blue.

"He's a...what?" Sylvia asks, distractedly.

"Dad's a *gamer*?" Zeke asks. "What planet are you on, Jeel?"

"What's a gamer?" Sylvia asks. "Whatever that is, it doesn't sound much like your dad."

"Mom, you really need to get a life," Zeke says.

"A gamer, Mom. Someone who plays games online, like, seriously," Jeannie says.

"You mean, like, video games?" Sylvia asks, frowning. "I can't picture your father wasting time on stuff like that. Jeannie, what are you talking about?"

"Card games," Jeannie says. "Maybe poker. I don't know. I'm not sure."

Zeke sits up. "Are you saying our father is a *hustler*?" he asks.

"When I came home, last night, he was...online. He looked really intense. He jumped when I walked in on him. And I saw..." *What did I see, really?*

"Your father has an awful lot on his plate, right now," Sylvia says. "We both do. But we don't want either of you to worry. We've got it all under control."

"You've got *what* under control?" Zeke asks.

"Oh," Sylvia says, waving her hand, "just grown-up stuff. Boring stuff."

"So...," Jeannie says, "you don't think it's weird that Dad plays card games online late at night?"

"I'm sure he's just blowing off steam. Just because he's over forty doesn't mean he can't goof off, once in a while."

Jeannie ponders this, then shrugs. "Okay." *Moving on. There are way bigger problems in the universe to worry about.* "I'm cold." Jeannie takes her bowl and goes inside. The sliding door clicks behind her. Sylvia drinks the last of her coffee, now also cold. Zeke leans forward.

"Mom."

"Hmm?"

"I've decided I'm not going to college in the fall. Even if I get in somewhere. I'm not going. Maybe later, but not now." He holds his breath, watching his mother's reaction.

Sylvia exhales and speaks softly. "I'm going to pretend you did not just say that. I don't think you understand..." She doesn't continue because her heart's not in her own point. Things are falling apart, everywhere. Is college an antidote to that? Maybe not. *God forgive me, but the thought of evading college tuition, especially now.*

Zeke, relieved and surprised that she didn't simply explode in righteous indignation, pushes on. "I'm an explorer, Mom. A certain type of explorer. And I can't explore the world if I'm stuck in a chair inside another classroom somewhere. Besides, why should you spend all that money if I don't want to be there, huh? Spend it on Jeannie. She's the intellectual in this family, anyway."

"I'll speak to your father," Sylvia says. "But don't sell yourself short. You have your brilliant moments."

"Well, anyway," Zeke says, heading inside, "I've made up my mind, and it's my life, and you guys can't tell me what to do." *Fuckin' A.* He disappears quickly, back to his room, before his mother can decide whether to prolong the discussion.

"What kind of explorer?" Sylvia calls out, belatedly.

Since neither child has thought to ask Sylvia how she plans to spend *her* day, she feels no obligation to fill them in on recent events. They will know what Carson knows, which is that she has decided to strike out on her own, but they will only be told when they need to be. In any case, since Jeannie has the day off, Sylvia decides to ask her to go to ShopFine to pick up some things. She sends Jeannie rather than Zeke because she knows that he'll come back with half a dozen non-essential items, such as a new pair of sharp scissors, or a chintzy mustache beer stein plucked from a bin of miscellaneous junk on sale, while forgetting half the stuff they really need. Jeannie will basically stick to the list, and if she needs tampons, well, that's essential too. Sylvia is still getting used to the fact that her children are edging toward adulthood, and even if they're not there emotionally—nowhere near—they are certainly old enough to take on adult-sized errands, leaving Sylvia more time to figure out what she's supposed to be doing now.

Jeannie refuses to drive her mother's red Audi. Too ostentatious. So she's in Carson's Ford pick-up. She likes riding high, but also driving a truck gives her a deep sense of belonging. *Whatever I end up doing, it's gonna require a truck.* She slowly noses the pick-up into a parking space at the far end of the ShopFine parking lot, to avoid any possible contact with other vehicles. She literally shivers every time she imagines putting a ding in her dad's truck, so she goes out of her way to avoid every scenario where that could happen. She drops down from the cab and shoulders a miscellaneous assortment of tote bags she brought for groceries. Jeannie made a point of asking her mother to round them up for her, while explaining why they should never use paper or plastic, and wondering aloud why her parents can't get it into their heads that the Earth's resources are limited, the oceans are clogged with garbage, and recycling is one small way we can all keep the planet from getting any worse. Sylvia waits out Jeannie's lecture, which she's heard before, and doesn't burden her with her own cynical views that recycling is a crock designed to make people feel better, and that as far as the environment goes, the horse has already left the barn. Nor does she point out to Jeannie that driving the truck burns more fossil fuel than the Audi. Being a teenager, Sylvia reflects, is a glorious opportunity to marry huge quantities of righteous certitude with an equally huge dearth of real-world perspective. *And that's Jeannie in a nutshell.* So she hands her the tote bags without a word.

Jeannie makes her way through the grocery list. She's in the checkout line, browsing her social feed filled with assorted crises, when she hears a voice so familiar, it may as well be her own. She looks up. It's Gina. Gina is the cashier. Gina, wearing a plum-colored ShopFine apron, her dark hair pulled back in a ponytail, is putting somebody's bananas on the scale and punching in the code. Thank you, Gina says to the customer, in a fake-happy, absent sort of voice. She looks suddenly older, and professional, and, Jeannie thinks, she looks sad.

Jeannie knows that Gina's large brown eyes have a way of narrowing when she's unhappy. And as Gina looks down at the register, handing change to her customer, her eyes are as narrow as Jeannie's ever seen them. Gina hasn't yet noticed Jeannie, who is still two customers away. A thought strikes Jeannie hard: Two years ago, Jeannie would already be waving, shouting, running over to embrace her best friend. They'd probably giggle. But everything's different now. *When did we both get so serious? Like, grown-up serious?* But it's more than that. Ever since the winter coat drive, and the SATs too, Jeannie can't shake the feeling that she's not the only one changing; everything is changing around her. Things feel unsteady, somehow. Wobbly, maybe. And her parents, too, are changing, though they don't seem willing to admit it. *Or maybe they don't see it?* Mom, staring off into space, more and more. Dad, doing God-knows-what on his computer in the middle of the night. *Oh, God. Not porn. He wasn't covering up porn. No, not my dad. He would never.* And now Gina: not who she used to be, but somebody else. *I guess that means I'm somebody else too. She can't leave me that far behind.* And then another thing really hits home: Jeannie didn't know Gina was working. She certainly didn't know she was working here, in the very grocery store they've been coming to since they were little kids. Back when it was still Grazinski's. Jeannie suddenly remembers her mom pushing the two of them in the cart together. They crouched in the basket because they were already too old to fit in the small section of the cart up front. Maybe first grade? It's almost unthinkable that Gina would keep a secret like this from her, that Jeannie wouldn't be the *first* person she'd tell.

Gina pulls Jeannie's cart forward for unloading on her side of the register. Jeannie rushes to get the first word in. "Hey," is all she can think to say. Gina jumps. "Sorry, didn't mean to—"

"No, it's—it's okay, it's fine, I just didn't—". Gina sends Jeannie's groceries through check-out.

"Why didn't you tell me?"

"I meant to," Gina says.

"At least let me—". Jeannie sets up her tote bags and begins packing groceries.

"No, really, it's faster if I do it," Gina says, quickly. She looks around to see if any managers are nearby. Jeannie steps back, suddenly nervous. She feels like she's performing a role she didn't have time to rehearse. Gina's performing a role too, and while she doesn't look happy about it, she doesn't look uncomfortable doing it, either. *Privilege makes me so stupid*, Jeannie thinks. *And useless.*

"Do you get a break?" Jeannie asks, because she doesn't know what else to say and because, maybe, if they can grab a few minutes to step outside together, they can get back to a "normal" footing.

"Not for, oh, a while. You shouldn't wait. That's $78.07. You saved $4 today."

Jeannie freezes, Gina's dead-professional voice slamming around in her head. It's like a body-snatcher movie, where they take the real Gina, the future social-worker-who's-gonna-save-the-world Gina, and put this plasticized machine in her place. Somebody waiting in line shuffles and coughs loudly. Jeannie hands over her mother's credit card. And then, without a chance to look behind her, or perhaps not looking because she can't bear to, she is outside, pushing the cart with the stuffed tote bags.

"Hey, chicken," a woman calls, as Jeannie begins angling the cart down the curb cut into the parking lot. "Hey, sweetie," the woman says, putting a hand on the side of Jeannie's cart. Jeannie stares at the hand: dirty, with long, ragged fingernails and swollen knuckles. "Are you the coat girl?"

"Am I the…". Jeannie looks at the woman, heavy-set, with wiry, unruly gray hair. Her face looks raw and wind-chapped, with lines radiating out from her eyes. She wears a long brown coat with a faux-fur collar. "Am I the…," Jeannie repeats.

"The coat girl," Winnie Suggs repeats. "You are, aren't you?"

Jeannie relaxes her grip on the grocery cart and smiles. "Yeah. But I had a lot of help, it wasn't just me."

"I wanna thank you," Winnie says, hugging the coat to her. "This been a life-saver. Cold winter, y'know?"

"I'm really, really glad. I'm really glad you found that coat. It looks great on you. You doin' okay?" Jeannie turns back to the cart, hating herself for wanting to turn away, to climb back up into the truck, and think about Gina. *Should I give her money? I only have $5. How insulting would that be?*

"Yeah, okay. Honey, I ain't gonna keep you. I just wanna know. When you were in the store." Winnie pauses. Jeannie watches the large-breasted woman's chest, rising and falling with each wheezy breath. "Did you see the new girl? The young one?"

"The new girl?"

"She's the only young one in there, now, but that'll change. Mr. Bill, I think he's weedin' out the old-timers. I got lucky—goin' first," Winnie laughs, then coughs. "What's that saying? Age before beauty? Somethin' like that." She lights a loose cigarette hiding in her coat pocket. Jeannie takes a step back away from the tobacco smoke, feeling like a silly little fool, even as she does so.

"I'm sorry," Jeannie says. "I'm really sorry. I don't know what you're asking me. I can be so stupid sometimes."

"It's all right, chicken. You maybe didn't even see her. The new girl at the register. Dark hair, I think." Jeannie's stomach does a flip. "I just wanna know she's doin' a good job, is all. I don't begrudge her. She don't know she's takin' somebody else's job. Wasn't my job no more, anyway, since he fired me. But still. They can't kill ya for bein' curious, can they? Maybe they can. I don't know."

"Um," Jeannie feels her face getting hot. She's suddenly in the middle of a situation, for which she feels morally unprepared, despite her best intentions—and which she never anticipated when she set off in the truck little more than an hour ago. "Well," she says, trying to choose her words carefully, not sure where the landmines are. "The new girl—I think she's just part-time...Does that count?"

Winnie laughs her smoker's laugh. Jeannie now realizes that if Winnie presses her on how she knows the "new girl" is part-time, she'll have to explain that they're friends, which, as Jeannie sees it, makes her complicit, somehow, in whatever was done to Winnie—not really, but sort of. But Winnie doesn't go there. "Well, then, they payin' her even less than me. Fillin' in with the part-timers, I guess. Hope she got a good home to go to, 'cause you can't make it out here on what they pay, even if you got the hours." Winnie shakes her head. "They are really somethin', huh?" Jeannie doesn't know whether or how to respond. "I let you go. You're a good girl, givin' out all those coats. I appreciate you."

Winnie Suggs walks away, a limp in her step, and lowers herself, slowly, to the cement, her back against the wall of the store, a few yards from the entrance. Jeannie watches her and thinks she's the only one to see her. *She's invisible. Down and out and done with. Nobody's problem.* Jeannie feels like she can't move. Like she shouldn't move. Like there's unfinished business here at ShopFine. She parks her cart, the ice cream only just beginning to soften around the edges in the chilly March air. *Fuck you, Jeannie King, if you can't do just one damn hard thing like you're supposed to.* She walks over to Winnie.

"I'm sorry, I don't know your name," Jeannie says, standing over her.

"Winnie Suggs, honey. You don't have to talk to me no more. You go on home now and get your groceries put away."

"Ms. Suggs, or Mrs. Suggs, or...do you need a place to stay tonight? Any night?" Jeannie's heart is racing with fear, with anxiety, with embarrassment, with a clear understanding that she's out of her depth but wants to get this right. If she stops to think it all through, she won't act. *Compassion is action.*

"I'm all right, chicken. Thank you." Winnie looks away. "Doin' just fine."

Now what, idiot? Make her feel like shit, or walk away and do nothing? She isn't doin' just fine. But what can I really do about it?

Jeannie nods. She reaches out her hand, to shake Winnie's hand. Winnie is turned away, her coat collar pulled up around her face. A March wind is picking up; the sky is gray. Jeannie can't bear to stand here another moment, facing failure like this, letting herself down, giving the lie to all the stories she tells herself about how she'll never turn away from injustice. *Yeah, right, you bougie bitch.* She tosses the groceries into the back seat of the truck, climbs up into the cab, sticks the key in the ignition, and then sits there. *I don't deserve to go home, like nothing happened.* She looks at Winnie from across the parking lot. From a distance, Winnie appears to be stock-still, sleeping, maybe, her coat pulled tightly around her. Or maybe she's thinking about her old job, which was taken away from her...why?...so the store could bring in younger help and pay them less? She watches the sliding door of the ShopFine and thinks about Gina standing there at the register, punching in numbers, sliding bags of frozen peas and potato chips and cartons of orange juice into Earth-killing plastic bags. Jeannie leans her head against the steering wheel to think.

CHAPTER TWENTY-ONE

```
Miller Brothers Auctioneers, Inc. His-
toric brick storefronts known as the Baker
Block, 608-622 Main St., Willing. Zoned
C-2 Commercial. May 19. 3:00pm. Qualified
bidders only.
```

Because of deep budget cut-backs, the Remington County Police Department cannot afford to patrol downtown Willing more than once a night, usually between midnight and 2 a.m. The district command is considering eliminating this patrol altogether, in order to shift scarce resources elsewhere. It's not as if anything is happening around Main Street at night, anyway. There's nobody on foot, so no one to rob, and hardly any stores left to break into; even a desperate thief would have to be stupid to bother. The town's commercial center is barely commercial, anymore. Nor can the county afford to remove all the weeds that have continued to sprout between the cracked sidewalks and among the broken patches of asphalt on Main Street itself. A hard winter created frost heaves that have caused sections of the street to crack and buckle—the better for weeds to take root. Repaving Main Street is out of the question; the county has already committed every penny of its meager transportation budget coming down from the state, and its own coffers are anemic. It's a constant triage situation, and downtown Willing—in fact, Greater Willing in general—is not the patient likeliest to be saved, at this point. That privilege is reserved for places like Linton Crossing, where something resembling a viable tax base still exists. So the old stone cornices and lintels that have given Willing its quaint character for more than a century continue to topple into the streets below, as ancient mortar is pried loose by rain and wind. There's nobody left on the public payroll to pick it up and cart it off to the dump. The chunks fall where they may, like ancient Rome collapsing in on itself.

For Zeke, Farrah, and Geronimo, the persistent air of desertion downtown means they are far more excited about their new little venture than they are worried about getting into trouble for trespassing. Still, they're taking some precautions this evening. The three of them, dressed alike in black T-shirts, jeans, and sneakers, are using duct tape to put heavy-duty black plastic trash bags across each of the street-facing windows of the long-empty second story apartment they've decided to take over. The light bulbs are burned out in roughly a third of the old-fashioned curved lampposts that line the street down below, so any light shining from above might catch the attention even of a sleepy patrol officer cruising Main Street in the dark. The four rooms are small and musty, but adequate for their purpose, with scarred old wooden floors, paint-chipped walls, and, in the two bedrooms, peeling wallpaper, revealing layers of cabbage roses and yellow stripes. There's no electricity or running water, but that's what the candles, camping lantern, and gallon water jugs are for. The water is for flushing the toilet, not for drinking. There's absolutely no trace of the immigrant Lithuanian family that lived here more than a century ago, eight of them crammed into four rooms, directly above the little dry goods shop they managed, right up until the first Great Depression. But Zeke, Farrah, and Geronimo wouldn't care about that, anyway. Ghosts of the past can do nothing for them. Only the present matters.

Zeke had told his mother he was an explorer. But now, he feels like an entrepreneur, like his dad. Ready to take on risks in exchange for rewards. He considers discovering this place to be proof of that. Another sign, in Zeke's mind, is that lately, his left hand feels like a 4, meaning pretty good flexibility. He's basically able to curl his left hand around the roll of duct tape, and rip with his right. It's been almost a year since the accident, and Zeke has not returned to Willing Enclave. He has no intention of working there this summer, and anyway, his dad hasn't invited him back. He figures, if he can make some money, they'll leave him be, for now. And making money is definitely part of their plan, but not, perhaps, even the most exciting part.

The space is now pitch black, except for the dim flare of the camp lantern, turned low to avoid attracting attention. But no light can escape now. Farrah turns up the brightness on the lantern. The sterile white LED light throws their shadows onto the wall opposite the blackened windows. The lantern emits a quiet hiss. The three of them stand in silence a moment, staring at their shadows—Geronimo tall and thin, almost scarecrow-like; Zeke, shorter and muscular, as he's filled out this past year; and Farrah, small and nimble, her nearly shaved head looking rounded and strange on the wall. Geronimo is still the coolest guy Zeke has ever met; he radiates an effortless beauty that mesmerizes Zeke, and the feeling has not worn off, even as they've gotten to know one another.

"So, Geronimo," Zeke says, mainly for the chance to catch the other boy's gaze.

"Yup?" Geronimo responds.

"Your name."

"Dude, I can't believe you waited this long to ask," Geronimo smiles. "I should give you a prize or some shit."

"So tell me," Zeke says. "Geronimo. . . GerONiMOOOO!"

"My grandpa was part-Apache or some shit. I'm not really sure." Zeke traces his finger along the ridge of Geronimo's cheek.

"That's why your cheekbones—"

"Nah, it's probably a bullshit story," Geronimo says. "But he was a cool Indian, y'know? Geronimo was. So I'm ok with that shit."

"I don't know shit about my family," Zeke says. "It's like, my parents came outta nowhere."

"Me, neither," Farrah says, fiddling with the lantern.

"At least you got a good story," Zeke says to Geronimo.

"I looked him up once, Geronimo," Geronimo says, "since he's my namesake and all. Figured I should check it out. He said some cool shit. He said, 'While I'm alive, I want to live well,' or some shit like that."

"Well that's perfect, isn't it?" Farrah says.

"Perfect," Zeke says. He looks around. "So what should we call this place?"

"Azkaban," Farrah says.

"*Los perdidos,*" Geronimo says. "The lost ones."

"Or how about we keep it simple, so people can remember. The Cave," Zeke suggests.

"The Cavern," Farrah says.

"I like that," Geronimo says. "The Cavern."

"Yeah," Zeke agrees. "That works."

With the light flickering on the crusty wall, Geronimo begins a fluid wave with his arms, and then begins dancing, gyrating, slowly, his gazed fixed on his own shadow. Zeke and Farrah begin moving around him. Their shadow limbs slide and tangle and blend together on the wall. *Like we're one beast, one strange animal, like nothing else anyone has ever seen,* Zeke thinks. *Deep in the Cavern.* Then their phones ping, almost simultaneously, and the spell is broken.

"Holy shit. We're up to 27," Zeke says.

"That's crazy town," Geronimo says.

"Yesterday, we didn't know if we'd get one," Farrah says.

Zeke rubs his knuckles on her scalp. "You mean *you* didn't think we'd get anybody."

"Is there, like, a cut-off?" Geronimo says. "I think there should be a cut-off because—"

"Because that makes us, like, exclusive," Zeke picks up, following Geronimo's line of thought. "We can charge more."

"Like a lot more," Farrah says.

"This is gonna be fucking awesome," Zeke says. Farrah pulls a joint and a lighter from her jeans. They sit with their backs to the window, passing it back and forth, watching their shadows on the far wall.

"I hope somebody brings beer," Zeke says.

"There's gonna be a shit-ton of beer, son." Farrah laughs.

An hour goes by in two minutes. There's nothing left to do. They've blown up the air mattresses and tossed them on the floor in the bedrooms. They've balanced a pair of small wireless speakers brought by Geronimo on the ledge of one of the wide window sills. Around 11, Zeke goes downstairs to crack open the heavy metal door tucked inconspicuously into the brick wall near the rear of the building, permanently shadowed by the narrow alley separating this building from the next. He discovered the door—and its willingness to open—a week ago, while on a solo scouting expedition just for this purpose, when tonight's apparent reality was still just a cool idea. He opens the door a few inches now, holding a flashlight facing downward, so there's no chance of flashing any light toward the street. Still buzzed, he listens to the darkness. He listens to Willing's particular brand of darkness, which feels to him like a combination of loss and death and loneliness—an ending—though to what, he is not quite sure. But at the same time, the darkness ripples through him in giddy waves, promising adventures, a chance for his soul to discover new territory, break new ground.

And then Zeke sees dark shapes coming towards him, moving against the dark itself, and he hears feet crunching on fragments of gravel, stone, and grass. *It's starting. Tomorrow will be nothing like today.* People begin clustering quietly at the door, some with six packs of beer, most with nothing but their own curiosity and craving for contact. The quiet is instinctual because it's understood this is a private party, as private as it gets. Invitation only, in a place where nobody is supposed to be right now. The bodies stand patiently, waiting to be waved in by the flick of Zeke's flashlight. They are white, black, brown, young and not so young. Male, female, hetero, queer, trans, nonbinary. One by one, they climb the old wooden stairs up to the immigrant family's former residence, where Farrah and Geronimo collect cash from each of them, until their pockets are bulging with the first profits of their new enterprise.

Chapter Twenty-Two

Sylvia, dressed in her sharpest navy blue business suit, drives her red Audi in silence. Carson, also in a dark suit, and wearing a WPC cap pulled down low, sits next to her, grim-faced. The Audi will be parked conspicuously in front of the house on display today. It's part of the shock-and-awe offensive, and while the Audi may not scream success like, say, the Bachmans' twin Porsches, the Kings can only deploy the assets they have. The silence is due, in part, to their shared view that if you cannot say something positive and uplifting, and cite clear evidence of progress, it is better left unsaid. There's nothing to be gained by dragging one another down. That's the unwritten but well understood rule of the Kings' private mutual aid and cheer society. Up to now, anyway. Sylvia turns on the windshield wipers, upping her aggravation level considerably, since an outdoor open house is practically a nonstarter if the rain really picks up. She mentally runs through the list of brokers, agents, former clients, and potential prospects she's been cultivating for two months now, specifically leading up to this. She can barely resist the temptation to auto-dial every single person to remind them about the event, and tell them the rain is expected to stop, though she has no idea if that is true. This is her maiden voyage as a solo practitioner. And even though she's done hundreds of deals over the last 20 years, she feels raw, hugely exposed, like a rookie hosting her first open house. And she hates herself for feeling this way.

Carson is thinking about the growing list of developments he has not shared with his wife—not yet, anyway—and whether the wisest plan is to continue to keep his own counsel. For starters, he used the last of the funds salvaged from aggressive online poker playing to buy lumber, electrical and plumbing supplies, and a week of labor from Bruno and Jorge, all for the one house receiving attention at Willing Enclave. He made that $25,000 over the course of three sleepless nights, after going into the red by nearly $50,000. The loss forced him to quickly buy a loan online at an exorbitant rate, which he paid back equally quickly after a much needed lucky streak. He was then left with the $25,000 that he plowed into contracting supplies and cheap muscle over the last several weeks. Sylvia has never felt a need to pry deeply into Carson's business affairs, so she doesn't know what Willing Prime Contractors has, or doesn't have, in the bank. She has gauged his success over the years by what got built. Essential to their pact—marital and otherwise—is their implicit faith in their mutual success, unless or until both are forced to look at strong evidence to the contrary. Darius and Vin know full well that Carson must have dipped into his own pocket, and they know there will have to be a reckoning. But the three agreed, after minimal discussion, that getting the house ready for potential buyers is the sole focus of their time and attention, in the short term, although their motives for doing so are not identical. Carson has had some time to think about the risks he's been taking, and the extent to which he is apparently willing to court disaster. He has concluded that "courting" is all he's done; disaster has not really moved in and taken up residence. The Baker Block is up for auction in a few days, after all, and Carson refuses to be counted out.

As Sylvia drives up the hill toward Willing Enclave, the construction site peeks out over the top of the rise. Sylvia sees instantly that there is no wow factor. Nothing screams *Buy me!* Or *Exclusive!* For so long now, Carson has talked about Willing Enclave as the new gateway to a small, highly desirable residential community that buyers will covet from all over. She had no reason to doubt him, based on past experience. On her visit with Jeannie last year, Sylvia could still plausibly imagine that everything Carson has been saying about this property would still come true. He just had to fight a little harder for it than he was used to. But now, months later, the whole site has a discouraged, disheveled air. The rise isn't high enough to command a view of anything in particular. The surrounding land doesn't show off any spectacular nature. It's quite ordinary, really; just another gash in the ground, created from an expectation that building something from nothing is a reliable way to make a profit. Sylvia imagines the houses themselves are embarrassed—not ready to step into the limelight because they are half-dressed and under-rehearsed. Two of the houses are still mainly just upright wooden matchsticks, with just a hint of subflooring and exterior Tyvek, loose pieces flapping in the wet breeze. The three empty foundations have now been empty for over a year, their once-clean edges beginning to lose definition with each passing season. And the house on which Carson has lavished his gambling funds, and where he, Darius, and Vin, with last-minute muscle from Bruno and Jorge, have spent all their time in recent months, looks, well, *blah*, Sylvia thinks. The front windows of the model home all lack shutters, and look naked without them. The huge, French country-style front door looks out of place—like Cinderella all decked out at the wrong ball. There are large bare patches in the row of hydrangeas that are meant to soften the front of the house. And the planned bluestone walkway leading up to the house is just a collection of loosely placed stones; nothing has been set in place yet. Nothing is *finished.*

Sylvia stands in front of the houses—or rather, the *suggestion* of houses—that she is supposed to sell today. She knows now she shouldn't have let her imagination run away with her without coming back out to the site. She shouldn't have spent $1,200 out-of-pocket on creating big color posters imagining the finished product—the sexy, chic, expensive-looking houses on the hill, reserved for the most discerning buyers who expect to live in sunshine every day of the year. The renditions are an embarrassing fiction next to the real thing. They show imposing edifices, lush front gardens, kids on bicycles, a backyard cook-out on a side deck. Pure fiction. Not remotely plausible, right now. *I'm supposed to sell the dream, and all he's given me is a shit show.*

Sylvia, vibrating with furious energy, yanks the posters out of her trunk and sets them up on the easels she brought. They look ridiculous—idyllic renderings dwarfed by the messy, muddy reality right in front of everybody. But what choice does she have now? Carson is yards away conferring with Darius and Vin. The three men stand with their WPC caps pulled down, hands stuffed in their pockets. All three wear suits, making them appear weirdly out of place on their own construction site. They trudge over toward Sylvia, standing by the renderings. Darius and Vin wear work boots, which look just silly, like boys playing at being men, Sylvia thinks. Carson wears dress shoes, but he's practically hopping to avoid all the mud.

"Do people show up on time at these things these days, or what?" Carson asks his wife. He looks toward the model home. "It's come a long way, right?" Darius and Vin nod.

"It depends," she says curtly.

"I've got a good feeling," Carson says, looking to his partners. "People can use their imaginations, can't they? Anybody coming out here for a look isn't stupid. They'll get it."

"Thank you, Sylvia, for all your hard work on this," Vin says.

"We appreciate the leap of faith," Darius says.

"I wouldn't call it a leap of faith," Carson says, irritated. "It's not a fucking magic show. We're not the first people to sell homes that aren't built yet. Jesus, Dizz."

A black Mercedes pulls up and all four look to see who it is. Sylvia is the only one to recognize Ann Likert, the last person she wants to see right now. The shame of getting booted out of Bachman Realty is lodged deep in her bones, and seeing her former colleague makes her whole body ache with it. But if Ann has come all the way back here from her new home turf in Linton Crossing, then perhaps she intends to bring buyers, which means Sylvia just has to suck it up. *The only way this day gets worse is if it pours.* The two women air kiss. Sylvia introduces Ann to the men, who immediately perk up. She wears a Burberry raincoat and high-heeled boots, and she steps daintily around the mud and debris. Ann glances at the posters, which Sylvia knows she considers completely irrelevant—and not remotely convincing.

"Walk her through the site," Sylvia tells the men. Even Darius and Vin suddenly become cheerleaders, and the three men talk brightly about the south-facing kitchens, the customizations available to buyers, and generally extol the extraordinary value to be found at Willing Enclave. Sylvia hangs back, despite being the broker of record for this property. She watches the men, out of earshot, gesticulating wildly and enthusiastically, as if all it takes to convince Ann Likert is to engage in a lot of arm-waving. Sylvia thought she wanted to lean in to this opportunity, but instead finds herself feeling oddly disconnected. What if this has been her last chance? What if everything she's not only worked for, but anticipated achieving for an endless stretch of months and years, has actually come to an end? And what if there's nothing she can do about it? Sylvia watches herself watching them disappear around to the backside of the house. She has a thought so anathema, so heretical to everything she's worked for, alongside her husband, that she wonders if she is truly ill, or about to get a big migraine.

I actually don't care if I never sell another house.

A second car pulls up the hill and parks next to Ann's Mercedes. A man in a dark blue business suit whom Sylvia has never seen approaches her, his eyes scanning the property. He holds out his hand. "Tom Jergens. Second National Bank." Tom takes a business card out of his breast pocket and hands it to Sylvia. "And you are?" Sylvia explains and directs him toward the house, where the tour is still going on. "No, that's okay," Tom says. "I don't know if you're aware, but we've been acquired by Contrails Capital. I'm just tying up loose ends before they ship me out to Phoenix next week. I thought I'd catch them…" He examines the houses. "This won't be half-bad…if it's ever finished." He chuckles.

"What do you mean, if?" Sylvia asks. While she has her own doubts, the word "if" from a banker sounds ominous. Tom takes a folded brown envelope out of his coat pocket and hands it to her. "Give them this." She takes it, but she doesn't ask what the envelope contains. She assumes it isn't good news, and bad news can always wait, even just a bit. Besides, whatever is in this envelope isn't meant to land on her. It's *their* problem. It's *their* bed and they'll have to lie in it. It'll be up to Carson to shield *her* and their family, from any direct blowback. *None of this is my fucking fault.*

Tom stands another moment, looking around. He shakes his head. "You know, people always want to blame the banks for everything that goes wrong with the economy. But this is way bigger than us. Way, way bigger. What's going on here," he waves his arm, "and pretty soon, everywhere, I'm afraid..." He trails off, still shaking his head. "Well, anyway, it's going to get ugly. Probably very ugly. At least Phoenix has lots of sunshine." Tom Jergens turns his back to Sylvia and walks toward his car.

Ann and the men return just after Tom has left. "Who was that?" Carson asks. "Why didn't you give them the tour, or send them back to us?"

"He wanted to give you this." Sylvia hands the brown envelope to Carson, who exchanges glances with Darius and Vin before pocketing it himself. All three see the bank's name on the envelope.

"So, Ann, what do you think?" Carson asks.

"Well," Ann says, checking her phone, "I think buyers are going to have a hard time seeing the possibilities until the model is completed finished and staged, and at least some of the landscaping is done. When will that be?" She looks to the men for answers, but her expression doesn't show much interest.

"Very soon," Carson responds quickly. "Early summer." Vin and Darius look down. Neither sees any point in contradicting him in front of the realtor.

"And I can tell you now, you'll need to lower the asking price," Ann adds, still scrolling through missed messages.

"Again?" Darius asks. "We already did, obviously."

Ann looks at him like he's a child. "It's all about the comps. You must know that. They're down. Way down." She looks at Sylvia. "It's not a seller's market. Look, I'm sorry. You've kind of gotten caught with your pants down, here." She checks her phone once more. "I've got to go. Thanks for the tour."

Ann walks away briskly in her high-heeled boots, already on the phone with a client—not a client for Willing Enclave, as Sylvia and her husband and partners all assume. And then a very heavy spring rain drenches everything, ruining all the signs before Sylvia can yank them off the easels.

"Where are all the buyers?" Carson asks, as they all begin racing to their cars. Sylvia does not give him an answer.

Chapter Twenty-Three

It's perpetual twilight inside the green nylon camping tent pitched in the Kings' backyard. The interior of the tent occupies a different space-time continuum from the outside world. Inside the tent, seconds, minutes, and hours are meaningless. Time is measured by the degrees of light and dark that filter in, and by the temperature, which ranges from steamy at mid-day to cold and clammy at night and in the early morning. And also by bursts of hunger, or a sudden urgency in the gut, which can strike any time at all. Sound travels differently, as well. A trapped mosquito is as loud as a B-2 bomber, and spring rain pelts with the sharp rap-rap-rap of a hailstorm.

Winnie Suggs, lying on a plastic air mattress inside this tent, looks up at a daddy longlegs climbing up toward the crest of the tent. She feels her life turning, like a log spinning around a bend in a river, and like the log, she has no idea where she's heading, or why, or how she is meant to *be.* But for now, and tomorrow, as far as she knows, this is home. Tucked in one corner of the tent is her brown winter coat serving as a kind of hold-all for other clothing—a few pairs of nylon underpants and bras, white tube socks, a few XXL polyester shifts with elastic at the neck and arms, and a pair of flip flops. A worn Ziploc bag holds a few toiletries. Over the last several months, without a stable place to call home, Winnie's possessions have dwindled down to the essentials. She lost track long ago of the other stuff she once owned, and took for granted; stuff that sat piled, stacked, hung, or hidden away in the studio apartment she rented for years. It's good to let go, she's decided, or at least, to accept her current unencumbered state, which just feels like the inevitable tide of her life, the log floating and twisting along the bends in the river, with little actual control over its own direction, or foreknowledge of its destination, until death asserts itself as the final decision maker. Winnie isn't afraid of death. She isn't afraid of much; she just takes it as it comes. Next to her little pile of stuff in the tent sits a cardboard box containing a pop-top tin of baked beans, a box of Saltines, two oranges, and a half-gallon jug of water, all courtesy of Jeannie King, "until we figure all this out," she'd said.

Winnie shifts her loosening bulk on the skimpy air mattress, preparing herself, mentally and physically, to get up and get out. The transition is hard for her. Maybe it will get easier as time goes on, she thinks, though she doesn't expect it will. Huddled in the doorway of the ShopFine, Winnie felt sheltered—like she was inside even when she was outside. And she knew exactly what surrounded her—every inch of concrete and steel, solid and stalwart, dependable as friends. She's trying to believe that inside the tent, though it's way wobblier than ShopFine, it's the same way, and that in time—if there is time—the tent will feel like a friendly place, and dependable too. It's not that she doesn't want to be here. Not exactly. She came willingly, after all, after a long conversation with Jeannie and her friend with the dark hair—the one Winnie knows took her place at the ShopFine register. The girls painted her a picture of a safe space. They were kind, and constantly apologizing, and trying so hard to please and respect her. Winnie knew they meant well, and the cold concrete was, in fact, beginning to send jagged pains shooting through her buttocks and spine. And so she said yes to the girls. And the looks on their faces—that alone was worth facing the unknown. Winnie believes that pleasing people is her one true talent, and she'll go a long way to put it to good use.

But outside the tent is another story. Outside, there is a vast, unsettling openness. A huge stretch of grass and wind and sky. She feels unsheltered, less tethered to her own life, and for a moment she misses the ShopFine fiercely. She thinks about what it really means to be *civilized.* Nights at the women's shelter, where the moment your take your eyes off of a possession, it disappears, were not civilized.

Living in her own tiny studio apartment, commuting to ShopFine for her shift every day, that was civilized, surely, though she didn't think of it that way at the time. And now this. Is she becoming less civilized, less defined as a person who belongs in the world? What is she? Who is she? Living in a tent offers a semi-indoor space, whereas the ShopFine is, Winnie admits, outdoors. So surely indoors is better than outdoors. And yet...there is still all this unpredictable wildness to contend with. It's not that she expects a bear or even a rabid raccoon to jump her by surprise. It's just the huge un-defined-ness of it. Direction-less space. There is the Kings' house, dozens of yards away, but it's too complicated to deal with right now. That's another kind of indoor space—the opposite of the women's shelter, where it's not clear what you *can* touch or claim. It's all very confusing.

But the moment has come when she must leave the tent. She unzips the flap and crawls out slowly, awkwardly, on all fours, her hands pressing on cold, wet grass. She stands slowly, stiffly, her back aching, her white-socked feet instantly soaked by the early morning dew. Next time, she'll put shoes on first. Then something appears in the corner of her vision and she is startled. She narrows her eyes to focus her vision. It's another tent. Not a wild animal, at least. A blue tent, almost exactly like hers. She does not know what to make of this. It never occurred to her that she wouldn't be all alone out here. She is puzzled, rather than comforted, and feels even more unsure of what she is doing here, what is to become of her, now that she has an actual neighbor. There is no sign of life from the other tent. And Winnie cannot wait any longer. She walks into the woods at the far end of the yard to relieve herself, using a packet of tissues to wipe her bottom. It's not the first time she's crapped outside, and she knows it won't be the last.

Gina has finally fallen asleep on the plastic air mattress in the blue tent, after a night spent tossing and turning, trying to find a comfortable position, curling like a fetus inside the sleeping bag she has borrowed from Jeannie. Gina has never gone camping before; she considers herself a city girl, far more concerned about being around people she understands how to help, whose problems seem somehow relatable, than immersing herself in whatever is going on in nature, which is too quiet, and which doesn't tell you what it's thinking. She finally drifts off just as the first gray light of the morning begins seeping into the tent, deepening and illuminating the shadows. By the time Winnie Suggs is unzipping her tent, Gina is sinking into REM sleep for the first time in two days. Both women are disoriented, their minds and bodies struggling to adjust to being inside and outside at the same time; each working hard to feel safe inside a floppy capsule that's buffeted by wind and rain.

Winnie walks back to her tent, still stiff and sore all over, feeling as if she's on the losing end of a boxing match. She bends, reluctantly, to reposition each of the plastic stakes jabbed into the soft, wet earth, just as Jeannie showed her yesterday. This shakes off the water that is pushing the sides of the tent into a concave position, returning the tent to a more taut position. What these kids know, Winnie thinks. Where does it come from? How many things have they done, and seen, and tried, that she's never been exposed to? Like camping and smoking marijuana and driving across the country and eating in a fancy restaurant where you don't even recognize the food on your plate. But she's the only person she knows who has slept at the ShopFine, she thinks, or knows the PLU code for rutabaga, whatever that is. Something has to be all mine, she thinks, and those experiences, at least, are all mine. The new girl can't possibly know all the codes. God, she would murder someone for a cigarette. Winnie crawls back into her tent and eats all the Saltines, then shakes the crumbs off her sleeping bag. Within an hour, a parade of tiny ants will make a trail to begin carting off those crumbs, but Winnie doesn't know this yet. She cannot imagine the arc of the day—this day or the next one. What's that place that's in between places? Limbo, she remembers. She's in limbo. So now what?

Gina sleeps until noon. She wakes up suddenly from a deep dream in which she's trying to fly across this yard, on her way to somewhere else, somewhere exciting, though she's been told it's a surprise, so she doesn't know where she's going. But she cannot get off the ground; instead she keeps kicking off from the grass in order to hover and skim for a few feet, just above the tip of the tent. Lifting off takes every ounce of her energy, like running a marathon. But still she cannot pull away. Her father is there, grabbing her by the ankle and yanking her back to earth, every time she tries to lift up and away. He looks angry, but also sad and scared. She wakes up feeling exhausted. She sits cross-legged on her sleeping bag, her long T-shirt sweaty and sticking to her back. She sucks down the last of her water. She's realizing this is all much trickier than she thought it would be, when she and Jeannie felt sure they were doing the right thing, the brave thing, by inviting Winnie Suggs to remove herself from the ShopFine premises. We didn't make her come, Gina thinks. She wanted to. It shouldn't matter that Gina is here for different reasons, or that Gina has a house she can return to, if she wants. The tents should be a great leveler; they're in this together. But that's not true, Gina realizes, and suddenly it's so complicated. Gina can so easily walk into the Kings' house, take a shower, borrow some clothes from Jeannie, help herself to orange juice and a bagel. In theory, Winnie can too—but really? Is this stranger with the sticking-up gray hair who nobody knows except to say hi to at the supermarket check-out counter...is this woman really going to waltz into the home of people she barely knows and act as if nothing is out of the ordinary? Or use the bathroom? My God, Gina thinks. Jeannie and I are idiots. Gina doesn't even know what Jeannie's told her parents about any of this, though two tents pitched in the Kings' backyard isn't something you can keep a secret. The tents are like a pair of mushrooms that swell up overnight. You can't hide the disfigurement. Not here, not on this vast, flat expanse of green.

Sylvia is transfixed. She sits on the deck, wrapped in sweat pants and a heavy wool sweater, drinking coffee. She cannot take her eyes off of the two tents. One blue. One green. *I'm seeing what I've already seen. How is that possible?* It's the vision that invaded her consciousness a year ago. A piece of it, anyway. Here it is, but is it real? *I'm fucking losing it. I have a brain tumor. I'm dying.* She has no idea how long she's been sitting here. She needs time to recover from the initial shock: walking out to the deck with her morning coffee, looking up...and then, this. The tents. No people. No cooking fires or laundry lines, but still.

The door slides open and Carson slips out onto the deck, looking like someone who hasn't slept in days. The skin around his eyes is folded and puffy. Sylvia wonders, briefly, if maybe they're *both* sick. If so, what would they tell the children? *Though they're not really children anymore, are they? Coming and going at all hours. Making their own decisions. Living lives that have nothing to do with either of us.* When is the last time the four of them did something normal, together, as a family? Sylvia can't remember. Carson and Zeke at the monster truck rally: That was a lifetime ago.

"What the fuck is that?" Carson asks. "What's going on, Sylvia?"

"I don't know," Sylvia says flatly. She does not see anything to be gained by telling Carson about her visions, months earlier. They still don't make sense to her, so she can't possibly explain them to him. She certainly doesn't want to voice her half-formed ideas about this—that the visions, from the beginning, she now realizes, marked the start of something just beyond her reach, something that is only now beginning to manifest. She's flooded with feelings she can't identify, triggered by the sight of these two tents, which materialized overnight. Like mushrooms. Or no, like fast-growing tumors. What she does know, what she can put her finger on, now, is that something around her has begun to shift, and has been shifting for a while. And that feeling, as well as the visions, are draining her like a car battery with the headlights left on too long.

"Well, who's out there? On our property?" Carson asks, testily. He half-wishes he owned a shotgun, because he'd haul that thing out here right now and fire a warning shot across the vast yard. *Get the fuck off my property.* But there is no gun. Instead, he cups his hands around his mouth and shouts out into the yard. "Hey!" There is no movement from either tent. He realizes his shout has died on the open air, well before it could reach them. *This is an encroachment,* he thinks, *and a violation. Shit's closing in. Not my fault. Not gonna take it lying down.* Carson wears an untucked flannel shirt and jeans, and he's barefoot. He walks out onto the grass, his feet instantly oozing with cold mud. Sylvia watches him trudge across the lawn. She feels a kind of paralysis creep over her; as though she has no free will, no will to actually do anything. This lump, this sedentary person, is someone she doesn't really recognize, yet here she is, clearly not taking matters—any matters—into her own hands, as an earlier version of Sylvia would do, she thinks. *I am a butterfly in reverse…crawling back into the chrysalis, instead of breaking free from it to explore the world on the wing.*

Carson approaches the green tent first, for no particular reason. Sylvia watches, shivering in the damp morning breeze. The faintest tingle of speech floats across the yard, unintelligible. She sees a head poking out of the green tent, but has no idea who it is, from this distance. Carson and the head speak to one another. The head disappears back into the tent. Carson appears agitated—Sylvia can recognize that much at almost any distance. Then the head emerges again, and they speak some more. The head disappears again, and Carson walks rapidly toward the blue tent. He says something, and a young woman emerges from the blue tent, in a long T-shirt and boxer shorts. Sylvia recognizes Gina by the shape of her body, the chunk of dark hair. *What is Gina doing here, in our yard, in a tent?* She watches as Carson puts a hand on her arm, briefly, and then he begins walking briskly back toward the deck. Gina goes back inside her tent.

Carson walks past Sylvia, shooting her a look that's both angry and puzzled, and he heads straight back into the house. He shouts, "Jeannie?! Jeannie!" He marches up to her room. Sylvia remains on the deck, hugging her arms for warmth, for comfort, waiting for all this to make sense, and for a sign telling her what to do about it.

"It's simple, Dad," Jeannie says, wide awake before he reaches the threshold to her room. "Don't make it into a big deal, when it's not."

"Simple how?" he asks, his voice a notch louder than normal.

"Winnie is the check-out lady from ShopFine. I mean, she used to be. Then they fired her for being old, or something, I'm not sure why. And she's been sleeping outside. And Gina and I—"

"What's Gina got to do with any of this? Why is she here—again? Why are they both here on our property? Why did you think any of this would be okay?" Carson fills the doorway to his daughter's room, his hands gripping either side of the door frame, as if he's propping up the entire house by himself.

Jeannie rolls her eyes. "What is your problem? Our yard is, like, a billion acres wide. They're not hurting anyone."

"That's not the point."

"Then what is the point?"

"They don't belong here."

"But I invited—"

"But *I* didn't," Carson snaps. "And neither did your mother—unless you're both hiding something from me."

"Oh my God, Dad. I don't know why you're so upset about two little tents in our ginormous backyard!" Jeannie pulls on sweat pants and a sweatshirt over her pajamas and jams on a pair of sneakers. "It's not like you're using it, or anything. You're never out there, except when you're pumping chemicals into the grass, killing off nature. It's like you don't want any living thing to touch your precious yard! That is so..." She fishes for the right word. "That is so...capitalist pig, Dad!" Jeannie ducks under her father's arm before he can say more, and bounds down the stairs. Carson stands in her doorway, trying to tamp down enormous waves of anger roiling his gut. *I'm just a fucking punching bag.* Carson goes to his own bedroom and sits on the edge of the bed, his hands spread on his knees. He's a tightly muscled man and right now, he hardly knows where to store, or else expend, the energy coiled inside him. The brown envelope that Tom Jergens had handed to Sylvia sits on top of his dresser, unopened, a triangular corner of the envelope jutting out—mocking him—over the edge of the bureau. He doesn't know what's in it, exactly, but he knows what it will mean, one way or another. And this afternoon, he and Dizz and Vin have no choice but to hash out their fate. Arrange their own firing squad, perhaps. Carson knows he's on a different page than his partners. And despite a nearly life-long track record of winning them over to his view on things—whether because he overpowers them with intellect, or logic, or just wears them down until they can't stand to listen to him anymore—this time, maybe for the first time, he isn't sure he'll succeed. Carson slips quietly downstairs to get his laptop. He brings it back up to the bedroom, flips it open, and dives into a high-stakes poker game. *Because somebody has to keep the wolf from the door.*

It's only 8:30 in the morning when the doorbell rings. Carson is so eye-glazingly deep into analyzing his opponent's poker strategy he doesn't really hear it. Zeke, who got in so late from the Cavern he's barely into a night's worth of sleep, is down for the count. Jeannie is delivering breakfast to Winnie and Gina—cinnamon rolls and to-go cups filled with tea. Sylvia can't imagine who would stop by like this on a Saturday morning. She opens the door a crack. There's a man, who appears neatly dressed but unshaven.

"Hello," he says, in lightly accented English. "I'm so sorry to disturb you so early, but I'm wondering...I'm hoping...is Gina here?"

Sylvia opens the door wider. "Mr. Martinez?" She hasn't laid eyes on him in years and immediately she sees the resemblance to his daughter, especially around the eyes. He is short and trim, nearly bald with a neat mustache. He wears a dark suit and an old-fashioned fedora. "Come in. You must have been so worried. I didn't realize myself until this morning...I assumed...I thought she would have let you know, or called you. They can be so thoughtless, sometimes, yes? Please, can I get you some coffee?"

"No, thank you. May I just...?" He looks uncomfortable, holding the hat with both hands.

"Follow me." Sylvia leads Javier Martinez through the kitchen out to the deck. She points to the blue tent. "She's in there. Or maybe I should say, *out* there." She can tell he is surprised by this. "As I say, I didn't know until this morning."

"But the ground is so damp," he says. Sylvia turns away, embarrassed and slightly annoyed. This isn't her doing; Gina isn't her responsibility. She didn't cook any of this up, and she doesn't like feeling she's somehow failing this sorrowful man who's never bothered to show up at his daughter's school functions, and who seems very un-fatherly. He's courtly, Sylvia thinks. What good is that to a teenage girl without a mother? "Of course, she's young. Nothing bothers the young," he says, as if sensing Sylvia's disgruntlement. "I will just..." He gestures toward the tent, as if seeking permission to tread across the overwhelmingly green, pristine perfection. Sylvia nods. She watches Javier stride across the yard, his shoulders hunched forward, the fedora back on his head. He looks like a man in a 1940s movie. Sylvia feels a flash of sympathy for Gina, growing up without a mother. But that doesn't mean she's prepared to take that on herself. She's suddenly weary of looking at the yard, at the tents. Perhaps some new law of nature will spring into action, and the tents, and the people in the tents, will simply vanish, taking their problems with them. But poor Gina, she thinks, guiltily. And poor Winnie. *Why is everything so complicated. I can't be expected...* She goes into the kitchen, eats half a cinnamon roll, stops herself, and then heads back upstairs to get dressed. She moves slowly because there doesn't seem to a point anymore to moving quickly. She's lost her taste for the chase. Assessing, measuring, evaluating, persuading, selling, putting a number to something that might be worthless in five years, or 10, or simply crumble into the earth a century on. It isn't real. But then, what is?

Sylvia sees her husband perched on the edge of the bed, his face pale and inches away from his laptop screen. He snaps the computer shut the instant he registers her presence and begins speaking rapidly, hoping to push on past the current moment.

"What's the situation out there?" he asks. Sylvia explains that Gina's father is speaking with his daughter this very minute, and presumably he will take her back home. "And the other one? Jeannie's pet project? We can't let that continue." Sylvia shrugs. "What if something happens to her while she's on our property? What if she dies out there? We could get sued. There'd be some kind of investigation. There'd be police and everybody else crawling all over the place—crawling all over our yard."

"Hah!" Sylvia laughs. "There's only one cop left on the payroll in this town, and I seriously doubt he'd make the trip out here, just to inspect our lawn."

Carson is standing now, pointing toward the window. "We need this shit like a hole in the head."

"Then *you* tell her to leave," Sylvia says. "I can't. I've seen her hanging around outside the market, like a ghost haunting its own house. I just can't."

Carson pauses and looks hard at his wife. "What's going on, Syl? I feel like I'm out here paddling pretty hard, and you're not paddling with me."

Sylvia sits on the edge of the bed. "I seem to have lost my paddle," she laughs, a catch in her throat.

"You ran away from Willing Enclave like it was on fire."

"I ran because it was pouring rain."

"You didn't..."

"I didn't produce. I didn't get the job done. That's what you want to say..." Her voice grows quiet. "So say it."

"Well. No. You didn't." Carson pauses. He takes the brown envelope off the bureau and fingers the edges. "You kind of fucked us, Sylvia."

"*I* fucked *you*?" Sylvia suddenly explodes. "Nobody can sell a pile of shit like that, Cap, I got news for you. Not even Ann Likert, who can do no wrong, it seems. You blew it. You and your half-assed partners. I don't know what the fuck you've been doing out there all these months, but nobody can put lipstick on that pig. So don't you dare—"

"Don't put this on me!" he yells back. "You agreed to the strategy! I didn't put a gun to your head! You agreed we'd try to pre-sell, that we'd try hard, so that we can raise some cash, and God knows, we need cash. A lot of cash."

Sylvia pauses. "How bad is it?" Carson doesn't answer, but she has a pretty good idea where they stand based on the whitish-gray tinge to his skin, and the jaw muscles he doesn't even realize he's clenching. She's fully capable of assessing the state of their joint bank account, but she's trying to ask him a larger question, to prod him toward a painful honesty that neither of them is eager to expose.

"I just..." she says.

"Just what?" Carson stands, rigid.

"I'm...I'm struggling to see the point."

"The point of *what*?"

"What's been driving us all these years—the glue holding us together. It's building a future, right, like it's an actual building that we're constructing from the ground up, brick by brick. And as that building rises, our lives get better, the rewards are bigger."

"We call that progress, don't we? What else is there?"

"Well, I don't..."

"Say it."

"I don't think so," she says, quietly now. "I don't think it works that way, anymore. I think...I think maybe progress is going extinct. Something like that. I can't really explain it. But I've, well, I've been seeing signs."

Carson picks up his laptop and puts his wallet and keys in his pants. He speaks quietly too, with menace in his voice, holding out the brown envelope from the late Second National Bank, now Contrails Capital. "I don't think this a good time for you to lose your shit, Sylvia. In fact, you couldn't have picked a worse time...Think about it."

"There are weeds growing on Main Street, Cap! We're dying, here!"

He leaves her there. She hears him pull his car out of the driveway. *I should never have said anything about the signs,* she thinks. *That was a mistake.*

By the time Sylvia returns downstairs, Javier Martinez is gone. Sylvia forces herself to walk out into the yard, but she cannot shake the feeling that she's treading on a field of bones and that her yard is a war zone in disguise. She is breathing rapidly, her nervous system inexplicably kicked into flight-or-fight mode by the time she reaches the blue tent, where Jeannie is playing gin rummy with Gina, the two of them sitting cross-legged and cozy like the little girls they once were. Sylvia suddenly realizes she's never had a close friend, like Gina is to Jeannie; she feels a pang of wistful envy.

Sylvia unzips the blue tent, uninvited. "Mom," Jeannie says, laying down cards. "Gina's grandma died last week. She just needs some space. Please."

"It's not my dad's fault," Gina says. "But I...I just can't be in that house right now."

"But he needs you, Gina," Sylvia says, crouching at the mouth of the tent flap. "I'm sure he does, at a time like this. I'm so sorry."

"He does better alone, Mrs. K.," Gina says. "He'd never say that, but he does. I'm just in the way."

"He came out here to get you, honey," Sylvia says. "He must be so lonely right now."

"Mom—" Jeannie says.

"No, Jeannie, it's okay," Gina says. "My dad doesn't have time to feel lonely. He doesn't feel much of anything, far as I can tell. And it's just…I can't…being in that house is like…" Gina's voice trails off. She looks away. Jeannie is aching for her. Sylvia sighs. She sees no easy way out of this. *Poor Gina. Poor everybody.* "Anyway," Gina says, softly, "I gotta get to work. Mind if I take a shower?"

"One week," Sylvia says. She zips them back into the tent and walks several yards over to the green tent. She pauses at the front flap. Winnie is snoring, though it's now nearly lunch time. She sleeps so deeply, she doesn't feel the trail of ants crawling across her, carrying Saltine crumbs back to the anthill. Sylvia doesn't see the point of waking her up just to kick her out. And she wants to see if Cap really has the guts to do it himself. This woman, kicked from pillar to post; adrift in her own town. How do these things happen to people? So for now, both tents, and their occupants, remain in the Kings' great big backyard.

Chapter Twenty-Four

Carson is determined to do the hard thing before he does the easy thing. Well, maybe not easy, but fun, in an adrenaline-pushing sort of way. The kind of thing that makes his blood rise like new sap; a replacement for sex with a new partner, exciting and scarily exposing. And he draws a bright line between these things. First, the partners meeting. Then the Baker Block auction. Which means first, the Haven. Ever since Willing Prime Contractors declined to renew their lease last winter on an under-used office in one of the aging strip malls just outside of town, they've had no choice but to meet either in one of their homes—not a good idea—or on familiar neutral territory, which only ever means one place. The drive down Main Street is more depressing and unsettling than ever. There isn't a single pedestrian on the sidewalk. Even the Sudsy appears deserted; the washers and dryers are cold and still. Maybe if people aren't working, they aren't bothering to do laundry either, Carson thinks. He drives past the building where Zeke and his friends are running the Cavern—a thriving, albeit illegal, private business that's part dance party, part hook-up space, where anything goes, as long as no one gets hurt. But Carson knows nothing about this. He knows nothing about the growing wads of cash that Zeke stashes in his room. And he has no idea that Zeke is on the verge of cutting a deal with a local drug dealer, who will supply him with molly that he can re-sell—at a mark-up—to the party-goers. Zeke thinks people will pay a convenience charge to be supplied on site, rather than scoring separately on their own. This was his idea, though Geronimo and Farrah readily agreed. The fact that Zeke isn't interested in taking the drug himself, but gets off on running the business with his best friends and figuring out what their customers want and need—well, perhaps on one level, Carson would admire this, if he knew.

In any case, before parking in front of the Haven—the only stretch of Main Street where cars still congregate—Carson swings south to the Baker Block. He's done his homework, having looked up the history of the block, and reviewed the map of the original plat showing how the land was divided for construction. And he knows now who Baker was: a grain mill owner whose family prospered in the 19th century, only to vanish from the public record shortly after 1929, when the stock market crashed. Carson draws comfort from this boom-and-bust story because it goes to show that history encompasses both ends of the story. If Willing and the rest of Remington County are in the middle of a bust cycle now, then a boom cycle is sure to follow, at some point. Or sure enough, anyway, as nothing is completely risk-free or foolproof. Carson will take those odds.

Still dreading the moment he must enter the Haven, Carson turns onto Berkely to see if anyone has rented Cyn's. The sign for Cyn's Café is still etched onto the front plate glass window, but the use of the space has morphed beyond recognition. It's hard to imagine entering this place now for a warm blueberry muffin and a cup of dark roast. A line of people trail from the doorway down the sidewalk and around the far corner. Carson doesn't need to see their faces to feel the waves of dejection radiating from them. They stand like cattle in a field, he thinks, waiting without expecting, living in the moment, with no plans for the future. Had he seen Jeannie's winter coat drive, he'd be having a déjà vu moment now. Men, women, and some children stand patiently in line, many wearing clothes that look like they belong on someone else—a wool sweater than knocks the knees of a small woman; a button-down Oxford shirt that gaps in the front on a man too large for it; a little boy wearing rubber boots, though it isn't raining. A hand-written cardboard sign in the window says "Berkely Family Ministry." Carson decides this is a polite way of saying it's a soup kitchen, without using the shameful Depression-era vocabulary. *They should fucking call it what it is,* he thinks. Downtown already reeks of failure, so it doesn't matter how you try and dress it up. In fact, he'd rather see a giant sign in the window that says "FREE FOOD FOR POOR PEOPLE," or blunt words to that effect. Because the worse it looks, the cheaper the nearby Baker Block will sell at auction later today. *And how did they let this happen?,* he wonders, watching the slow-moving line through his rolled-up truck window. By "they," he means the people themselves, not the various forces acting upon them—the shed jobs, shuttered businesses, lack of capital and cash, and so forth. "Grow a pair!" he yells out loud, to no one but himself. *Apathy is the loser's last refuge.*

Inside the Haven, the air is gummy and stale; spilled beer leaves a permanently sticky residue on the shellac-coated high tops. There are no women inside the bar today, only men who look to Carson like their next stop is the bread line down the street. Every face seems vaguely familiar: guys Carson might've gone to school with decades ago, or guys who worked in Willing's last family-owned hardware store, which failed late last year. Maybe some of them are just local grease monkeys Carson's seen forever at the Mobil or the Texaco, without really noticing them. Dizz and Vin, looking down, looking glum, blend in more than they should, Carson thinks. Whatever is going on among the three of them, and whatever is to come, Carson cannot imagine lumping them in with the real losers in the bar. The guys who can't seem to find a place to land as it gets harder to land anywhere. Carson knows he's late, and he knows this will push his partners' last buttons. *Maybe that's what I want,* he thinks, *for Dizz and Vin to be on the edge of unhinged, giving me the rational advantage.*

Carson brings a beer to the table and slaps the brown envelope down.

"You didn't open it," Vin says.

"Nope. Didn't need to."

"It says 'game over,'" Darius says in a flat voice.

"I guess it does," Carson says. He sees he misjudged his partners' moods. They're not even close to unhinged. They're skipping over all that, and heading straight to defeated.

"We had a good run," Vin says, "and a long winning streak. You gotta admit, we did a lot better than we thought we could, when we started out. And you know," he adds, slowly, as if reluctant to share his true thoughts, "sometimes, the smart play is knowing when to call it quits."

"We did better than our parents," Darius says. "But I don't think our kids will. I think winning streaks in general are over. And I gotta say, that bothers me even more than the fact that we're bankrupt. At least we had our shot. But my son Greg? I'm worried. I can't see forward, anymore, like I used to. Like *we* used to. And my God, how we took that for granted. Like it was meant to go on forever."

"For Christ's sake, we're not dying," Carson says. "We're not actually, physically dying." He waves the envelope.

"You know what, Cap?" Darius says. "I'm really tired of your Pollyanna bullshit. You always think that if you say 'the sky isn't blue, it's green,' and if you say it loud and often, then it must be true. This time, reality wins. And you can't spin it. And if you try and spin it, I'm calling you on it."

"Something *has* died, Cap," Vin says. "Look at us. We're not the same. We'll never be the same. We're done—what we were, together. What we built. The way we walked around wearing our company hats like we owned the place. Like everything we touched would turn to gold because we were the smartest guys on the wood pile. That's dead. The bank calling in our loans—that's the funeral."

"It's that fucking piece of shit land on the hill," Darius says. 'Willing Enclave,' my ass. We should've seen it coming. I'm gonna tear down those fucking houses with my bare hands."

"Say something, Cap," Vin says.

Carson sidles off the high-top bar stool and stands up. "You know what I'd do differently if we had a chance to do it all over again?" he asks. "Nothing. I wouldn't change a fucking thing. Including Willing Enclave. It's a great name, and a great property, and both of you should man up."

Darius stands. "Man up?! Is that what you think this is about? We're just your wussy partners and you're a fucking action hero riding in to save the town? You know, Cap, you've always been obnoxious, and we loved you, anyway. But now—you're just delusional, and I'm done."

"We're bankrupt, Cap," Vin says. "There's no back-peddling here. Let's just do what we gotta do and hope we come out of this with a roof over our own heads, for Christ's sake. I don't wanna drag this out. It's time to move on."

"I wanna hear you say it, Cap," Darius says. "I want to hear you say, out loud, 'Willing Prime Contractors is bankrupt.' Go on, say it." Carson takes a long swig of beer. The three men observe a tight silence. "We're leaving," Darius says, finally, running his hand through his thick black hair. "Elena, Greg, and I. We're moving to Arizona. As soon as we wrap this up, we're going."

"Shit, Dizz," Vin says. "You're really gonna walk away? Just like that?"

Carson opens the envelope and takes out the bank papers. "Go on. Sign them. You want out so badly, so get out."

"Do *you*?" Vin asks. "Want out?"

Carson smiles. "I always get what I want. You know that." Darius signs. Then Vin. Carson collects the signed papers and puts them back in the envelope. "Bankruptcy isn't the end," he says. "It's a license to start over. You should know that. But you'd both rather cave, it seems. I'm done arguing about it. I can lead your sorry asses to water, but I can't make you drink."

"You're the ass, Cap," Darius says, loudly. "Always have been. Always will be."

"Dizz," Vin says, as if to ratchet him down, while recognizing it's pointless to try. Carson begins to walk away. "Cap, wait."

"What?"

"It's not your fault," Vin says.

"I never thought it was," Cap says.

"You do what you gotta do, Cap," Darius says. "And I'll do what I gotta do. That's all there is to it."

"I'll get the paperwork to Contrails," Carson says, his back to his friends. "You don't have to lift a finger."

"Don't do anything really stupid," Darius calls after him. They watch Carson walk out of the Haven, both wondering when they'll see him again—or if the three of them will ever go back to being what they were, which was friends for life. Darius turns to Vin. "I need another drink."

The Baker Block auction takes place on the sidewalk, mid-way down the block. A large red-and-white auction sign is tented on the crumbling sidewalk. A small table has been set up, as well as a rickety podium. Carson is one of only three bidders, in addition to the auctioneer. He's got a certified check for $25,000 in his breast pocket, without which he cannot make an earnest bid for the property. He got the funds not from gambling, where he's currently hovering at the break-even point (after a precipitous dip followed by a hasty, and very lucky, recovery), but from the IRA account he and Sylvia set up when they were just starting out. He raided it without hesitation, since this is a rare opportunity to develop a new line of business. He took the rest of the meager college savings account, too. Once things develop a bit further, he'll tell Sylvia. Of course.

The bidding is desultory. The auctioneer, a clean-cut man in his mid-forties, wearing a black down parka, does not speak in the ultra-rapid, clipped tones that auctioneers use on TV or in the movies. The proceeding feels to Carson as if it's unfolding in slow motion. The auctioneer recites the physical condition of the buildings in detail, yet only to a degree—since the documentation also comes with a repeated warning that the buyer accepts the buildings in as-is condition. Carson looks up at the magnificent stone facades, the detailed crenellations, the large plated glass windows designed to invite passersby to gaze longingly at the enticing displays of goods—shoes, bonnets, pastries, radios, sheet music...almost anything anybody needed. He can see for himself that some of the cornice work at the top of several buildings has broken off. Chunks of wood and lathe and plaster litter the sidewalk where the pieces have crashed while no one was looking, while the weeds were growing in the cracked pavement, and while the stores stood empty, witnessing their own decline in helpless silence.

The auctioneer concludes his performance. The prospective buyers mill around, looking at the buildings, skimming the paperwork. Carson is surprised that he doesn't recognize the two men and one woman who are his competition. Perhaps they're from out of town, he thinks. Perhaps they're flunkies sent by anonymous corporate bidders to scoop up these properties on the sly, assuming they know something that others—like Carson—don't know. *Arrogant fuckers.* He is dead certain this is the right move, at the right time. Finally, the auctioneer removes a padlock from one of buildings, and the small group tramps in to inspect the premises first-hand. They will not be let into every building; only this one. The buyer-beware clause is intended to cover a multitude of sins. And besides, this kind of transaction isn't for the faint of heart. Carson sees what he needs to see—and what he wants to see. When the tour is over, the small group returns outside. The auctioneer opens up the formal bidding process; only written, sealed bids may be submitted on the forms provided, and then tucked into little envelopes. Carson watches his competition walk off in separate directions to jump on their cell phones. *I knew it: they are just lackeys doing someone else's bidding from afar.* He decides not to wait to see what they do, as he already knows what he plans to do. And he figures he's got the true home advantage. He completes the form, which includes writing down his total bid for the buildings, inserts the form with his certified check, and hands the envelope to the auctioneer, slowly and casually. Five minutes later, the whole thing is over. The other bidders have walked away without submitting anything. The auctioneer tells Carson he has submitted the winning bid. Additional paperwork will follow by registered mail. They shake hands. The auctioneer puts his gear into the back of a white van parked in the street and drives away.

Carson stands alone in the middle of Main Street, staring up at his new property. He smiles, feeling elated, balloon-light, in a way he hasn't felt in a very long time. The last time he felt this good, in fact, was the day he and Dizz and Vin purchased the Willing Enclave property, which felt at the time like a fantastic coup that would translate into a large profit—and which would bring something new and beautiful into the world, in the form of gorgeous houses where happy families would make memories for generations to come. *That's what they've never understood, and why I've beaten my head against the wall all these years. You can't judge the world by how it looks now, but by how it* will *look when you're through changing it. That's the secret to all of it.* Carson walks up to one of his buildings on the Baker Block and rubs his hands along the crumbly brown stone, allowing the rough texture to scratch his palms a bit. His hands are coated in centuries-old stone dust, settled car exhaust, and the hopes and dreams of two centuries of merchants. Finally, he gets into his car and heads for home, looking in the rear view mirror for one last glimpse of his new prize possession. He has absolutely no idea how he intends to pay for it all, and make necessary improvements. But for now, possession is all that matters. And possession is nine-tenths of the law.

The Third Winter

Chapter Twenty-Five

Notice. The Town of Willing announces the following changes to curbside garbage and recycling pickup for all residents, effective immediately: Twice-weekly garbage pick-up is now suspended; residents are required to transport all sealed trash to the Remington Trash & Recycling Facility. Curbside recycling has also been eliminated.

*

Notice. The Remington County Public Library announces a service reduction, effective immediately. The North Willing branch will reduce operating hours from 7 days a week to 1. The branch will be open from 10:00 am to 2:00 pm, Mondays only. The South Willing branch is now closed until further notice.

*

Estate sale. 4225 German Drive, Willing Heights. Everything must go. No reasonable offers refused. Vintage glassware, dinner service for 12, luxury watches, jewelry, electronics, more. Rare opportunity in Willing's most selective neighborhood.

Nick French rolls his midnight blue BMW to a slow stop and checks his mirrors. The street is deserted, which is good. He isn't usually this brazen—making a buy in the middle of the day. But the pressure is finally getting to him, and to keep on going, he needs to find some release, some way to relax. His big baby, Touchstone

Construction, is morphing into a salvage operation—literally; his earth movers no longer dig foundations. Instead, they shovel scrap, for which Touchstone is paid by the ton. Most months, he's no longer breaking even. His last half-decent construction job was a gut reno in Willing Heights, but that's long finished, and now that goddamn house is sitting empty, slowly rotting, as the owners fled when Contrails Capital put it up for a short sale for which there is no buyer in sight. Nick knows there's a metaphor in there somewhere, but he doesn't want to think about it. He also knows, and takes a small amount of satisfaction from knowing, that he held things together longer than that asshole Carson King. He's lost track of King, recently, but he's pretty sure he'd know if Willing Prime Contractors was doing any work of note. Meanwhile, it sickens Nick to watch his own company move farther and farther away from its first life, its intended life, as a gold-plated residential building contractor with every CEO, politician, loan officer, and building site inspector in Greater Willing on speed dial. Now, the CEOs have fled and their companies have moved or folded. Bank loans aren't even a real thing, anymore. It doesn't matter, Nick thinks bitterly, how much upside you gave the bank, year after year. That's all washed away and forgotten. What's more, the only official site inspector within 100 miles is so deeply on the take that he's pricing himself out of what's left of the market. And the pols are holed up somewhere in their shabby offices, hitting the links in Linton Crossing, or hunkering far away in the state Capitol, wanting as little to do as possible with the shit show that Willing has become. And not just Willing the town, but almost everything within a 50-mile radius, or more, as if the entire area had been sprayed with Agent Orange, triggering a die-off, a withering of everything down-wind of ground zero. Only the ugly, spiky weeds sprouting along Main Street, in cracked sidewalks, and between crumbling mortar joints of several buildings seem to be thriving, even in the dead of winter, as if they're feeding off desolation itself.

Nick looks around again, to make sure he's alone, parked outside this traditional colonial house on a nondescript suburban street. It's one of those tired neighborhoods you'd never notice, Nick thinks, and he couldn't imagine living here, with his own family, in bland anonymity.

His own house, near the crest of Willing Heights, is a damn site better than any of this. If things were different, he thinks, he'd put a deal together to buy out every house on this street, build half as many contemporaries on spacious lots, put in a lot more trees, and then sell the shit out of it. If things were different… Nick calls the number he was given and waits. A few minutes later, someone approaches the car from around the corner. A girl? No, it's a guy, short, well-muscled, with curly blond hair below his shoulders. Nick rolls down his window. A blast of ice-cold air surges into the car.

"Hey," Zeke King says, looking him over. "Can I help you?" Nick tells Zeke what he's looking for: oxy, maybe some hash. Zeke nods and disappears around the corner. Nick figures he's not supposed to see how these deals are sourced—or where. He doesn't care, anyway, as long as this gets done fast, so he can get out of this bullshit Beaver Cleaver neighborhood. Zeke returns, hands Nick a couple of plastic baggies, and Nick, in turn, pokes a wad of cash out the passenger-side window. Zeke takes the money and walks away, turning out of sight. He'd make a hell of a builder, that kid, Nick thinks; clearly he's got a high tolerance for risk. He tucks his stash, checks his mirrors once more, and drives away.

Zeke walks the short distance back to the Kings' colonial, which is nearly identical to the one where Nick waited for him, except for the yard, of course. He goes to up to his room, where he keeps a small, portable safe hidden at the back of his closet. He puts Nick French's cash inside the innocuous ivory-colored lock box—the kind of household safe that usually holds passports, mortgages, wills, and so forth. This one is stuffed entirely with cash. It's one of 15 identical mini-safes stashed in various locations. Some are at the Cavern, tucked behind a false wall that Zeke and Geronimo put up in one of the small back bedrooms. Each of them has several identical boxes, and Zeke has nearly filled this one. Their personal banking network is almost getting too big to handle, Zeke thinks. He's thought about buying a metal garden shed at the Home Depot out by Linton Crossing, which he can set up in plain sight on one of the last patches of open yard, near the back deck. He likes the idea of hiding money in plain sight.

The shed would be padlocked, of course, and Zeke would make sure that the only ones who knew what was inside were on a need-to-know basis. He makes a note to check in with G and Farrah about this idea; they consult one another on almost all decisions now. The Cavern is a reliable cash cow now. They're raking in enough to feed and clothe themselves. Geronimo bought himself a hoopty—an '88 Cadillac. And they've hired a bouncer—basically, someone to mind the door, collect the cash, and keep an eye out for any threats. They knew they'd need to find someone they could trust 100 percent. Farrah suggested Carol—big, friendly, but with just the right amount of menacing swagger. Carol, who needs funds for transition surgery, came on board without hesitation, and things have been running smoothly ever since. She's helped to expand the Cavern's clientele, and she even started a movie night—mostly weird indie shit that flickers on the wall, often with the sound turned off. It just works.

On his way back out to the yard, Zeke looks in on his mother. She is in her bedroom under the covers, watching something on her laptop. Her brown curls, generously flecked with gray, droop onto her shoulders. She wears a wooly infinity scarf looped thickly around her neck, nearly hiding the lower half of her face.

"You need anything?" Zeke asks. Sylvia forces herself to look up.

"I'm fine, honey. Thanks. Have you seen your father today?"

"Nope," Zeke says. "Not today, or yesterday, either."

"Well, he'll turn up, I'm sure," Sylvia says. "He always does, right?"

"Yeah," Zeke says, turning away quickly. It never stops hurting, seeing his go-getting, profit-chasing mother virtually confined to her bed—for no particular reason, as far as he can tell. Zeke doesn't know about Sylvia's night walks.

Zeke walks out to the back deck, his breath visible on a cold, gray afternoon. He checks his phone: terse text messages from his main supplier and surprisingly, his dad. *Later.* He looks out across the yard and sees what his mother saw on a sunny spring morning nearly two years ago. Back then, it was all in her mind—a vision so real, so disturbing and compelling, she is still wrestling with the impact and the path that vision set her on. Zeke is looking at the real thing: over an acre of land crammed with tents, improvised laundry lines, garbage-can fires (for heating as well as cooking), water stations. There is a steady, thrum in the air: people talking and arguing, fires crackling and hissing, babies crying. *Tent City,* he calls it. *My city*, he thinks. *They're mine now.* Men, women, and children warm their hands over the fires, weave in and among the tents, pull half-frozen clothes off of lines strung between tents. A group of kids keep warm by kicking a soccer ball between rows of tents. There's no room to play properly, so they've adapted. Old-fashioned battery-powered boom boxes are cranked up here and there, pushing competing waves of music and staticky talk radio out across the yard. Zeke has stopped analyzing why he feels unfazed by what's happening. He's stopped wondering if something is wrong with him. Instead, he's embraced the *now*, and takes real pleasure in figuring out the angles of the situation: how to manipulate the circumstances to suit him, both commercially and personally, which increasingly are one and the same thing. And so far, it's all working out just fine, as if all this were tailor-made for his particular talents and interests. For him, the icing on the cake is that the two people he loves more than his own family, Geronimo and Farrah, are in it with him. It's as if the three of them couldn't wait to shake off the conventional lives they were born into, leave high school in the dust, and set out a proverbial shingle. *You want it or need it? We've got it or we'll get it...for a price.*

Zeke sees Jeannie weaving her way toward him. He cannot get used to seeing her without her thick brown hair. She recently cut it all off herself with scissors, and what's left is weirdly patchy and spiky. He hasn't asked her why she did it, and she hasn't volunteered a reason. Jeannie looks up at Zeke on the deck. The occupants of Tent City have been remarkably respectful, up to now, by tacitly agreeing not to encroach on the house itself, including the deck.

"You check up on mom?" Jeannie asks.

"Yeah," Zeke says.

"Anything to report?"

"Nope," he says. "You want my coat?" Jeannie, thin as a stick, is under-dressed for the cold.

"I'm fine," she shrugs.

"You look miserable. It's freezing out here."

"I said I'm fine. You talk to dad?"

"He texted."

"What did he say? Do you know where he is?" Jeannie wipes her nose with her sleeve.

"Nah. I'll find out later. I'm busy."

"Well. Guess I'll see you around." She turns and disappears back among the tents, a wraith who barely takes up any space. Zeke watches her briefly, shaking his head. He sleeps indoors every night, in a warm bed with a soft pillow, often surrounded by the friends of his choosing. Jeannie has been living outside for months now, alone in the tent she had once loaned to Gina. He shakes his head again, anger welling up suddenly. *She's an idiot.*

Chapter Twenty-Six

Bruno Fernandez isn't sure this is a good idea. He's had doubts from the moment he heard about it. Now, as soon as he steps onto the edge of the yard, he stops so abruptly his wife, Paula, runs into him. Irritated, he nudges her aside. Bruno and Paula are both numb and sweating at the same time, after walking six miles across Willing in unforgiving cold. Their third-hand Honda finally quit on them, and bus service is nonexistent, these days. For many people, getting anywhere means hailing a gypsy cab (if you see one) or hoofing it. Paula says thank God they left the kids at home with her sister. They're probably glued to Nickelodeon, she thinks. She wants to call and check on them, but she knows they need to conserve minutes on their phone card. The cell phone is for emergencies only. Bruno squints across the yard. The grass has been trampled to dirt. He can't imagine living out here. How would they manage? Is it even safe? Paula squeezes his hand, but says nothing. Bruno knows what they're both thinking: Never did they expect to see in America something like this: crowded, dirty, overrun, like the Sinaloan slums of their childhood. Even Sinaloa is better than *this,* now. Bruno suddenly feels as though he's been traveling in circles for years, always ending up where he started, never quite managing to break that circle so that he's able to set out on his own straight line—a line that leads to a new way of living, and a clean break from the past. He wishes Jorge could see this and commiserate, but Jorge pulled up stakes a few months ago, leaving Bruno with an empty, rudderless feeling. Jorge scraped up enough money for bus tickets to get his family to Portland, Oregon, where a cousin told him there's pick-up construction work to be had. Jorge pleaded with Bruno to come with him, but Paula did not want to pull the kids out of school and start over in a place where there weren't really any guarantees that things would be better, or easier. And Bruno couldn't really promise her otherwise.

But the thing that keeps Bruno and Paula standing at the edge of the yard now is the inescapable fact that they can live here for free and come and go as they please. Or so they've heard. Paula suspects that in a place like this, everybody barters, and as she's a whiz with needle, thread, and a BeDazzler, surely she can sew clothing in exchange for other things they need—whether that's beans and rice or new shoes for the kids. Giving up a real roof and indoor plumbing for this public maelstrom might seem crazy, but living jammed into a tiny, crappy two-bedroom, one bathroom apartment with fractious relatives, as the Fernandez family has been doing for over a year, is not a happy-ever-after situation, either.

The couple are still standing at the edge of the yard, taking it all in, making private calculations about what the future really looks like here, when Jeannie approaches them, a worn backpack slung over her shoulder. She has made it her job (one of many jobs, actually) to monitor the borders of Tent City—her brother's name, not hers. If Jeannie were to put up a sign for this place, for what her family's backyard has become, she'd need a really big sign. In her mind, it's the *Willing Community Encampment for Economic Refugees and all Displaced Persons,* or something like that. And there'd be a huge "*All are Welcome!*" sign too. If she had her way. Which she doesn't. But she's figuring how to exert power even while powerless. She tries to welcome every arrival, even those arriving in the middle of the night, which means she's trained herself to sleep lightly, her tent strategically located near the busiest "border"—where the yard ends and the sidewalk begins, on the west side of the property. That's where Bruno and Paula stand now, shaking her outstretched hand. She's done this so many times, she's developed a semi-formal orientation. At least four feet between tents...No open fires...There's a roster for chores, including hauling away garbage and the port-a-potty tanks...Anyone caught stealing will be kicked out... Jeannie also lists a number of planned improvements—planned in her own mind, anyway—as if she were in her mother's business, trying to talk a potential new buyer into making an offer on a property. A first-aid tent, she tells them, should be up and running shortly. Also, a lost and found. And maybe some type of deal with a local gypsy cab, willing to charge a flat two bucks for a ride to the ShopFine or the 7-Eleven. There aren't too many other places left in Willing worth going to, and nobody in Tent City has more than a few bucks to spend on any given day, anyway. Bruno and Paula just nod.

"Any questions?" Jeannie asks.

"We're just looking," Bruno says, glancing at Paula.

"Our kids—they're at my sister's," Paula says nervously. She's felt Americanized for years, but here, suddenly, she has no idea how she's expected to behave.

"Well, we're running out of room," Jeannie says, matter-of-factly. "So if you're in a jam, don't wait too long." She's seen this before: people come by sometimes just to gawk. She knows the gawkers probably have somewhere else to go, somewhere better. Like a real home. She suspects Bruno and Paula are not gawkers, however. *They're probably just trying to figure out how this all works. And if it works for them.* "I'm sorry. That sounded harsh. Of course you're welcome to join us—with your kids." Jeannie smiles. "Here." She digs into her backpack and takes out a small Baggie filled with Cheez-Its. "For the road." It's the first food Bruno and Paula have seen all day. They thank her, and watch her disappear among the tents and the smoky fires that send white wisps into the gray winter air. "See you soon?" Jeannie calls after them. Bruno just waves, and they walk away, cold and foot-sore.

A few hours later, Carson is taking a break. He hates admitting that his lower back is screaming for relief. His body is not allowed to complain, he thinks. There's too much still to do. You might say it's *endless,* but Carson turns that around in his head, so it's *endless opportunity.* That's far more energizing and he's going to make it true, in any case. But he's six months behind schedule. First, there was unexpected red tape around securing the deed to the Baker Block. Then there is

Willing Enclave, which has slowed him down even more. Darius made good on his threat: he took his family to Arizona, although they've been unable to find a buyer for their house in Willing. The only communication between them since then came in the form of a postcard of the Grand Canyon three weeks after they left, addressed to the King family. Carson tore it into pieces and threw it in the trash. He feels a deeply settled, permanent sort of anger toward Darius. But toward Vin, he is so furious he can't even put words to it. Vin has been jobbing for Nick French. *Fucking, lying ass-licker Nick French!* When Vin finally told him, on one of the last days they were on site together at Willing Enclave, Carson looked at him coldly and said, "You've always been weak, Vin. But this is low—even for you." Vin smiled slowly, sadly.

"I've lost everything, Cap," he said. "I put everything I had into *us.* Yeah, you, me, Dizz. I put everything I am, everything I ever wanted to be, into *us.* I don't really have a fucking life. You've always thought *you* were the only one who was really committed, but you've always been wrong. *This,*" he waved his hand at the Willing Enclave mess, "*this* is what I'm about, what my *life* has been about, for 20 years, Cap. So you wanna call me weak? Go ahead. But that's only because you're too stupid and pig-headed to see what's really in front of you. And work with what you've got, not what you think you want."

The two men stood together on drying mud, in front of a decaying building site that was nothing more than a gaping money pit at that point. Carson continues to believe that they could have sold the incomplete houses on spec, at least some of them, if Sylvia had done her job, if Ann Likert hadn't been such a stuck-up bitch, if it hadn't rained, if Bruno and Jorge had been kept on longer...if...if...Standing there, in muddy work boots, neither Carson nor Vin knew if they would ever see each other, or speak to each other, again.

Now, finally, Carson has what he's always wanted, what he's been craving. *All mine, so nobody else can fuck it up.* Weak daylight filters through the grimy second-story windows of the middle building of the Baker Block. He chose to start here, at last, because this one is in somewhat better shape than the others. The ground-floor retail space is empty, even if the wood pillars in the center are rotting. The second story, a future apartment for a pioneering retailer, or maybe office space for an eager start-up, is also empty, while the other buildings are crammed with odds and ends that will need to be removed. A thin mattress with a blanket is pushed to a corner of the room. A plastic bag with beer and soda and a couple of roast beef sandwiches sits nearby. Carson has stripped the walls down to the studs and is beginning to rewire the electrical lines to meet code. He's had to remove a huge amount of early 20th century knob-and-tube wiring, and it's taking far longer than he'd hoped. He's miscalculated how much slower this kind of work progresses when there's only one pair of hands to do everything. *I AM Willing Prime Contractors—THE Willing Prime Contractors,* he thinks, bitter and bemused at the same time. *Those turkeys.* Carson massages his lower back with his palms, while admiring the original wide-plank oak floors, which aren't in terrible shape, thanks to a century or so of hiding under the ugliest linoleum ever made—every tile of which now sits, broken and dusty, in a couple of cartons nearby, ready to be hauled out on a dolly that Carson will need to bump down the stairs himself, unless Zeke deigns to call him back. Carson is pretty sure Zeke will keep his mouth shut about all this, if he asks him to. *You can't get flooring like this, anymore. They'd kill for this in Linton Crossing.* Of course, he isn't in Linton Crossing. Nowhere near. But this is the Baker Block—the beginning of the *new and improved* Baker Block.

Carson's phone rings and he hope's it's Zeke, but it's Sylvia.

"Hey," he says, noncommittally.

"The kids are wondering where you are," Sylvia says. "Cap?"

"Yeah."

"What's going on?"

Carson looks around, wincing as he torques his back. "I'm working."

Sylvia, still in bed, tugs at the infinity scarf on her neck. "Really," she says. She knows him. You don't get what you want by pushing; you have to wait him out. *Like coaxing a wild animal out into the open, one cautious, quiet step at a time.* There's a brief silence, while Carson decides what to tell her—how much—and how he can tell her the truth without telling her about the auction and everything that goes with it.

"I'm rehabbing, actually," he says, which is true, as far as it goes.

"That's great!" she says. "Where? Outside Willing, I assume? Is that why you didn't come home? Why didn't you just tell me? Is it really such a secret?" So much for gentle coaxing. She'd much rather prod. And poke. Preferably with something sharp.

"Yeah, I'm sorry, Syl. I got so caught up—and then I was so exhausted. I didn't mean to worry you."

"I wasn't worried, Cap. But the kids—"

"I texted Zeke. Haven't heard back. What are they up to?"

"Why don't you come home and find out for yourself?" she says.

"Look, I want to surprise you. Since things have been a little rough...I want to bring us good news, like before. Like always. So, give me a little more time." Carson hopes this approach buys him several more days, at least. He intends to go hard-core on this. Sylvia isn't really buying it. She believes he's run away, temporarily, because he can't stand to look at what his property has morphed into—something so far outside of his control, it's a raging insult. More than that, she thinks he can't stomach what's become of *them,* what's become of *progress.* It's almost as if they'd made it all up, years ago, as if they'd been living a fantasy for more than 20 years—something they cooked up to feel good about themselves, about everything. And now, only now, has their real life, and their real marriage, begun. And what is there to hold it together? To hold *them* together, besides the twins? Is she crazy? Sylvia doesn't know what crazy is, at this point. It's a sliding scale.

"Sure," she says to the phone. "Don't forget to eat." She hangs up. He didn't even bother to ask her what she was doing while he was away.

Chapter Twenty-Seven

Javier Martinez, wearing his one good suit, sits in a plush chair, turning his hat in his hands. His hands are nothing like his father's, he thinks, but for the short fingers and hairy knuckles they share. What would my *padre* make of my hands? No callouses, no cuts, no swollen joints. Would he mistake me for a wealthy man of leisure? Or a stupid *vago,* a lazy bum, who does not know the real meaning of hard work? He would not understand that the story is not in my hands, and neither is my fate. That is not the American way.

Javier's name is called. He picks up his slim briefcase and enters a windowless, beige office belonging to a bank employee he has never met. He feels doomed from the start. Business is about relationships, he thinks, and this woman does not look like someone he can ever connect with. But he will try. He must try. Once the bank was taken over by a huge conglomerate—a monster that surely has more in common with MedCan than with a small businessman like him—he knew he'd be reduced to just a number. And while banks care a great deal about numbers, they do not give a fuck about a blip, a mere footnote, like him. He knows this. And still he must try to convince this woman, a loan officer with Contrails Capital who was dropped down here from the sky, with no apparent ties to any person or any particular place that matters to Javier Martinez.

The nameplate on the desk says Julie Crawford. "Good morning, Miss Crawford," Javier says.

"Good morning, Mr. Martinez," Julie replies, scanning his life on her computer screen. He tries to peer into her eyes, to see if any familiar numbers are reflected there, but all he sees are her blue irises. "Or do you prefer to be called Señor Martinez?" she adds, forcing a smile.

"I am an American citizen, Miss Crawford."

"Mister, then."

"Yes. But you may call me Javier, if you like." Only here, he thinks, in the grip of this institution, would I invite a stranger to call me by *mi primer nombre.*

"Mr. Martinez, what brings you in today?" Julie asks. *You know this already,* he thinks. *So am I now simply the mouse again, and you are the cat, toying with me until you grow bored? How much more of this?*

Javier clears his throat and forces himself to sound self-assured. "I require a $100,000 line of credit to address certain...challenges...that have arisen over the last 18 months."

"I see," she nods, clicking her way across several screens. "You appear to carry no debt on your balance sheet."

"That is correct."

"Good for you." Javier wonders if this is a good sign, or merely a placeholder for what's to come. "But I also see that you've sold off most of your assets, rather than keeping them on your books for depreciation value. Why?" She looks directly at him. He pauses a moment.

"It is how I survive." He hopes that doesn't come across as aggrieved.

"But as a business, Mr. Martinez, surely you don't want to merely survive?" Julie asks, leaning back in her chair.

"You have heard of MedCan?" he asks. She nods.

"They've cleaned your clock, haven't they?" Julie says. Javier is not familiar with this expression. He looks at her. "You've been under-bid, I'm guessing," she adds. "Drastically."

"Yes." That is what it comes down to: He has been under-bid. The thousands of hours he has put in over decades, the planning, the long hours, countless decisions, making his business a priority ahead of his family, which of course he did for them...no...he did it for himself, to prove his own worth, to prove that he is not a laborer barely scraping by like his father, but something more, something advanced, something better than what came before him...But Eugenia died, anyway.

His mother died, anyway. And the light of his life, Gina, has left him behind, as he did his own father. And for what? Where does it get them?

"If you would give me the opportunity," Javier says, slowly and courteously, "I know that I can rebuild Vida and she will be stronger and better than before." He knows he is not speaking the language of business. But he hopes that speaking from his heart will add to what Julie Crawford already knows, as she knows everything about the business.

Julie taps a pen on her blotter and purses her lips. "I'm afraid, Mr. Martinez…" *She knew before I walked in*, Javier thinks bitterly. *Of course she did.* "I'm afraid, Mr. Martinez, we cannot approve your request for a line of credit."

Javier learns why, but it does not matter. No is no, whatever the reason. Contrails Capital has decided, in its infinite wisdom, to eliminate its inherited positions in tiny enterprises like Javier's and to focus instead on its $100 million-plus loan portfolio. That means none of the commercial business the bank now handles is based in, or has any real ties to, Willing or even Remington County. The brick-and-mortar bank is like an incomplete erasure mark on a piece of paper: you can still see the outlines, but the thing itself isn't really there. And one day soon, as Contrails ticks through the adjustments required of its acquisition plan, the building itself will cease to be a bank at all, and the erasure will be complete.

The night is cold and clear, but that does not matter. Even on cloudy nights, or when a cold rain or sleet is falling, Sylvia embarks on her nightly walk through Tent City. Like Jeannie and Zeke, she too has a private name for this place, a name she intends to keep to herself. *New Hell*. A private joke: New Hell is a tony residential development somewhere in a pristine corner of Willing, the kind of place where she'd sell every house at full ask, without breaking a sweat. In New Hell, Sylvia thinks, the residents have agreed to strict covenants to protect the natural beauty of the place and protect the value of their investment...Has everything she defined as "success" been merely an accidental collision of time and space and her physical body—all merely in the right place at the right time? And if so, does that mean she, Sylvia, has no discernible or innate talent or ability whatsoever? *Am I purely a byproduct of luck? And when the luck runs out—as it surely has—then what?* Sylvia huddles inside Carson's big, black down parka, the hood pulled so far over her face, she looks like a phantom picking its way in furry boots among the tents, stumbling occasionally over tent stakes poking up from the frozen soil. Her original vision sprang upon her in daylight, and she pushed it aside as quickly as she could, barely allowing the unbidden images to register—and taking no time at all to find meaning in any of it. She never imagined the whole damn thing would actually come true. Who, or what, did that to her? And why? And what's expected of her now that it's so real? In the absence of any answers, she is drained by the questions that will not stop rolling around inside her head.

And so she assigns herself a nightly task, which helps her feel tethered to practical realities. She roams the grounds picking up trash—juice cartons, empty toilet paper rolls, crushed cigarette packs—and puts them into a large black garbage bag, which she deposits at the curb each night. There's always a mountain of bagged trash. Twice a week, based on the roster, somebody borrows somebody's pick-up and makes a trip to the dump on the far south side of Remington County.

After crisscrossing the yard in a somewhat methodical fashion, Sylvia looks out on the dark at a sea of tents that extends all the way to edge of trees, where the yard ends and the stream begins. The tents look like miniature pyramids; some glow from within, lit by flashlights. Standing still, and quieting her own breathing, she can hear others breathing in their tents, talking in their sleep, rolling over uncomfortably in thin sleeping bags, barely shielded from the frozen ground beneath them. Tonight, several small children are coughing hard—a barking cough that Sylvia imagines must rattle their little bones. But what can she do? She didn't invite these people here, she only let it happen, and not really even that. It just happened. Winnie Suggs was the first. Then Gina, for awhile. Long lost Gina, Sylvia thinks. Her thoughts turn to Jeannie. She knows she's out here somewhere. *Not coughing, please.* Sylvia does not know exactly where her daughter's tent is pitched. She just knows she's here, close by, and she tells herself that Jeannie has loads of common sense, and can take of herself. She's run out of ideas—and bribes—to entice Jeannie back inside. *At some point, you just have to let them be who they are. They're both stubborn, like their father.* She recalls a time when the twins were seven, and she told them they could not have brownies until they ate their broccoli. They sat at the table together for over an hour, banging their spoons and demanding dessert. Sylvia does not remember how it ended, but she thinks Carson eventually yanked the spoons away from them.

She climbs onto the porch and sits in a rocker that's encrusted with ice. The cold, at least, is real, undeniable. She sighs deeply, mournfully. She wonders, suddenly, if she'll live to be a grandmother. It's unimaginable, right now. It feels far more likely to Sylvia, at this moment, that anything and everything she and Carson ever thought they were working toward is not just gone, but also totally irrelevant. Like forcing kids to eat broccoli before brownies, as if it made a difference. The future, she believes, no longer exists, which makes everything leading up to this moment feel pointless.

About an hour after Sylvia finally heads back inside, as the sky begins changing from pitch black to faint gray, a two-year-old girl living in a dark blue tent in the middle of the yard with her mother and uncle, who once owned and operated Willing's small dry cleaning store, dies of whooping cough.

Part III

The Third Summer

CHAPTER TWENTY-EIGHT

UNITED STATES BANKRUPTCY COURT

DISTRICT OF REMINGTON COUNTY

IN RE

CONTRAILS CAPITAL INC. VS WILLING PRIME CONTRACTORS LLC

Carson G.King
Sylvia B. King
1003 High Court Drive
Willing, PA 15840

This letter is a formal notification that you are in default of your obligation to make payments on your home loan, account #2498574. This current account holds the sum of $12,980.72, payable by August 1, 2025.

This amount has been overdue since June 1, 2025 and you have ignored multiple requests to make a payment or reconsolidate your debt.

Unless the full amount is received within 15 days, we have no choice but to begin the foreclosure process on your home.

Fran Hauser has come to believe that Jeannie King is a saint, a real saint, not a proverbial one, and that she, Fran, will be admitted to Heaven if Jeannie blesses her. Fran has known that Jeannie is special ever since the thing with the free coats, a couple of years ago. Fran doesn't remember when it was, exactly, just as she's forgotten how long it's been since Javier Martinez fired her from his oxygen supply company. Whatever it was called. None of that is real, now. But Jeannie King is real as only a saint can be: ever present, ever a source of hope. So Fran makes it her main business every day to serve Jeannie, as best she can. Sometimes, that means scrounging used Baggies for Jeannie to fill with Cheez-Its. Sometimes, it means refilling Jeannie's water bottle with fresh water because Jeannie forgets to eat and drink much of the time, Fran has observed. Fran believes that even when she's stealing somebody else's water, she's doing the right thing because she's serving a higher cause—Saint Jeannie. Saints require upkeep, just like everybody else, as long as they're still here with us on Earth. These days, Fran can be seen in her dirty white blouse, skirt, and flipflops trailing several yards behind Jeannie, ready to do whatever she is asked. Jeannie rarely asks, but she appreciates Fran's good nature. Right now, however, Fran is agitated and out of breath, after zigzagging across Tent City looking for her.

"I think you'd better come," Fran heaves, "right away."

"Can it wait, Fran?" Jeannie says. In other circumstances, say, a classroom or an office, "Fran," who is old enough to be Jeannie's grandmother, would be "Ms. Hauser" to Jeannie, but not here. "I promised Winnie I'd look in on her. She's not doing well, and I'm feeling really guilty about—"

"No, Jeannie. All due respect, I don't think it can wait."

Jeannie closes her eyes and takes a few deep breaths. She is covered with summer grime; her hair, which she keeps hacking off with scissors, is stiff with oil and dirt; and her collar bones reveal deep hollows. "Okay," she says, bone-weary. "Lead the way."

Fran leads Jeannie between rows of tents jammed so close together, many share stakes. There is no grass, only flat, dry dirt that kicks up dust as they walk. A small crowd has gathered around a small plastic cooler, and they're all looking down at it. They step aside when Jeannie arrives.

"Oh, no," Jeannie says. "No, no, no, no, no." The cooler lid is open, and inside lies a newborn lying on a thin towel, its umbilical cord still dangling. Jeannie does without thinking what everyone else was either afraid to do or else didn't do because they were afraid they'd be forced to take responsibility, and nobody in Tent City wants to handle more than they're already handling. Jeannie lifts up the infant and cradles it. It's a girl. She is very still, but Jeannie puts her ear to the baby's face, and she feels a faint, warm breath. "She's alive. I need some twine and a pair of scissors," she says. Someone hands her both. She wraps the cord tightly about an inch from the navel and snips the rest. Fran retrieves the cut cord. She will wrap it, dry it, and keep it as the first holy relic created by Saint Jeannie.

Jeannie King is a 19-year-old holding a tiny infant for the first time in her life, and in reality, she has no idea what to do with it. First, she brings her into her own tent (after suggesting to Fran that she start asking around to figure out who the mother might be). Jeannie gently swabs the baby with a dampened cloth and then wraps it in the cleanest towel she has, which is only slightly cleaner than the one she was found in. She knows she doesn't have a lot of time to save the baby's life; she knows it needs nourishment and a diaper, and she isn't sure what else. And then she knows exactly where to bring the baby: to her mother. Her mother will know exactly what to do.

Jeannie looks up at the house. She does not want to enter. She has not entered in a long, long time. *I have put away childish things.* She and Sylvia have had a series of curt conversations over the last several months, but only at night, when Sylvia is on her walk. More than once, Jeannie has stood outside her own tent, watching her mother in silhouette picking her way among the tents, bending to pick up trash. Sylvia doesn't do that anymore, although she still walks at night. The trash problem, which Jeannie is sick about, along with so much else she can't solve, is overwhelming. And so is the stench. But the infant must come first. Jeannie cradles the baby to her chest and weaves her way toward the house. She tries not to look at any one feature of the house itself, but it is impossible to keep the high, wide back deck from filling her vision. The deck where she used to slurp cereal in the mornings, wrapped in a blanket, while her parents sat drinking coffee, planning their days. Did that really happen? *What if all my memories are false, and someone, or something, is trying to tempt me away from the path...* She shakes her head. *No. Do the work. Do what you have to do. Keep your promise, keep the snake happy.* She reaches the wide wooden steps that connect the deck to the yard. Jeannie and Zeke used to play a game where they'd jump from the bottom step onto the grass, roll themselves gently down the first slope of the lawn, and then get up and do it again. And there was lemonade, Jeannie remembers. Cold and sweet, in a clean glass beaded with moisture. She is suddenly, desperately thirsty. Clutching the baby, she heads to the side of the house and turns on the spigot that's meant for a garden hose. The water splutters out and she crouches to catch it in her mouth without splashing the baby. Jeannie does not know that within a week, Remington County will turn off the water to the house because the utility bills haven't been paid.

The tacit agreement among tent-dwellers to leave the house and deck alone, to let the family retain some sense of ownership and privacy, was violated months ago. The breakdown began when an old VW bus pulled up to the house, discharged 19 people clutching sleeping bags and garbage bags holding their possessions, and then sped off. Bruno and Paula Fernandez and their two little girls were in that VW. They almost didn't come, but when Paula's brother-in-law set one of the beds on fire with a lit cigarette, she and Bruno realized they'd run out of options. The VW was followed by a cavalcade of drive-by's—battered minivans, decommissioned (or stolen) delivery vans, and orange school buses with the school names blacked out with spray paint. At least one of the buses obviously belonged to Willing High. Zeke was around when one of those pulled up; he laughed. These vehicles discharged dozens and dozens of men, women, and children at the end of their rope—physically, emotionally, and certainly economically.

The Kings' back deck is now covered by ratty sleeping bags, boxes, and black garbage bags that hold everybody's junk, or their garbage, or both. A portion of the railing has been torn down, though it's not clear why. Perhaps for firewood. Or maybe somebody just couldn't stand to see something nice in the midst of so much misery, so it just made sense to even things out a bit. A real house with a roof, a kitchen, and a bathroom (!) is like a slap in the face to someone who doesn't have any of this anymore, which is almost everybody, it seems. Jeannie doesn't begrudge them. It's nobody's fault, she believes. Larger forces, invisible forces, have been at work for a long while now, and it's hard to see a beginning, middle, or ending to any of it. Still, she cannot completely ignore the vestiges of her own personal history: this is where she once felt safe and cared for. Even when her parents were at their most distracted, when her dad spent long days on construction sites, and her mom was showing houses at all hours of the day and night, even then, she never questioned that she belonged somewhere, that meals would regularly appear on the table, and it was all good and effortless.

Jeannie enters the house through the deck's sliding glass doors, which are now cracked. Sylvia had tried keeping all the doors locked all the time, but she gave up when it became clear that a small band of rowdy tenters were going to break the doors down if she didn't open them. So she did, and since then, she's barricaded herself into the master bedroom. She kept well out of the way the first few days that people began crashing in the house. Fights over territory broke out every day. There was a lot of pushing, shoving, and yelling. She heard later about several knife fights as well. Now, the damage is done. Carson and Zeke both come and go; Sylvia never knows when either of them will be there, so she has forced herself to stop listening for their footsteps outside her door. Jeannie never comes in. So when she hears the deck doors open now, she assumes it's just a tenter returning to the few square feet of floor space he or she has staked out and now desperately wants to preserve. When fights break out over indoor turf, as they frequently still do, Sylvia turns up the sound on her bedroom TV, or her laptop. Not her fight. Not her problem.

"Mom?" Jeannie stands in the doorway of Sylvia's bedroom. The room is unbearably hot, even with the window wide open. Running the A/C is out of the question. Jeannie can smell the rankly sour sheets. The washer and dryer broke down months ago, from over-use and abuse.

"Jeannie! My God, Jeannie!" Sylvia is overcome by a rush of deep feelings she has nearly forgotten how to feel. Love. Sadness. Regret. Shame. All at once, emotions pierce the thick armor of dullness she has built up to shield her from the unfolding horror and her responsibility for it, which continues to rub her like a sore that never heals. "What are you—" Jeannie holds out the baby. "Whose?"

"We don't know. We found her in a cooler."

"They're animals, Jeannie. I wish you'd—"

"No, Mom. They're not animals. They're desperate. And hurting. You see that, don't you?"

"Fucking tenters," Sylvia says harshly.

"Don't say that!" Jeannie yells. "This is why—!"

"I'm sorry." Sylvia reaches for her daughter. "Jeannie, I'm sorry. You did the right thing—bringing her to me. But she's too quiet. We need formula. Can you get some?" Jeannie nods and turns to leave. "There might still be some sugar in the kitchen, if the animals—if the tenters—haven't used it all up. I'll go find it and mix up some sugar water. You'll hurry back, yes?" Jeannie nods again and leaves. Sylvia cradles the infant, trying not to let herself get attached to a creature that may not live. But she feels grateful to it, nonetheless, for bringing her own daughter back to her. She wets her pinky finger and puts it in the infant's mouth. The reflexive suckling, though weak, floods her with memories from another life.

Chapter Twenty-Nine

The white tent that Zeke shares with Geronimo and Farrah is used only to transact business. None of them sleeps there. They never want to shit where they eat, as the saying goes, and they can't understand why anybody would. Sometimes they sleep together at the Cavern, on nights when they feel like partying. Around 4 a.m., after everyone leaves, they unlock the back bedroom where some of the small safes are stacked, and tangle up together on the king-sized futon they've installed. Other times, they crash (and do laundry) at Farrah's. Her mother, Corinne, doesn't actually live there anymore, but she still sends Farrah money every month. When Sturgis Memorial Hospital in Willing drastically cut back on beds, Corinne scrambled to find another nursing job. She found one at the community hospital in Linton Crossing, and now she rents a tiny room in a house out there, while still paying down her mortgage on the small house in Willing. Corinne, for her part, lives like an impoverished nun. Farrah's been more or less on her own for so long, her mother is at this point more of a casual friend than a parent, and there are no hard feelings. She knows her mother did what she had to do, and she does not feel neglected. It's understood that her mother simply has nothing extra to spare. So Farrah covers her own daily living expenses and incidentals with cash thrown off by her business interests with Zeke and Geronimo. Necessity truly is the mother of invention, for all three of them.

The tent is white for a reason. It's the only white tent in all of Tent City, and the only white tent that is permitted. As everyone knows by the large red cross painted on both sides of this tent, it's the de facto first-aid station. Tenters go there to pick up Band-aids, steri-pads and surgical tape, antibiotic ointments and creams, sanitary pads, generic Tylenol and Motrin. A heavy-duty tarp is pitched over the tent to help keep the inside as dry as possible. Zeke, Farrah, and Geronimo stock the basics for everyone's convenience. The supplies are stored in clear plastic boxes, all neatly labeled. The three of them pay tenters to guard this tent 24/7 and to keep their mouths shut. The first-aid station is just a front, however, for the thriving drug operation run by the three friends, now partners. The place is so jammed with tenters now, there's no need to service outside customers like Nick French. All the customers are in-house—meaning, they either live at Tent City or play at the Cavern. There's some overlap, but not much. Zeke, who loves negotiating, handles the back end—supply and procurement—which is why his real family doesn't see him that often. He's on the go. Geronimo and Farrah deploy their charm and charisma to find new customers and up-sell existing customers. They move a ton of weed and oxy, but also many "flavors" of fentanyl: Tango and Cash. Dance Fever. Apache. Goodfella. They draw the line at heroin, to the extent they can keep their fentanyl supply clean; heroin's just too Goddamn much trouble. No PCP, either. Nobody's looking to start a war here. Jeannie is a frequent visitor to the first-aid tent—strictly for medical supplies. Zeke doesn't know what she knows. And he doesn't want to know. He has a vague idea that she spends all her time trying to help other tenters in need, which is everybody, and he doesn't really see the point of that. Nothing's going to change, no matter how many Band-aids she picks up. The twins say hi when they cross paths. Once in a while, "Hey, Jeel." And sometimes, a quick hug. But they run in different circles, now more than ever, even though they're treading the same acreage every day.

It's two o'clock in the afternoon and it's 98 degrees inside the white tent. But the three partners never miss a standing business meeting. It dawned on Zeke recently that maybe he's re-invented his father's business dynamic: three partners, a thriving business, congenial collective decision-making, a high tolerance for risk. He has the impression this is how Carson and his uncs Darius and Vin operated for a long time. Until they didn't, for reasons that aren't quite clear to Zeke, unless they're simply economic. But he suspects there's more to it, and maybe someday he'll ask his dad to explain it. Zeke watches Geronimo's tall, slim silhouette glide along the outside wall of the tent. Geronimo still sometimes has the same effect on him as the first time they met properly, at Farrah's. Zeke experiences a nervous flutter in his gut, followed by a heightened energy, as if he's been zapped by an invisible life force. It doesn't happen all the time. But now, just now, as Geronimo pops his head into the over-heated tent, his T-shirt clinging to his thinly muscled body, Zeke experiences this physical reaction. They are easy with each other; their friendship occupies a broad spectrum: friends, lovers, partners.

"Hey, keeper of magical shit," Geronimo says to Zeke, "got any ice cold beer stashed here, somewhere?"

"I wish," Zeke smiles. "What was the take at the Cavern last night?"

"Carol called me this morning. Around $600, she said."

"Damn," Zeke says. "You ever wonder where people are getting the cash?"

"Who cares, as long as they keep showing up?" Geronimo shrugs. "Nobody's working legit, anymore, so whatever it takes, y'know."

Farrah enters the tent. "Shit," she says. A long cut on her arm is bleeding. Zeke rifles through one of the first-aid boxes for Neosporin and bandages. "Must be the heat," she says. "Makes people ornery as shit. I had to avoid three fights on my way over here. People punching the shit out of each other, arguing about, I don't know, like, hot dogs, or something. Fucking tenters. They're screaming up at the house, too. You can hear it half-way across the yard." Zeke registers a flicker of concern about his mother, but he figures that by now, she can handle herself, especially if she just stays in her room. "I got nicked, anyway."

"Hey, Z, I'm low on oxy," Geronimo says. "Goofballs too." Zeke pulls out a small metal box that's buried beneath a stack of Army surplus blankets in a corner of the tent. He hands Geronimo a couple of small Baggies.

"You?" Zeke asks Farrah.

"Benzos, weed, the usual shit," Farrah says. "Whatever you got,

I'll sell it. A lot of people are coming to the Cavern just to buy. They don't want to dance or fuck."

"Losers," Geronimo says. "Life's too short to be so fucking serious. If you haven't figured that out by now..." He shakes his head, as if in pity.

"Well, we'll keep carping the shit out of the dee-em, yeah?" Zeke says, tucking the box away under the blankets. They all laugh. The three of them are users too—but not of drugs. They're bound, in part, by a natural inclination to use other people, to manipulate them, mainly benignly, so that they get exactly what they want or need, which includes money, but also sexual adventure. They don't do it consciously, not really; it's the way they've always approached the world, separately and now together, and it's a foundation of their mutual attractions.

"I got a proposal," Farrah says. "I've been thinking about it awhile, and today, these assholes made my point." She touches her bandaged arm. "Private security. Like, our own police force. We pay some of the ones who have their shit together to patrol the grounds for us. We can fold our tent security into the same operation. The best part is, we control them. They go where we tell them, do what we say. Whaddya think?" Farrah's eyes are intensely green. She radiates an almost feral energy that makes both Zeke and Geronimo feel like hunters.

"I like it. But how do we make money off that shit?" Geronimo asks.

"Through favors, right?" Zeke says quickly. "You know, little stuff at first. Like, suppose your neighbor's throwing garbage in front of your tent. You tell a security guard, they take care of it, one way or another, and then you—the tenter, I mean—show your gratitude." The others nod, thinking about this.

"And pretty soon, there's bigger shit to do, right?" Geronimo says. "Like, say a bunch of tenters get together and decide they wanna kick somebody out for picking too many fights, or stealing, or some other annoying shit. But they don't wanna get their hands dirty."

"So they ask security to do it for them," Farrah says, "and negotiate a fair price for services rendered."

"Exactly," Zeke says. "And we get a cut of everything."

"What kind of weapons are we talking about?" Geronimo asks.

"What leverage would the guards have?"

"Guns are too risky," Zeke says, "and we don't have the resources or the manpower for all that. What about baseball bats? Cheap and effective."

"And tasers," Geronimo says. "We can buy everything online."

"And pick it all up in Linton Crossing," Farrah says.

"What should we call these goons?" Zeke asks. He likes branding his enterprises. First, the Cavern, and now... "How about, the Enforcers?" Farrah and Geronimo nod. Within a week, after making discrete inquiries and observing a variety of tenters, the three of them have privately recruited the best candidates—the ones who don't like taking shit from anybody else and who are really, really hard up for money. The field was wide open.

Chapter Thirty

Nobody walks around Tent City this summer without a bandana or some kind of wet cloth tied around their noses and mouths. The stench is overpowering. People have been seen retching and vomiting when they get a strong whiff of Tent City perfume—any bag of garbage mixed with excrement left rotting in the sun. The chore roster fell apart when the vans started dumping people *en masse*. The port-a-potties have long since given out, so depositing and moving human excrement is miserable and time-consuming and involves tossing bags of the stuff into the aptly named shit pit dug at the perimeter of the stream. Jeannie is just about the only person left who goes around bare-faced. She holds her breath when absolutely necessary. Hers days now consist mainly of making rounds, visiting folks in their tents, to see what they need or if she can help in some way. Fran continues to fill the role of self-appointed sycophant, which in practice means she picks up useful information to share with Jeannie—who's ill, who needs first aid, who's really hungry. Wherever Jeannie goes, tenters offer to feed her, even if it's only a handful of pretzels or a day-old cooked hotdog. It's as though she's a respected foreign dignitary and the tenters are Bedouins, bound by custom to make her feel welcome and cared for. The tenters have no idea that this bony, quiet, friendly young woman is connected to the big house, and she never divulges this information. Jeannie never refuses whatever she is offered, even when it takes all her willpower to keep from gagging at whatever morsel is handed to her, often in a crumpled napkin or sagging on a much-used paper plate. She doesn't let any of it bother her. She believes she is right where she's supposed to be, doing what she's supposed to be doing. Going to college could not possibly have offered a clearer path, in the alternate universe that was her life.

The weather has been intensely hot for weeks, with no rain. The yard is more dust than dirt, except where people sprinkle water to keep the dust down. Before the water crisis began, toddlers often spent hours sitting just outside the family tent, slapping little mud puddles dug for their amusement, and to cool off. But now, everyone has been conserving water, taking every opportunity to fill bottles, jugs, even empty garbage cans that have been lined with clean plastic garbage bags, which also are not easy to come by. The main water line to the Kings' house is shut off. Remington Gas & Electric has been peppering area residents with cut-off notices for nonpayment, triggering a round of austerity measures at the utility itself, which has now had to lay off some of its own long-time employees as ratepayer revenues decline. Ironically, a few former Remington G&E workers—not anybody from the executive suite, of course, but the hourly folks, including some of the entry-level admin assistants, along with cafeteria and custodial staff who were direct employees of the utility—are now tenters on the grounds of one of the very households that's no longer paying its utility bills. It's a full-circle moment, whether anyone recognizes it or not.

Necessity is now behind increasingly rare acts of cooperation. Tenters scrounged (stole) garden hoses, connected them, and somehow got hold of assorted valves and couplers to create a leaky, makeshift water conduit stretching from a fire hydrant nearly two blocks away, across and between other houses, all the way to Tent City. Laundry, as well as personal hygiene, mainly consists of a quick dip, a hard squeeze or a shake to return some water to its receptacle, and then a quick air dry. By the time the dried clothing comes down, it's already coated in brown dust and tiny insects. For much of the day, tenters stand in line waiting for a chance to open the hose and fill whatever water receptacles they've got. Adults send their adolescents to wait in line, and so the line has become an unexpected place to see and be seen, to flirt, to find a snack (somebody's always trying to sell something), and to gossip.

Some of the older folks look at the line and think way back to the gasoline shortages of the 1970s, when cars lined up at gas stations, waiting sometimes for hours to fill their tanks. Then, as now, it's a social occasion marked by outbursts of vicious, venal fights and arguments. Joe Wenkowicz, a young guy in his twenties who assumed he would one day manage Willing's Ace Hardware store, has stood in the hose line under a broiling sun for two hours when he sees a woman twice his age cut in line right in front of him. He doesn't know or care that she used to teach in a cosmetology school until the student loan program that enabled students to borrow copious amounts of money to learn the art of hairdressing dried up, leaving her with nothing to fall back on. Joe's premature beer gut has all but disappeared since he landed in Tent City. "Get back in the fucking line!" he yells at the woman in front of him. She yells back, insisting *he* was always behind *her,* not the other way around. Others in line quickly join in the argument, taking sides, mainly out of boredom, not really caring who's right. It doesn't matter. Nothing much matters from one minute to the next, one day to the next. It's just about enduring now; waiting and hoping for something to happen, something to change, for someone to flip a switch so everything can return to normal, to the way things used to be. An Enforcer hears raised voices and comes over to see what's going on. The Enforcer, Dottie Crandall, is a 32-year-old woman wearing a black polo and tan shorts. She's big and wields a smooth, fat baseball bat like she was born with it. She keeps her taser holstered, waiting for an even better opportunity to deploy it. Just the sight of her is enough to calm everybody down. Besides, it's too damn hot to argue. Everybody takes a step closer to the hose, creating the illusion of progress.

Nobody living inside Tent City can see what Tent City has done to the surrounding neighborhood. Or perhaps it's the other way around. Many of the Kings' neighbors, who were never really friends anyway, have moved away. Unable to sell their homes, they settled for renters and whatever paltry dent the rent helps them make in their never-ending mortgages. Many of those renters have since had to rent out rooms in their own rented houses, just to make ends meet. Nobody cares what the law says about this; it doesn't register. When Nick French parked outside of one of these homes around the corner to buy drugs, nearly every house on that block was in transition, with owners getting ready to move out or renters just moving in. The reason the tenters have been able to snake their long water rig across these properties is because the renters and sub-renters don't give a damn. As long as the water still flows into *their* homes, who cares what anybody else is doing? It's only by pooling their minimal resources each month that the renters are able to pay their water bills, anyway.

Every six-year-old in Tent City knows what the basic problem is. Mom and Dad don't have jobs. So nobody pays them. So there's no money to buy stuff like they used to. That's the part that's easy to understand. Hundreds of adults spend summer evenings—most evenings, in fact—huddled in small groups outside one tent or another trying to figure out the rest. Why did this happen? Who started it? Who's really in charge—of Willing, of the banks, of the state, hell, the frickin' country? And why isn't anybody fixing what's clearly so broken? Several conspiracy theories are making the rounds: Russia has overtaken the U.S. government and is spreading its Communistic tentacles into cities and towns like Willing, breaking the back of the economy so that people will be forced to forget all about capitalism and accept Communism. Others are convinced the U.S. government is engineering a take-down to turn everybody into weak sheep. The ultra-rich, the 1 percent of the 1 percent, are buying up all the property and all of the companies, and they're going to consolidate their power over everything and everyone. And all the jobs in the future will be based on a patronage system—as if a super-Boss Tweed were in charge of the whole shebang. And then there are those in Tent City who say the Jews are to blame for everything that's happening, and the sooner we get rid of the Jews, the better off everyone will be.

Jeannie has heard the one about the Jews. More than once. And every time she hears it, she thinks about the brass menorah that she brought out from under her bed and into her tent way back when all this was getting started. She still isn't sure who it belonged to, among her ancestors, or what she should do with it, but it's the only thing she's decided to hold onto from before. Someday, when things are different, she vows to figure out what it means…or if it means anything at all.

Fran catches up to Jeannie. "Winnie's been asking for you," she says.

"I know," Jeannie says. "It's been crazy."

"Sure, of course." Fran yanks a loose thread off of Jeannie's T-shirt and puts it in her own pocket. She thinks Jeannie has been avoiding Winnie, which is unlike her, and she doesn't know why. But she also does not ask Jeannie questions, because it just doesn't seem right. And because Jeannie rarely answers a personal question. "So, do you want me to give Winnie a message?"

"No, I'll go."

"Now?" Fran asks. Jeannie bites her lip, practicing the restraint she has worked so hard to incorporate as a part of her truest self. Jeannie *has* been avoiding Winnie. *Not avoiding,* she tells herself. *More like not giving her special treatment. Like I did in the old days.* Way back at the beginning, when Jeannie brought a tent out to be next to Gina, who was next to Winnie. And the two of them did everything they could think of to help Winnie feel welcomed and comfortable, which was tricky, since Winnie refused to set foot in the house. She was nice about it, always apologetic, but the girls could not persuade her to come inside to use the toilet or take a shower. And so for weeks they checked in on her several times a day, making sure she had food, clean water and towels, rolls of toilet paper, a flashlight and batteries, magazines to read. Jeannie even brought down a portable mini-vacuum every couple of days to clean out the floor of the tent and chase out the beetles and spiders that had settled into the corners. Fran, Jeannie's self-appointed eyes and ears, has been sharing updates on Winnie, who Fran knows is special to Jeannie for reasons that she, Fran, is not privy to. And the news, for many weeks, has not been good, yet still Jeannie has not included Winnie on her daily rounds.

The day Jeannie forced herself to enter the house, to bring the baby to her mother, was a tough day. But visiting Winnie will be tougher, and Jeannie, despite months and months of schooling herself to be as disciplined as a drill sergeant, has allowed herself to make excuses every day for not going to Winnie.

"I will go," Jeannie says. "I really will. But I have to do something else first. On my own." Fran knows she's being told to hang back. She nods, hiding her disappointment. Fran never expects to see another paycheck in her life, and the next best thing—the thing that makes her feel good—is to serve Saint Jeannie. She finds purpose in this, which helps her make peace with everything that's come to pass. Fran just wishes Jeannie would let her in a little more. She could be so helpful, if Jeannie would trust her. But not today, apparently. Fran watches Jeannie head toward the house. She doesn't know what's going on in Jeannie's head, or what awaits her up at the house. Yet she does not dare follow her.

Jeannie has heard rumors about a never-ending poker game going on at the house. She's watched a variety of people making their way up to the mud room door on the side of the house. From there, it's a few steps into the den…where she and Zeke played Monopoly on the floor, eating a big bowl of popcorn…*Leave it alone…*She's pretty sure they're not all camping out in there, as there's not an inch of room left. And if they were fighting over floor space, she'd know about it, or see Enforcers dealing with it. Then yesterday, two middle-aged guys—one of whom she recognized as Cyn's former cook, Joe Finnegan—were talking about it. Finnegan wondered aloud if any game where the dealer is also running the cards could possibly be fair, but the other guy just shrugged. Jeannie knows, without being told, who's running the poker games, but she wants to see for herself.

Jeannie turns the knob on the mud room door, which has a screen door behind it. It's locked. But this door is never locked, she thinks. She sees herself in snow boots, stomping off snow on the landing, then putting a slippery mittened hand onto the knob and entering the mud room. She knows there is hot chocolate waiting… Jeannie shakes her head. "No!" she says out loud. She bangs on the door. She waits, then bangs again. She hears a lock bolt sliding. The screen door has been removed. And then he's there, facing her from inside the mud room, and for a fraction of a second, they do not recognize one another. Carson King wears his long gray-blond hair in a ponytail that trails to a wisp down his back. His face is weathered and deeply lined, and thinner than Jeannie's ever seen it. Paler, too.

"Hey," Carson says. "Honey. Hi."

"Hi." Jeannie looks past her father, who does not step aside for her to enter. She sees that the mud room has been sealed off from the den. It's a separate, enclosed space, now. The only way in and out is through this one door, which now locks, heavily, from the inside. *Who is he hiding from?* But then she sees he is not hiding, exactly. He's carved out a private space, which is unheard of in Tent City. Three men and a woman sit at a folding table. They're holding cards and look at Jeannie with undisguised irritation.

"Cap?" one of the players says, impatiently. Jeannie feels as though she's been slapped. A stranger, a tenter, is calling her father by his nickname, the name that only close friends and family use. A name that belongs now in a box, on a shelf, where only a few people know how to find it. *But why should that matter now?* races through Jeannie's mind. *He isn't really mine, anymore. He's anyone's. We all belong to all of us, and none of us…I belong to no one, now….*

"Jeannie Bean," Carson says, quietly, "I'm in the middle of something. Is anything wrong?"

"No," Jeannie says. "Nothing is wrong…Cap. Everything's fine."

"Then…"

"Nothing. Catch you later." Jeannie turns and walks away from the house, dodging tents and debris as quickly as she can.

"A round of hole cards," Carson says, dealing.

He is ruled by his methods and his means. For about 12 hours out of every 24, he runs a continuous poker game from the mud room of the house that he fully expects to reclaim as his home one day, after the tide turns back in his favor. Because he is a better than average player, he wins often. A number of tenters have established a kind of syndicate; they pool their limited resources, stake their best players, and put them against Carson. This suits everybody because it raises the stakes, which translates into bigger winnings. The players are constantly shifting because the syndicate is impatient; one disastrous winning hand, or two, and you're out. And there's no shortage of tenters waiting to try their luck, each of them thinking they're going to rake in the pot, because after all, how long can anyone's unlucky streak really last? It's got to break your way, at some point. Carson runs the operation, and plays every game, so he benefits the most from the entire arrangement. He benefits in other ways, too—thanks to Zeke.

One day, Carson stopped by the white tent when he heard Zeke would be there. He found his son working the calculator on his cell phone. Carson does not ask Zeke how he manages his affairs, and Zeke doesn't tell him. Carson considers both his children to be launched at this point, and it's a damn good thing they're both smart enough to look after themselves. *We didn't do such a bad job, after all.*

"Hey, Pop." Zeke looks up from his phone. "Need a Band-aid?"

"How's your hand?" Carson asks. Zeke flexes his left hand, which remains stiff.

"It works, most of the time. Long as I don't try to connect with a left hook." They laugh.

"Actually," Carson says, "I could use one of your Enforcers, up at the house."

"What's going on?"

"Nothing. The usual assholes being assholes, but nothing major. It's for me. I need protection."

"You in trouble, Pop?"

"No, nothing like that. More of a precaution, really." Zeke nods, thinking. "I'll give you a cut—a little each month. Does that work? The rest is committed elsewhere."

"We can figure something out." The two stand silently in the tent, looking at each other as men to be reckoned with. In another time and place, Carson might tell his son he's proud of him, even call him a chip off the old block. But he lets it go, unsaid. "I'll send somebody up to the house tomorrow. That work?" Carson nods. They shake hands.

Carson is half-way out of the tent before he stops and turns back around, casually. "Oh," he says. "I almost forgot. Some Benzedrine would be appreciated. As a favor to your old man." Zeke nods several times, taking this in. He remembers riding on his father's shoulders as a small boy: like he was astride the tallest, most powerful giant in the world. And they were both invincible.

When he's not dealing or counting cards, Carson is back at the Baker Block. Every dollar he earns at cards that is not spent, begrudgingly, on feeding himself goes back into the endless rehab work. Before leaving the house each night, he visits Sylvia in her—their—bedroom. He has come to understand that he must seek her out before her night walks. She no longer performs any chores when she goes out, which seem pointless, but continually tries to take stock. She works at making it all seem real. She has tried counting tents, but gave up somewhere north of 200. They're pitched every which way; there are no neat rows. Some face southeast, to catch the morning light, while others face west, as if to inviting the darkness to descend sooner at the end of each day. Some nights, she'll see a couple humping against a tree at the far end of the yard. Frequently, she steps around people shuffling in a drugged stupor. And once, she found a little boy, alone and crying. He had wandered out of his tent and couldn't find his way back. She spent half the night searching for his parents, who didn't realize he was gone. There is always a line for water, but it is shorter at night, and that's when Sylvia, in a ratty T-shirt and an old pair of capris and sneakers, waits to fill her own buckets and a water bottle she keeps by her bed. As a rule, she does not talk to tenters, which means she hardly speaks at all. She carts her own bagged excrement to the shit pit.

Her night walks, which began in fits of sleeplessness, are now also the only time she can steal a few hours, while the baby sleeps. The baby's mother never came forward, and as there is always more than one pregnant woman in Tent City, and many are there on their own, the answer isn't obvious. Fran continues making inquiries, nosing around in people's tents as often as she dares, but she has drawn a blank, as has Jeannie. It's common knowledge that the house has taken in an infant. But so far, nobody seems to care. Nobody has come by asking for her. Every day that Sylvia cares for the child, she thinks it could—and should—be her last. The baby's true mother will be overwhelmed with guilt and wish to reclaim her, she thinks. *You don't really believe that, do you? That's the kind of thing you like to think you used to believe. You used to think the world worked that way. But now you know it doesn't.* Jeannie has not been by since dropping off the infant. She sent someone Sylvia does not know—not Fran, whom Sylvia recognizes as Jeannie's loyal shadow—to drop off a case of formula, source unknown, outside the bedroom door. For a long while now, Zeke is the one she counts on to bring food for her and the baby, diapers, soap, and other bare necessities. She is disgusted by her helplessness, by her premature reliance on her own child to care for her, and yet she cannot see any other way to survive right now.

Carson disapproves of the unknown infant. He nearly jumped the first time he saw the baby in her arms, on one of his evening visits. He has told Sylvia to offload it to a tenter. There must be a single woman out there, he said, who has always wanted a child, and now she can have one, no questions asked. You know it doesn't work like that, she told him. Besides, how will a tenter care for a newborn? The way they all do, he replied. By begging, borrowing, or stealing.

Chapter Thirty-One

Carson knocks before entering. The baby is asleep in a dresser drawer—one of his drawers—that has been pulled out of the bureau, lined with a blanket, and placed on the floor. He steps around the drawer and sits on the edge of the bed. His hands, extremely rough and calloused, pull up small threads on the bedspread. He has spent the last several months sanding—by hand, on his knees—the ground floor of the middle building of the Baker Block. He no longer owns a floor sander, but sandpaper is still easy to come by. He has stained the floor, as well, and now it gleams. In recent days, he has stood outside the plate glass window (which he cleaned by using up an entire bottle of Windex), peering in, admiring the gleaming oak floors, the polished wooden beams, and the clean, new promise that beckons from within.

Carson waited six months after the auction to tell Sylvia about the Baker Block. Every day, he thought about telling her. He knew he *should* tell her. He knew that keeping a secret like this went against everything they had worked for in their old life together—their sense of shared purpose and momentum. But every day, he also told himself that if he could just get a handle on the repairs, and get at least some of the property back into some kind of shape, *then* he could go to Sylvia with good news, and a plan. *Why bring her a problem, when I can instead bring her a solution?* When he began spending nights out of the house, he told her he was worried about thieves stealing copper pipe from Willing Enclave, and that he needed to spend nights up there, to guard the property. Where will you sleep? she asked, only half-believing him. In the truck, he told her. She let it go because probing any further might unravel whatever was left of the fabric holding them—holding some sort of life—together at that point, and that was more than she wanted to face.

So Carson continued spending nights inside the Baker Block building on Main Street, working as far through the night as he could, with a boost from the benzos he was getting from Zeke. His was the only light shining in a window on Main Street, save for the faint flickers trickling out from the nearby Cavern night after night, about which Carson was completely unaware. By the time he told her about the building and the project, he'd roughed in the new electrical and replaced most of the damaged plaster with new drywall, which he purchased a few sheets at a time with poker winnings. By that point, their family finances were in complete shambles, and as they hadn't had a proper conversation about any of that, the Baker Block purchase seemed to Sylvia to be more theoretical than real. But now, Carson is making his reality hers.

"We're ready," he says without preamble.

"Ready for what?" Sylvia asks. *Night after night, he comes to me with nothing but the dreams in his head.*

"A tenant."

"You're joking."

"Jesus, Sylvia!" he says. "You might at least try—for once! You can't hole up here, doing nothing, forever!" *Like dead weight.*

"I'm not doing nothing," she says, evenly.

"I want my partner back."

"Spend the night," she says, yet not really sure she wants him to.

"I can't! I've got to get the place finished. There's still a lot to do."

"Cap," she looks at him closely. *His pupils are pinpoints.* "It can wait, can't it? Nobody's coming to see it any time soon, are they?"

"That's not the point." He paces. "You know how it goes."

"How does it go?" *Say something rational, please.*

"Let's get it on the market! The sooner the better! *You* know!"

"Cap, there is no market. Not right now."

"There's *always* a market! You lost your damn job because you stopped looking for the market, didn't you!"

"Who do you imagine going in there?" *I cannot tell you what you want to hear.*

"A café. Maybe a wine bar. Maybe, I don't know, a children's clothing store. The space is very adaptable. You should get off your butt and come down and see for yourself."

Sylvia already knows what she will see if she goes into downtown Willing. And it is not what her husband sees. She never imagined that their shared capacity to picture the future, together—to will the future they both wanted into existence—would turn back on her, on *them*.

"Let's go away," she says. "We'll bring the kids with us. We'll find a place where we can start over. Someplace where we still matter, where our talent, our potential, won't be wasted. Someplace easier."

"We're not quitters, Sylvia."

"That's not what I'm saying."

"In case you haven't noticed, I've never stopped working—for us. And I'm not going to pull up stakes on a whim, or because you're sick of trying to work things out." They turn quiet, looking away from each other.

"We're caught in a vortex, aren't we?" Sylvia says, almost to herself.

"What?" he asks, irritated. "Will you please focus!"

"It's like we're swirling, faster and faster, around this…thing… this…vacuum that's in the center of everything…sucking everything down…and we can't climb out, no matter how hard we try. We're stuck, and now we just have to see it through."

"If you aren't going to help me, Sylvia, then all you're doing is hurting me. Hurting *us.*" He puts his hand on the door.

"I'm sorry I can't give you what you want, Cap."

"Sorry won't cut it," he says, his back to her. *I will cut you loose in order to save you,* he tells himself. But there is so much more he does not tell her—like how much trouble he went through to find bolt cutters strong enough to remove the padlock that Contrails Capital placed on the front door of his Baker Block building.

CHAPTER THIRTY-TWO

Tent City is a colony: a living, breathing organism that expands and contracts the way an animal pants in the heat, thirsty all the time, surviving on instincts and chances. In this summer's never-ending heat, it is a collection of men, women, and children living lives they did not expect, in conditions that inspire shame and anger and feelings of overwhelming inadequacy. As the conspiracy theories about how and why this is happening wax and wane in popularity, a subterranean deep-seated despair takes hold and remains largely unspoken. But that does not mean such feelings are invisible. Tent City is seething all the time now. On a Thursday afternoon in July, 14 newcomers show up at the edge of the yard. No one is there to welcome them or explain anything. Jeannie is on the far side of the yard blowing up balloons with a handful of six- and seven-year-olds; no one knows where the balloons came from, and no one is going to ask. They will all take whatever small graces come their way, even Jeannie. The new arrivals try weaving their way onto the grounds—and quickly find themselves surrounded by tenters and Enforcers whose shared body language is clearly saying: Fuck off. We're full up. These would-be tenters put their heads down and press on, despite being shoved and spat on, until they come to the stand of pin oaks alongside the stream. Here, they cannot pitch tents, only unfurl sleeping bags on hard ground lumpy with tree roots. Nobody cares. The stench of the shit pit would make this space a non-starter under normal circumstances, but circumstances are anything but normal.

Sylvia drags herself out at night. A deep-seated exhaustion pervades her bones, despite having slept for most of the day, tending to the unnamed baby's most essential needs in between. Each evening, Carson asks her, in tones tinged with anger and anxiety, to come see his progress at the Baker Block. And each evening she refuses. Sylvia can see in her mind's eye the weed-strewn stretch of Main Street where the Baker Block stands, the broken sidewalks, the cracked, burned-out street lamps, and the dark, faceless buildings staring emptily into Willing's void. No, she tells him every evening. I'm needed here. Her husband scoffs and shakes his head. Tonight, Sylvia sweats in the heat and humidity, wandering without purpose among the tents. She will fill her water bucket tonight on the way back inside, where the air is just as oppressive and as ripe with stale ideas. *I cannot end here. This can't be all that's left to me.* She thinks back on Carson's refusal to move away—a last-ditch effort to end this nightmare. And she realizes what she must do, on her own, if she wants to do more than survive. She must leave—go far away from here. Someone else will have to take the baby. Her husband will have to manage on his own. And her own children...The twins lost their first front teeth on the same day, and she remembers how they greedily searched for quarters under their pillows the next morning, and how they laughed about being rich...She pulled sheets off both their beds that told new stories about their journeys toward adulthood...spots of blood on Jeannie's, spunk on Zeke's...Her children are adapting, have adapted, in fact, to a reality that she as a parent could never have prepared them for, and never wanted to. They are coping—more than coping, especially Zeke—and there is little she can do for them, at this point. *Maybe I was forewarned, so I'd have time to adjust.* She stops walking, stops seeing, as the thought of leaving sinks in as the last sane response. *How will I tell them?*

A loud scream shatters Sylvia's trance. She hears a second scream, very close by, and bodies thumping, and a man speaking softly but urgently. Sylvia looks around for an Enforcer, but she is deep in the center of Tent City, and Enforcers tend to patrol the perimeter at this time of night. Sylvia does not have her daughter's courage or her son's bravado; she would never run toward a fight with an intent to do something. But as she moves a few feet to her left she enters a kind of alleyway between tents, which is marked off by fat garbage cans. She sees a woman forced into a bent-over position between the garbage cans. There are two men. One holds the front of the woman in place, her head smashed into his chest, while the other man, his pants down around his ankles, rapes her from behind. Her screams are now muffled by the shirt of the man holding her. Both men are speaking nonstop, saying obscene things, while egging each other on. A flashlight lies on the ground, casting sharp light and shadows on the scene. Sylvia freezes. *Why doesn't somebody come out and do something?* She thinks she sees heads popping out of tent flaps, yet no one emerges. "No!" she yells. "No!" Her brain feels stuck; she cannot figure out what to do or say to make this stop. The rape seems to go on forever, and she feels as though it's happening to her. "You fucking animals!" She looks around for anything she might threaten them with, anything to end this. She sweeps the flashlight off the ground and shines it directly in each man's eyes. "Get away!" She doesn't hit them with it; she can't bring herself to do it. But her presence, and the light, force them out of the moment.

"Fuck off!" they yell.

"Leave her alone!" she yells back, shaking, waving the flashlight from one to the other. Both look under-fed, with scraggly beards.

"Shit!" one of the men says. "Let's get the fuck outta here."

The men weave their way between tents, vanishing into the dark maw of Tent City. The young woman collapses to the ground, sobbing and shaking. Sylvia gets on the ground and wraps her arms around her. A moment later, a woman with long gray hair crawls slowly out of a nearby tent and hands Sylvia a blanket and a bottle of water—for the shock, she says, as if she performs this duty on a nightly basis—then crawls back into her own tent without another word. Sylvia covers her with the blanket, despite the heat, and rocks her gently. *Not Jeannie. Not Jeannie. Not Jeannie.*

"What's your name?" Sylvia asks softly.

"Alison," the young woman whispers. Sylvia looks down at her face, streaked with dirt and tears, and she knows who this is. Alison Hart. Cynthia Hart's niece. Jeannie's former classmate, the girl who whined about her Aunt Cyn moving into her bedroom and squeezing her out. *The kind of thing we used to waste time worrying about. Why did it matter so much?* She can't remember. *But what if this happens to Jeannie? What if it already did?* Her thoughts scatter in a million directions and she cannot reign them in. *This girl shouldn't even be here.* Sylvia strokes Alison's light brown hair, matted with small sticks and dirt. She holds the water bottle to Alison's lips and encourages her to take small sips.

This is not the first rape to occur in Tent City. But it's the only rape that Sylvia has ever witnessed. *Did Baby Doe come from rape?* Deeply sickened and disgusted, she walks Alison to Jeannie's tent, both of them stumbling along the way. Jeannie is awake, though it's nearly three in the morning. She takes one look at Alison and sizes up the situation.

"Come," Jeannie says gently. "Lie down." She points to her own sleeping bag, which sits on a thin foam pad. "Let's get you cleaned up." Jeannie looks at her mother.

"I tried," Sylvia says, shakily. "I didn't know how…I should have…I wanted to…" They do not speak further, as Tent City has reduced both of them to near-silence for long stretches. Jeannie begins gently sponging Alison, who is crying hard, silently. Sylvia feels a hot lump in her throat and tears roll down her cheeks. She can't bear the thought of leaving without Jeannie, but she is suddenly terrified that if she doesn't get out soon, she will shrivel up and blow away. The old Sylvia would power through this, somehow, but that Sylvia is long gone. And she hates herself for it, for all of it.

Sylvia does not sleep at all that night. She walks back to the house slowly, without her water bucket, which she lost somewhere. She remembers to check in on the baby, who is sleeping soundly in the dresser drawer. Shortly after dawn, she calls Zeke, waking him from a tangled sleep with Farrah at her house. She tells him about Alison and asks if there's something he can do about it. Can he find the guys who did it? She has come to accept, almost without thinking about it, that her son is powerful, in some way, and is able to get things done. She remembers, ages ago, he told her he wanted to become an explorer. She didn't understand him at the time, and chalked it up to some temporary adolescent fancy. She still doesn't quite understand him, but she sees that he has a way of barreling through obstacles and mastering situations—much as his father used to do.

"Yeah," Zeke says sleepily, matter-of-factly.

"What do you mean, 'yeah'?"

"Do you know how many people—not just girls—are getting raped or assaulted out there? It's happening every day."

"No," Sylvia says. "No, that can't be true." She can't see Zeke's wry smile.

"We're trying to beef up security, but it isn't easy. I mean, we can't just give everybody a taser and hope for the best."

"What about Jeannie?"

"What about her?"

"Is she safe? I mean, can you assign her an Enforcer, or something? You know she doesn't care about herself, at all."

"I already did, Ma, weeks ago. She fought me on it, but I told her I was gonna do it, anyway. Jeannie's fine. She's getting by."

"What about those fucking rapists? Can you find them and punish them?"

"Listen to you," Zeke says, laughing. "What do you think? Should we hang them in the town square, put them in the stocks, or burn them at the stake? Take your pick."

"I prefer drawn and quartered," Sylvia says, bitterly. "My God, Zeke. What's happening?"

"What do you mean?"

"Where will it end?"

"I don't know, Ma. How did it start in the first place? All I know is, it wasn't my fault." Sylvia closes her eyes and the original vision returns—smoky, crammed, dirty, dusty Tent City overlaid on her enormous green yard. It's horrible. And still, she does not understand how or why. Losses piling upon losses seem unaccountable—literally, un-countable—and cannot be explained away by sheer logic. Willing's economy has been collapsing in upon itself like a black hole, sucking and vacuuming everything into its dark, impenetrable center. Sylvia feels that she and Carson have been gripping the rim of this black hole, doing everything they can to avoid getting sucked in. *The vortex.*

It's exhausting, and by now, Sylvia feels a sense of inevitability, as her ability to reverse course—or wake from this nightmare—slips away. She does not share these feelings with Carson because she does not want to hear him say something so far removed from her own take on reality that he may as well have moved a million miles away. She doesn't want to hear him talk about how much their own destiny remains in their hands. She doesn't want him to tell her, perhaps accuse her, of not holding up her side of their lifelong bargain. This argument, once begun, will not end well, and she doesn't want to endure that.

In the days and weeks that follow, Enforcers are everywhere. There are twice as many monitoring the hose line, which is getting rowdier, as tenters grow even more weary of the hot, daily grind. Joe Wenkowicz, the young would-be hardware store manager who got riled up when he thought someone was cutting in line a few weeks earlier, does the same thing again, even though the same person has been ahead of him for an hour. Maybe he's just so bored, he needs to make something happen. He starts yelling. He shoves the teenage girl in front of him for no apparent reason. She swings her water bucket at him, socking him in the jaw. He pulls her hair. Dottie Crandall, the Enforcer, relishes the opportunity to pull out a long black taser rod and let Joe have it. Dottie smiles as she pokes the electrified rod into his ribs. Ages ago, she worked as an elementary school crossing guard. That job never covered her bills, and this job pays even less. But deep down, she is feeling fulfilled, at last. Only in adversity has Dottie found her true calling. Joe falls to the ground, screaming. Dottie threatens the girl, too, but just the sight of the tip of the black taser rod quiets her down. Dottie turns and faces the line, feet apart, braced for conflict.

Fights break out all over, about everything. Somebody stole somebody's matches. Somebody is accused of stealing food, or diapers, or clean underwear drying on a laundry line strung between tents. People aren't bringing their bags to the shit pit fast enough. The thin man who brokered calm between two women fighting over winter coats at Jeannie's coat drive a few years earlier tries to destroy his neighbor's tent, pulling out stakes and flinging them away. He yells that his neighbor snores so loudly, he can't sleep, and it's driving him crazy. The men begin fighting, tearing at each other's ragged clothes. The man from the coat drive tries to drive a tent stake through his neighbor's heart. A crowd gathers to watch and cheer on one side or the other. Bets are called and placed. Two Enforces lurch into the scene, tase both the men, and then point their weapons toward the crowd, yelling at them to break it up.

The old woman with long gray hair spits at the Enforcers. "Nazis!" she shouts.

"Shut up, bitch!" someone yells at her. "They're here to protect you!"

Zeke suggests to his mother that she should stop walking around by herself at night. He cannot guarantee her safety. The Enforcers are already stretched thin. She refuses. It's still my property—our property, she tells him. Zeke doesn't see any point in arguing. Sylvia is on the verge of telling him she's going to leave soon, anyway, and her night walks are becoming a farewell ritual. But she's not ready to say this out loud. She hasn't told Carson, either.

Chapter Thirty-Three

Jeannie knows she cannot put the task off any longer. Her conscience speaks to her, urgently, without let-up. She has named her conscience Themis, Greek goddess of moral order. This is what she remembers from a fifth-grade unit on Greek mythology. This is the one that stuck with her all these years. *Because I was only ever meant to be this person that I have become. Themis has lived inside me from the moment I was conceived. Themis tames the snake.* Thoughts along these lines have begun crowding in upon the practicalities that otherwise rule Jeannie's days and help her push aside thoughts of hunger, fatigue, and deepening loneliness. Such thoughts are all beside the point, she tells herself, and Themis agrees. Themis helps Jeannie, and is the source of her torment as well.

She has tended to Alison for several days, scouring Tent City for rare morsels like a peach—a peach!—to tempt her to eat, while she, Jeannie, sucks on the pit when Alison is finished. Jeannie also sends Fran on time-consuming missions, looking for this and that—a new broom, a water bottle that doesn't leak. This is how Jeannie tries to honor Fran, to acknowledge her indispensability, while also creating some distance between them. Jeannie has worn herself down to a nub, but there is no room to do things differently. Finally, one day, she escorts Alison back to her own tent and settles her in.

"I'm scared," Alison says, as Jeannie zips her in. "What if they come back? What if they find me? What if they want to finish what they started?" Alison looks at Jeannie with wide eyes. Jeannie remembers the day in school when Alison complained, long and loudly, about her aunt Cyn booting her out of her own bedroom, and forcing her to sleep in a small back room. She wonders if Alison wishes she could curl up in that back room forever, now, safe and sound. But it would be cruel to bring up the past, in any form.

"They won't," Jeannie says.

"How do you know?" Alison asks.

"Because..." Jeannie says. *Because everything that happens here is random. The violence is random. The acts of kindness are random. There is no 'if-then' in this place.* "Because," she says, "they lost interest. They've moved on." *Tonight, they will rape somebody else.* "I'll ask Zeke to send an Enforcer to check on you." She does not say *I'll ask my brother,* as *brother* sounds too intimate in this place, promises too much connection.

"Okay," Alison says, forlornly. Jeannie is outside the tent, looking back at Alison's dark silhouette through the tent-flap mesh. "Thanks a lot. I don't know why we weren't better friends when..."

"Yeah," Jeannie says. "Me too." She walks away quickly. Themis is lecturing her for not really caring much about Alison—not even liking her, really—but acting instead out of cold obligation. *Is that really the way you want to play this, from now on?* A compulsion to do the right thing drives her forward every day, but it's become grim work; she has lost the sense of pleasure she used to feel by serving others.

And now the moment has arrived when Jeannie cannot live in her own skin if she does not visit Winnie Suggs. Winnie lives in the same green tent, in the exact same spot where she first landed. Winnie occupies Ground Zero within Tent City. The King family are the only ones who know this, for sure. Winnie's tent is not easy to find, now, as it is lost amid dozens of crooked rows of tents, deep in the center of Tent City, which haphazardly surrounded Winnie's tent in the confusion of days and weeks that unfolded early on in the unplanned evolution of this homeland for economic refugees. The first few new tenters, rather than seeking to surround themselves with an artificial ring of privacy—open lawn—sought safety in numbers, which meant creating a compact little neighborhood of tents, where people lived practically on top of one another.

Jeannie navigates her way to Winnie's tent based on sense memories—her distance from and angle to a particular stand of trees at the back of the yard; her distance from, and angle toward, the back deck. These are the indelible wayfinders Jeannie relies on, without even realizing it, to get around the over-featured yard that once appeared virtually featureless. She stops a few yards away from the front flap of Winnie's tent. The tent itself looks exactly as it did the first day. Jeannie does not expect Winnie to look the same. She has not laid eyes on her in months; it is quite easy to avoid running into someone in Tent City, as people keep odd hours, scavenge and scrounge in unpredictable patterns, and Winnie was never one to do things straightforwardly, anyway. But now she cannot bring herself to walk the last few yards to the tent, or to call to Winnie, or to rub her palm on a tent sidewall—a common greeting in Tent City, a way to let someone know you have arrived in a place where there are no doorbells. She isn't afraid of Winnie, not exactly, but of what Winnie will do to her—not physically, but in other ways, in the ways that hurt the most. Winnie's presence brings Gina's absence too close.

For nearly six weeks, the first pair of blue and green tents poking up from the Kings' vast yard sat there like two ink stains on a white cloth: permanently altering the landscape, never blending, yet, as the weeks passed, increasingly difficult to picture the yard without. Winnie, Gina (who didn't leave after a week, as Carson asked), and Jeannie developed a manageable routine that was also secretly pleasurable. As the awkwardness and newness of the situation faded, the Genes took on shared responsibility for Winnie, as both felt they owed it to her to make this work, since they had set it in motion in the first place, in the parking lot of the ShopFine. They fed her, did laundry for her, even erected a short fence, using scraps of old fence posts they found down by the stream, so that Winnie would have privacy to pee and defecate near the trees. She refused to enter the house, and after a while, the teens stopped asking. They brought down hot water from the house by the pailful, and on warmer days Winnie used the garden hose hooked up to the side of the house.

Sylvia was agitated and spooked by all of it—but she didn't know how to talk about that, and how it was all tied up with the visions. Some nights, she paced the living room, staring out through the sliding glass doors at the yard, waiting for something—but she couldn't say what. She couldn't know this was the prelude to her night walks. Carson was vocal about his disgust. They're trespassing, he said, over and over. They're killing the grass. They've got to go. Like Sylvia, Carson couldn't say what he really meant. *What's mine is not theirs.* Carson directed his anger at Jeannie; he considered her the architect of these unwanted alterations. And he told her every day he expected her to fix it. Jeannie began spending more time in the tent with Gina, and less time in the house. She walked around with her stomach in knots, caught between worlds and duties. This is when Themis first made herself known, or perhaps, simply began to speak up so that Jeannie would have to listen.

At the time, Jeannie thought that Gina had made peace with her father, and vice versa. Gina walked home to eat dinner with him one night a week. (He never returned to the Kings' house after that initial visit.) Gina could not bear spending much time in her father's house—it no longer felt like *her* house. Her abuela's absence left the place cold, and she felt, some evenings, as though the ghosts of her mother and grandmother were both urging her, in silent whispers, to get out, to go away. She could see that Javier was trying, but his way of trying didn't make her feel grounded or even welcomed. He made her hamburgers with American cheese. She saw that he barely ate. His face had taken on a waxen look and his mustache, now all gray, drooped unevenly. The Vida van was parked in front of the house. Javier had sold his own car for ready cash, and now used the van for everything.

"Papá," Gina said, "what is happening with your business?" She debated asking him this question on the way over, but decided she would ask, and show him she was no longer a child, that she could think for herself, and that she cared about the wider world.

"When are you coming home?" Javier replied.

"Why won't you talk to me?"

"I have nothing to say that would interest you."

"This is why…this is why I can't live here with you anymore. I'm a person, but you can't see that. I can't live here, and be a... a...*thing.*" She pushed her plate away.

"*Querido,* I'm sorry. I want...I only want you to be happy. Your mother would know how to do for you, but I seem to know nothing. I am stupid." Javier rose from the table. "A stupid, stupid man. And I cannot even keep a daughter!" Javier swept their dinner plates into the sink with such force, both broke into pieces. Gina immediately turned to the wall, where her father had punched a hole. She did not know this man, who this man had become. And she did not want to live under his roof. Javier saw he had frightened her and rushed to wrap her in his arms. He had not touched her, had not held her, in a long, long time. He stroked her hair and told her he loved her. He told her he was sorry, for everything.

"*Lo siento, lo siento, lo siento,*" he murmured over and over.

"I know," she said, crying softly. "I know. But I can't...I can't breathe in this house." Javier stepped away from her and sat down heavily.

"You're going to leave me, too," he said softly. He covered his face with his hands. Gina could not bear to watch him. She couldn't let herself believe that *she* was the cause of this misery; he'd been miserable for a long time, and she only had an inkling as to why, and what had been happening. But if he isn't going to confide in me, she told herself, then he has no right to keep me.

"You left home when you were my age, didn't you?" she asked. He looked up at her, tears in his eyes. "Now it's my turn—to find something better." Javier shook his head.

"*This*, all *this*, was supposed to be better," he said. He could not tell her: *I am about lose everything I made for you and your mother*. To tell her would make it more real than he could stand.

"For *you,*" Gina replied. "But not for me." She kissed the top of his head and walked out of the only house she had ever known, breaking into a run down the steps and into the street, because if she did not act quickly right then, she knew she might never be able to act at all. *Perhaps*, Javier thought, watching her disappear down the street, *she can save herself, for I am lost*.

Gina spent most of that night lying awake, flat on her back, in her tent. Jeannie lay on a sleeping bag next to her, tossing and moaning in her sleep. Gina felt strong enough to leave her father, but she struggled to make peace with leaving Jeannie behind alone to deal with Winnie and everything that seemed to be happening, or might happen. It was hard to tell what was going on, exactly. The two of them had done so much together up to now that it seemed strange to Gina, and certainly disloyal, to think only of herself, and her own future. She and Jeannie had long shared an unspoken feeling that they were both meant to *make a difference.* And while neither was sure yet what that would look like, they knew, even when they weren't seeing each other as often as they used to, that *destiny* meant something; they heard a calling, and together and separately, they were trying to decipher its meaning. Toward daylight, Gina drifted off, exhausted and unresolved as to how she would manage. Jeannie left her sleeping and went up to the house for a shower and food. Jeannie was still using the house on a regular, though limited, basis at that time. When she came back out, she looked in on Winnie first, who was playing solitaire, her legs splayed. Winnie smiled and told Jeannie everything was fine, and thanked her for the hot tea. She told Jeannie that she was a blessing.

When Jeannie opened the flap to Gina's tent, she saw her own sleeping bag and nothing else. Gina's sleeping bag was gone, along with her knapsack and her mother Eugenia's canvas carry-all. Jeannie put down the bagels she was carrying and stood up in the tent, her head pushing against the nylon ceiling. She looked around as if Gina and her things were hiding, which of course was impossible. She came outside and called for her. There was nowhere to hide in the Kings' yard, and there was no one in sight. Jeannie's heart rate sped up and her breathing grew shallow. She felt a fight-or-flight urge, yet had no idea where to go, or what to do. She doesn't remember what she did over the next few hours but towards evening, she got a text message from Gina. Within three weeks, Jeannie would stop using a cell phone altogether, but that night, she was still attuned to the alert *ping* of her phone.

> J, sorry. couldn't figure out what to say. had to go. will explain when i figure it out myself. i'll be ok. xxoo. g

Jeannie stares at Winnie's tent now, wishing hard that she could unzip it and Gina would be there instead of Winnie. Or maybe the two of them playing gin rummy. Winnie could play cards for hours on end and had taught both girls how to play. Themis tells her sternly to stop wishing. *If wishes were fishes.* She heard that somewhere, a long time ago, back when making a joke wasn't something you even had to think about, it just happened. *Get over yourself.* Jeannie rubs her palm on Winnie's side wall. There is no response. The front fly is zipped closed. She slowly unzips it, careful not to startle Winnie or awaken her. As the zipper comes down, a horrible stench escapes from the tent, forcing Jeannie to gag. She takes a step back.

"Winnie?" There is no response, but Jeannie thinks she hears a rustling in the tent, which she wants to take as a good sign. "Winnie, you doin' ok in there? Need anything?" *Don't be a fucking coward. Do what you're supposed to do.* Jeannie removes a bandana from around her neck and ties it over her mouth. For once, she looks like almost everybody else walking around Tent City this summer. She unzips the flap and steps into the tent. Her eyes need a moment to adjust to the dark. Once they do, she needs a few more seconds to understand what she is looking at, and then she backs out of the tent quickly, zips it up, and vomits the meager contents of her stomach all over the dirt. Winnie is dead, a bloated corpse lying on its side. A rat has begun gnawing at her face and a dense swarm of insects is feasting on the remains of her last meal.

Chapter Thirty-Four

When Jeannie does not leave her tent for a whole day and night, Fran is not too worried. She thinks that perhaps, Jeannie is at last taking a "day off" and getting a bit of the rest she continually denies herself, while urging everyone else to take care of themselves. (She does not yet know what Jeannie found, and it will be another day before the corpse is wrapped in garbage bags and carted to the shit pit by tenters paid by Zeke. No one moves a muscle in Tent City without compensation, unless it is strictly in their own interests to do so.) Fran is always touched when this young woman who could be her own daughter, perhaps her granddaughter, counsels her on making sure she eats and sleeps enough, and drinks plenty of water. Fran knows that's who Jeannie is, and she rejoices in that. But when Jeannie is still lying curled up in a little ball for a second day in a row, then Fran begins to worry. Nothing she says or does seems to reach Jeannie, who appears to Fran like a frail and helpless kitten. Still a saint, but increasingly, a saint in trouble. Jeannie will not speak or eat or drink. Fran's reverence for her increases in proportion to her own feelings of inadequacy and even impatience, as it's clear she, Fran, does not know how to help. So finally, toward evening on the second day of Jeannie's self-imposed exile, Fran takes the only option left: She goes up to the house to find Sylvia. Even though many tenters are unaware, Fran figured out a long time ago that Sylvia is Jeannie's mother.

Fran picks her way gingerly through the ground floor of the house. It's crowded with sleeping bags and debris of all sorts. It's a pigsty,

Fran thinks in disgust, and the smell is awful. At least a dozen men, women, and children are simply sitting on the ground, or draped on beat-up furniture, looking glazed and spent. It's as if they have forgotten how to move, how to act, how to initiate anything beyond meeting the barest requirements of life. They have all given up, Fran thinks. What's to become of them—of any of us? She vows to keep moving, to stay in Jeannie's orbit, no matter what. Giving up is dying, she thinks, and I'm not ready for that. Let me not be taken any time soon, for there is work to be done. Fran asks the room at large how to find Sylvia. Someone points a finger toward the ceiling. Fran finds the stairs and walks timidly past the twins' old bedrooms (Jeannie's was claimed long ago, and is now an unrecognizable hovel, but Zeke keeps his own room very locked), until she comes to the closed door to the master bedroom. She knocks quietly, but there is no answer. After a moment, Fran opens the door. Jeannie is in trouble, and this gives her courage. Sylvia is asleep in the rumpled bed. The baby is fussing quietly in the drawer. Fran, keeping her eyes forward, willing herself not to pry, tiptoes over to Sylvia and shakes her gently until she wakes up. Fran quickly explains and in under a minute, Sylvia has pulled on pants and shoes and they're out the door.

Sylvia squints in the daylight. She has not been outside, in sunlight, in a very long time. The light triggers an instant migraine, but she ignores it. Fran does not think Jeannie has moved in several hours. Sylvia sits by her sleeping bag and rubs her daughter's back. Jeannie rolls over, slowly.

"Hey," Sylvia whispers. Jeannie closes her eyes and tears slide down the sides of her face.

"Winnie's dead," Jeannie says.

"Oh, honey, I'm sorry."

"I killed her."

"That's not true," Fran says quickly.

"I know," Sylvia says. "Of course it's not true."

"It *is* true!" Jeannie says, her voice cracking.

"Honey," Sylvia says, "Winnie was sick when she got here. You know that, don't you?"

Jeannie sits up, and Sylvia is alarmed by how thin she is, with dark circles under her eyes. There is short gray hair sprouting on her haphazardly shorn head. A buried memory stirs in Sylvia—a story she heard as a little girl, about a relative, a great-aunt, who barely survived Auschwitz. Someone showed her a faded brown photograph. *I had nightmares.* Sylvia imagines, for an instant, that Jeannie resembles her great-aunt. The left side of her head screams in pain.

"Winnie was fine!" Jeannie croaks. "But I ignored her. I didn't help her when she needed help. She wouldn't ask for it, but I knew. I knew. And I pretended I didn't. Themis told me, and I wouldn't listen!" Sylvia and Fran exchange a look of alarm. Jeannie leans over and grabs a tin cup—part of a long-lost set of camping gear—and begins banging it against her head. Sylvia and Fran lunge at her together, take the cup away, and gently hold her arms.

"Fran, I'm going to keep her still," Sylvia asks. Fran nods. "Go up to the house and get Carson. I don't think we can carry her out of here without help." Fran nods again and tries to soothe Jeannie, who is weeping openly now, and almost too weak to struggle.

Fran bangs on the mud room door, but no one answers. She hears shouting, and chairs scraping.

"Go ahead, say it," Carson says evenly, seated at the rickety card table in the airless, enclosed mud room, which smells of cigarettes and flop sweat. "You want to say it, so say it."

"You're a fucking cheater," Bucky Preston says. He's bald with a pot belly and a pockmarked face. His hands are soft. Bucky used to sell cars at Remington's largest dealership until it folded, quickly, sickeningly, as if all the air had gone out of the hokey, over-sized arm-waving character balloon that undulated in the wind to attract customers' attention to the lot. His commissions were barely enough to cover his *own* car payments, and he didn't have enough to start over someplace else. So he stayed in Willing, and gradually made his way to Tent City—the last stop for many who swore it could never come to this. "You always cheat." Two other players nodded, their cards still fanned in their hands.

"I never cheat," Carson says, his voice still steady. "I don't have to. I'm just a better player."

"You're the fucking house, King," Bucky says, "and the house always wins, doesn't it?" The same men nod again. "I'm sick of this shit." Bucky looks at the two men who nodded. What happens next is clearly pre-arranged. The Enforcer who had been posted at the poker games, as Carson requested, was assigned elsewhere weeks ago. Tent City's rag-tag security force is a finite commodity, and Zeke is constantly forced to play whack-a-mole, as new trouble spots arise daily. Carson said nothing when the Enforcer stopped showing up; he's not about to signal to his son that he is weak or frightened, because he's not. One of players moves quickly behind Carson's chair and pins his arms, painfully, behind his back. The other pulls out a knife and holds it to Carson's throat. Carson clenches his jaw. *These motherfuckers.* "So we're changing up the game. First, we're gonna even things up by taking back the money you stole from us."

"Won off you, you mean," Carson says.

"No, you fucking stole it," Bucky says, "and that stops now, today. You think you're somethin', lording it up here in your big house, but you're drowning just like the rest of us, aren't you? Or you wouldn't be here."

"It's my fucking house," Carson says. "Why would I leave?"

"It's shit, now," Bucky says. "Where's your stash?" The man holding the knife to Carson's throat, who is one of the two men who did not finish raping Alison Hart, digs the point in just enough to draw a scratch of blood. The woman at the card table, Evelyn Fitzgerald, a quiet steady player who is tolerated by the men—for in spite of everything, the men would prefer a unisex game—leaves the mud room quickly, before the others can react. She bumps into Fran on the way out.

"Don't go in there," Evelyn says. She is about Fran's age, but hard around the edges where Fran is soft. "It's not safe."

"But—" Fran says.

"Don't!" Evelyn says. Fran knocks again, but no one answers. She doesn't want to go back to Jeannie's tent empty-handed. Evelyn returns with Zeke and two Enforcers. All three carry tasers as well as baseball bats. They smash the lock to the mud room door and kick it open. Thirty seconds later, Bucky and the other two men are on the ground, clutching their balls and their guts. Zeke and one of the men he trounced are staring at each other, fishing for an uneasy memory. *Bud. The married dude who cheated on his wife. At Willing Enclave.* Bud recognizes Zeke too and looks away, humiliation washing over him in sick waves. Carson is standing, wiping blood off his neck. He hardly recognizes his son, dressed in black leather, made of compacted muscle, with a knowing, watchful look in his eyes—a hyper-alertness that seems to take everything in at once. Carson suddenly feels old for the first time ever. He hates it.

"I could've fucking handled it," he says to Zeke.

"Sure," Zeke says. "Yeah, of course. But, you know, we try to stop this shit before something else happens, before word spreads." Violence in Tent City is like a contagious virus—easy to catch, hard to cure.

"Well," Carson says. He looks at the broken door and wonders if he'll ever own this space again. He begins calculating where he can move the game to, and how he can increase the stakes. Then he kicks Bucky Preston in the ribs. "And fuck you, Bud," he says.

Fran pokes her head into the mud room. Carson and Zeke both give her the same annoyed look. "Uh," she says, "it's Jeannie."

Chapter Thirty-Five

Carson hates second-guessing himself; he's not in the habit of doing it. He's always believed it's a sign of weakness that afflicts people who are indecisive, unsure of themselves, and lacking in a guiding vision—a plan for life. And that's not Carson. How else could he have gotten this far? In their last year of working together, Darius and Vin both did a lot of second-guessing, and that brought Carson to the verge of despising them, which was plain to all of them. And he's still wrestling with the extent to which they—not he—are responsible for the thinning and fading away of Willing Prime Contractors. When you get right down to it, a thriving business is equal parts guts, opportunity, and luck, and when any one of those is running low, you stoke the other ingredients to make up for any shortfall or fundamental weakness. Carson thought for years they all saw things this way; it wasn't the kind of thing you needed to spell out. But maybe that was never actually the case. *Still, I always played for keeps.*

For some time now, Carson has struggled to quiet an inner voice torturing him with self-doubt. *Why didn't I barricade the house when the first intruders arrived? Why didn't I buy a gun so I could shoot them on sight? Why did I let these vermin infect us? Why didn't I stop it before it began?* Carson has no good answers—just as Sylvia has no explanation for her visions; and yet the two have never compared notes on this. And at this point, Carson is disgusted with himself for not getting out ahead of this whole situation—define it how you will, he thinks—and disgusted by the sense of helplessness that the situation has engendered. And the only way he can handle this, and still live with himself, is to create a kind of antidote—an opposite and equal reaction, as if the rules of physics themselves were dictating his actions. This means pressing on with the Baker Block building renovation. Bringing this dying old structure in the abandoned heart of Willing back to life seems like the only thing that makes sense in his life right now. It's the only thing he can do that reeks of *progress, action,* and some form of momentum that speaks to a future where his home, his property, and his family are not irretrievably lost. He's frustrated by his failure—hopefully only temporary—to keep Sylvia on his side. They both do better when they're on the same side. But for a while now, he has felt as though they are fighting for opposite things, or do they only seem to be? What's real, now, as opposed to simply felt?

Carson has not seen his family, or the inside of his house, since the day of the mud room fight three weeks ago. He lives off of greasy wrapped food from the 7-Eleven and a Styrofoam cooler of beer. He sleeps on the thin mattress on the second floor of his center building. And he works almost nonstop with the aid of the uppers that Zeke gives him for free. Zeke and his posse are helping him in another key way. Zeke knew his father depended on the steady cash he won at poker. So, after conferring with Farrah and Geronimo, Zeke offered his father a room in the Cavern to run his game. The three partners agreed that gambling was a natural adjunct to the fun and business already booming there. If it panned out well, perhaps this would be something they could expand upon.

Carson looked around with curiosity when Zeke, Farrah, and Geronimo took him to the Cavern for the first time. It was daytime, so the room looked quite drab and ordinary. The windows remained blacked out, so only a gloomy, gray light filtered in. A makeshift bar, huge metal ice buckets, an enormous pair of black speakers, and some canister lights gave him some idea of the nighttime ambience. They walked past a room with mattresses on the floor and variety of paraphernalia that Carson had never seen before: rubber tubes and pulleys, bungie cords, a swing suspended from the ceiling, a black leather harness. *What the hell is my son into?* At the same time, he was studying the space with a developer's eye. *There's potential here. We could do something with this.* He did not ask any questions; he did not really want to know, and did not feel he needed to know. Zeke seemed remarkably self-possessed for a 19-year-old; Carson couldn't argue with that. The partners offered him no explanation, in any case, but passed on to show him the smaller of the two bedrooms. It was empty—or had been emptied for his benefit. They offered to replace the card table that had been broken during the mud room fight. They told him they'd take a cut of all action, and he agreed that was only fair. Carson thought Farrah and Geronimo were weird, but if Zeke respected them, then so would he. And he'd keep his thoughts about that, and everything else he'd seen, to himself. *Whatever it takes.*

So now, with his poker game re-established (and a refreshed clientele, thanks to the different mix of people who frequent the Cavern), he's scraped together enough money to buy the rest of the drywall he needs to finish the walls on both floors. The heat is thick and oppressive, and sweat drips from his whole body as he pounds nails. But Carson hardly notices. His head is thrumming with a drumbeat of expectation. The space is taking on new life, and life attracts life. Willing is not going to disappear off the face of the earth. He's always known it's just a matter of waiting it out. He feels like a lion stalking its prey, carefully, slowly, cautiously—certain that he will get what he wants in the end. There was a time when Sylvia felt this way too. Maybe that will happen again. Maybe his lioness will rejoin the herd, a herd of only two, perhaps, but a herd, as he sees it, nonetheless.

Chapter Thirty-Six

Zeke is reentering Tent City from a garden shed two blocks away, at one of the houses that's been rented and sub-rented until nobody cares who comes and goes. The shed is where he regularly meets one of his suppliers. The night is oppressively hot and humid. Zeke slaps mosquitoes attacking his damp neck. He's thinking about his dad, and how he looked in the mud room, with a knife pricking the pale blue artery thrumming in his taught neck. Zeke had never seen that expression on his father's face before, and never wants to see it again. His dad looked human, *too human. Like somebody right at the edge of breaking.* All those backyard barbecues years ago, when the uncs would come over. The men would stand around the grill, joking, arguing about sports, and politics, skimming over work as though it were their very own third rail, just for a few hours on a summer Sunday. Zeke often stood nearby, watching the men, nursing a Coke. When he was 12, he began noticing that Darius and Vin looked at Carson in a way Carson never looked at them. *Dad's the boss,* he thought, *and they know it.* He decided one day *he'd* be a boss; he wouldn't settle for anything less. By the time he set off on his adventures with Farrah and Geronimo, Zeke had forgotten all about being a boss—intent, instead, on getting out of going to college and getting out from under the parental eye, which was pretty easy to do, especially once everything around them started falling apart.

But now, as Zeke makes his way back from the garden shed, his hand resting lightly on the taser hooked to his belt, he realizes he *is* a boss, after all. He didn't plan it, exactly, but it happened anyway. And when he broke into the mud room the day Evelyn ran to tell him there was trouble, Zeke felt something shift between his father and him. Not a passing of the torch, exactly; more like a shift in how each of them stood with respect to time. Zeke suddenly saw his father not simply as vulnerable, but as a man who had already spent most of his power. And in that moment, as the Enforcers were zapping his father's assailants, Zeke felt his own power locking in. He knew who he was, what he was doing, and how he would do it—not for the rest of his life, but in moments that counted. In this way, father and son were quite different, though neither thought about it consciously, and they would never discuss it openly. Carson lives for the future; the power behind his drive comes from an overwhelming need to push on, and never stop pushing. Zeke has no faith in a future you can't see; his gut, his emotions, his intellect are all rooted in the present, and in gauging each moment, each hour, so as to mine its possibilities.

As he steps back onto his family's property, he pauses at the threshold, his feet straddling the curb. He slaps his bitten neck. Lights twinkle randomly across Tent City—flashlights, cigarette tips, even some barrel fires, despite the heat, for it's the only way to cook food. He cannot see his house from here; it is obscured by the vast sea of tents, and the house is mainly dark at night now, in any case. The heat has slowed everyone down, and yet this place is never actually quiet. Laughter and shouting reach him across the yard in random waves. Coughing, scraping, the flapping of towels and blankets, the splash of dirty water onto the parched ground, static-filled radios… all contribute to the live current of the place. In this moment, Zeke cannot imagine another life for himself. All the parts of him feel tied together, here, in this chaotic, unplanned, ad hoc village of strangers who left or lost their old lives behind. *Not random at all.*

He steps toward the first crooked rim of tents when two men surge unseen from his left and right, put him in a chokehold and pull the taser from its holster. They force him onto the ground, an elbow digging sharply into his back. He strains to hold his face a half-inch above the dry summer dirt and sharp twigs. He cannot see his attackers. He rapidly ticks through a list of people who may have it out for him: A supplier he didn't pay on time? The old poker gang? Enforcers demanding a bigger take? None of these seems likely. Zeke is incredibly careful, and he knows Farrah and Geronimo are also fastidious; they're risk-takers but they hate loose ends. That's how they've all gotten as far as they have.

"What the fuck?" Zeke says to the dirt, trying to twist his head to get a look at the men.

"Do you know Abby Goodwin?" one of the men asks. Zeke tries to remember this voice: low, gravelly, shouldn't be hard to recognize.

"No," Zeke says. "You jumped the wrong guy."

"Don't think so," says the second man, a nasal tenor.

"If you're looking for money, there are easier ways," Zeke says. "Let's talk about it."

"I don't want your fucking blood money," the man with the deep voice says, twisting Zeke's right arm hard. His left arm is also in a tight grip; his injured left hand is throbbing. He waits for more, clenching his jaws.

"You sold drugs to my niece, you fucking scumbag," says the second man. "Whaddya think happens when you sell drugs to a 14-year-old girl?"

The first man, who now has his knee, rather than his elbow, deep in Zeke's back, begins to sob. "Motherfucker!" he yells in a strangled voice. "I'm gonna kill him, Frank, I'm gonna kill him!" With Zeke still pinned painfully to the ground, Frank argues with his brother, called Tom. The plan, apparently, is not to kill him, but Frank knew Tom would not want to hold back once they had him.

"Just tase him, Tom. Then we'll tie him up and throw him in the woods, like we planned. You don't wanna mess with a body. We send a message, yeah?"

"Wait," Zeke says, looking for an out, or at least time. "What happened to Abby? What do you think I did? I never met her."

"You fed her drugs," Tom hisses in Zeke's ear. "You didn't give a shit, did you?"

"I don't sell drugs to kids," Zeke says. "I wouldn't do that. My sister's a kid. I wouldn't."

"You're lying," Frank says. He jabs the taser into Zeke's ribcage. Zeke bucks sharply as pain zigzags through his body.

"You gave her drugs like it was candy," Tom says. "She was bored. This fucking hell-hole. She was just a kid. And she had no fucking idea, did she?" Tom spits in Zeke's ear. He leans his weight on him and Zeke hears his right arm snap; it sounds like a branch cracking off a tree somewhere deep in the woods. *That stupid nail gun...*A jolt, a walloping surge, and then darkness.

When Zeke opens his eyes, the first thing he sees is a blurry gray-pink dawn. He is convinced that his head has been severed from his body, but that somehow, he is permitted still to see and think. He can swivel his gaze, but the rest of his trunk feels severed, which is to say, simply not there. *This is fucked up...a talking head?...How will I get around...? But I am alive, and that's something.* He blinks and furry shapes appear. *The trees move. Of course. I can't move but the trees can. Compensation. An eye for an eye. Is that how it goes?*

"Oh my God. Oh my fucking God." Farrah sees him first. She and Geronimo have searched all night. When Zeke didn't return from his supply run, they knew something was wrong. He was due back at the white tent by 12:30 last night. When he didn't show by 2:00 that morning, they set out, combing every inch of Tent City, methodically. They retraced his steps to and from the garden shed around the corner twice. They agreed to split up for an hour, to cover more ground, and then meet up at the white tent at 4:00 a.m. Both were blanched with exhaustion and worried beyond speaking. Sure, Zeke can take care of himself, but they know better than anyone that this place is unpredictable—and growing more so every day. They had sent six Enforcers out looking too, but felt it would be unwise to sidetrack more of them, as they were needed to quell the fights, often brutal fights, that broke out every night now. The Enforcers also came back with nothing, but both Farrah and Geronimo knew they hadn't looked all that hard. They just didn't really care all that much—people vanished from Tent

City without any explanation all the time—and playing hide and seek wasn't the job they'd agreed to do in the first place.

Farrah grabs Geronimo and they bend over Zeke's body, wrapped awkwardly in twine. Frank and Tom had rolled him like a log into the woods near the stream, which no longer burbles as it's been starved for water this summer. The shit pit invades their nostrils; they're accustomed to it, tamping down the gag reflex. This is the very end of the Kings' property, the place where the glory of the yard completely peters out amid a broad stand of pin oaks and other thin-limbed trees that blot out the sun. Farrah strokes Zeke's head and carefully tips some water into his mouth while Geronimo starts on the knots with a jackknife. They both bend down to kiss him on the cheek. Their salty tears mingle—all three of them. Farrah squeezes Zeke's left hand and he groans. But when the twine comes off and his right arm is no longer cradled, then Zeke passes out from the pain.

Chapter Thirty-Seven

For the first time in over a year, all four members of the King family are in the house at the same time. They are in the master bedroom, which is the only room they still "own" in the entire house. There have been many nights when Sylvia was convinced a group of tenters were storming up the stairs to evict her and claim the space as their own. After all, why should she have an entire room to herself, when families larger than hers were crammed into flimsy two-person tents for months on end? But this is one disaster that did not materialize, and once Zeke posted a roster of Enforcers outside his mother's room, the chances of any "occupy" action diminished dramatically.

Zeke lies uncomfortably in the king-sized bed. His entire right arm is encased in a home-made plaster cast; his left hand is wrapped in an ace bandage; and his ribcage is a deep black-and-purple. Jeannie lies on an air mattress on the floor. She told Sylvia she wouldn't stay a single night in the house unless she remained close to the ground. She is still weak with malnutrition and lack of sleep, and she's tortured by thoughts of *Winnie, Winnie, Winnie.* She couldn't put up much of a fight, but she did try. Sylvia catches a few hours of sleep in the middle of the day in an upholstered chair; she still walks at night, despite the generally lawless atmosphere that pervades Tent City. Carson never stays over, but he's here now. And Baby Doe, who spent her first few weeks in the lined dresser drawer, has been farmed out to Fran Hauser who has agreed, for now, to take care of her. Fran was thrilled to be asked; she is infused with the glow of service to others. And she wants to prove her worth to Jeannie, despite the difference in their ages.

Carson and Sylvia are literally watching their children sleep now. The room is quiet for a long stretch, though the rise and fall of other voices in the house are inescapable. "They'll be okay," Sylvia says softly, as much to herself as to her husband.

"Yeah," Carson says. "They're pretty tough."

Sylvia looks at him. "I'm leaving." *I'm leaving you.*

"Why?" he asks sharply. "Why would you do that?"

"Because…"

"You'd never leave *them.*"

"They refuse to come with me. I can't make them. Maybe one day—"

"But why?" he asks again. Sylvia shakes her head. *He never asks the right questions.* "Okay, so we've gone down some blind alleys. I know that. We got off track. I know that too. But you can't give up, Sylvia. *I* won't give up, just because we've hit a roadblock." Carson paces in the few feet of clear floor space available. *The cold air return still needs work. I should re-seal the front windows. Gotta get back to it.* "I should have stopped it."

"You couldn't."

"I should have tried. I should have ripped those tents right out of the ground, the first day they appeared." *I failed you. Say it.*

"It's not your fault. Any of it," Sylvia says. She puts a hand on his arm, to still him.

"I should've fucking killed the first stranger who set foot on our property. That stupid old woman. What was she doing here? Why did we let Jeannie have her own way? We're doing everything wrong, Syl. We used to do everything right."

"I don't think like that anymore."

"Well, what *do* you think—about anything—Sylvia? What do you think is going to happen? To us? To them? To all of this." He waves his arm. Sylvia shrugs. "We used to work together. A well-oiled machine, remember? I'd be finished by now if you'd help me, instead of barricading yourself in this stinking room."

"*Our* room."

"Not in a long time. Not now. And if you leave, then not ever. Is that what you really want?"

"Do *you*?"

Zeke moans in his sleep and Jeannie rolls over. Twin radar. Sylvia and Carson, standing apart, look at their children together. "They'll be okay," he says. "They have to be." He walks out of the room, closing the door behind him.

Chapter Thirty-Eight

The dry heat wave continues well into August. Pockets of old black tar form bubbles along cracked patches of Main Street in downtown Willing. More than half the streetlights have burned-out bulbs. There is no one left on the municipal payroll assigned to maintain them, and the handful of local government employees remaining are so full of inertia—the less there is to do, the longer it takes them to do it—they cannot be bothered and they never go downtown anymore, anyway. The traffic lights dotting Main Street flash red in unison. The traffic is so sparse, there's no point in coming to a full stop at an intersection; a soft touch of the brake will do. Three more decorative building cornices carved by Italian immigrants in 1905 have fallen down and smashed onto the sidewalk. No one was injured because no one was there, but portions of the sidewalk are nearly impassable now, littered with chunks of stone the size of ragged bowling balls. The gold letters on Cyn's Café are mostly worn off by now. A passerby would have no idea that the place was once full of life. The last whiffs of coffee and blueberry muffins are long gone; even the last little crumbs on the floor were gobbled by mice months ago.

As the town atrophies, the decrepitude spreads like a cancer into the surrounding neighborhoods. The modest aluminum-sided houses closest to the once-noisy Main Street traffic are either empty or filled with illegal squatters. Several of the former owners who defaulted on mortgages they could barely afford in good times are now in Tent City, and not one of them can face going back to visit the rung of the ladder they'd been forced to release—pushed off, is how it feels. Besides, their front doors are heavily padlocked, the windows boarded up. The frontage road leading from Willing out to the cinderblock building that houses Javier Martinez' moribund business, Vida, is so quiet now, families of rabbits sit safely in the center of the road, munching on patches of grass poking up through the asphalt. The low-slung industrial office park where Sandy Tipper's family has run a building supply business for three generations is almost entirely vacant, the angled parking spaces nearly all empty, day after day. Sandy had to let his receptionist go; she lives in Tent City now, in a second-hand orange tent with her aging father. Sandy sits day after day in his dark paneled office stinking up the room with cigars. His computer is untouched. The stacks of trade periodicals and brochures gather dust, also untouched except for the pile that Carson King kicked over several months earlier. Sandy straightened those in a neat stack. The last time Nick French paid a call on Sandy Tipper, Nick stared at him with pinpoint pupils, his leg jiggling, his car keys pitching from palm to palm. Sandy sold him an order so small, it was barely worth recording on the ledger. Nick wouldn't tell him where the job was, or for whom. Sandy didn't press him. In truth, he couldn't wait for Nick to leave.

So ironic. Sandy, Carson, and Nick have more in common than they realize: in their own ways, each is waiting, hunkering down, convinced that there are still fresh innings to be played, and determined to be ready to step up to bat when the game resumes and the rules are back in place.

Carson is at the Baker Block building, on the ground floor, which is, in his mind, the designated Class A commercial space—office or retail. He's stripped and refinished the Romanesque wooden pillars so they gleam, as do the handsome, wide-plank floors. He still believes that if Sylvia would just come look, she'd catch his fire; she'd grasp the intrinsic value begging to be messaged, marketed, displayed. They haven't spoken in a week. And now, he's lying on the floor on his side, his right arm shoved as far as it will go into an air duct shaft. He's finger-screwing a metal duct panel that had come loose, rattling noisily when he tested the heating system. He tries pushing thoughts of

Sylvia away by running through poker hands in his head. He'll take his seat at the card table at the Cavern late tonight, as usual, and fight for every dollar, every lucky draw, every counted card he possibly can. He'll study his opponents, watch for their tics and tells, and show them no mercy. Carson pulls his arm out of the shaft and lies on his floor on his back, looking up at the white pressed-tin ceiling, recalling how he pushed his paint brush into every crenellation and groove in the square tin panels, hundreds of them, his neck aching from the strain of looking up, his face splattered with paint. *Somebody out there wants to pay for this.* His eyes close for a moment, and then a bright white flash cuts into the darkness behind his eyelids, followed by a loud crash. He startles awake, sits up, and looks around to see what has fallen, what has come undone, what he must fix until it is once again perfect. Another flash, followed by a crash, and he realizes a summer storm is coming. The late afternoon sunlight has turned to milky gray, as storm clouds thicken outside. Carson is suddenly so tired he cannot move. *Must get a refill from Zeke.* He lies back down on the hard wooden floor and falls asleep instantly. When he wakes up—he'll never be sure whether it was moments or hours later—black smoke is billowing from the air duct, there's a loud crackling sound above him, and dry lightning and thunder are rattling the old windows.

Like a long scream of pent-up frustration that's suddenly released, the summer lightning is everywhere, all at once. Long jagged purple lines of it, sky-filling white pans of it, are everywhere. The only place in all of Tent City where the ground holds any moisture is around the mouth of the communal hose. Otherwise, the encampment is a dry tinderbox. This isn't news to anyone, but what could anybody do about it? It's hard enough scrounging for food, medicine, and fresh water each day, without worrying about fire hazards. A thick shard of lightning strikes two pin oaks growing near each other at the far end of the yard. They begin to burn, the fire's oxygen causing the upper boughs to sway vigorously as the fire consumes them and works its way down the trunks. The ground-dwellers living back there grab their sleeping bags and run from the burning trees as far and as fast as they can. Flying cinders set one of the sleeping bags on fire, and it takes three people stomping on it to put it out, leaving clumps of burnt nylon and foam padding on the ground. Tenters gather to watch and everyone is making the same calculations: Will the fire reach the tents? When? What can we do? As the trees burn, several people try yanking the hose, but the yard is too big and the water's arc cannot reach the trees. A bucket brigade forms rapidly, cooperative energy surging through the throng. Alison Hart, Fran Hauser, Joe Wenkowicz, Bucky Preston, and dozens more tenters, as well as Enforcers, including Dottie Crandall, try getting water to the fire any way they can. But the existing water bottles are ineffectual, the main hose takes too long to fill anything, and the distance to the trees is too great. Several people get as close to the trees as they can to wet the ground by dumping pails of water on the dirt, in the hopes of creating a kind of fire break. But the heat building around the trees is intense; the fire is leaping to other pin oaks nearby, and within 10 minutes of the lightning strike, a row of trees is ablaze. The first trunks fall and because the ground is so dry, the fire begins crawling across the yard, feeding on dry leaves, twigs, and garbage as it creeps toward the tents. The lightning flashes again, followed by booming thunder, and still there is no rain. Everyone in Tent City is now standing outside, watching the fire progress, rooted in place as they wait for their brains to issue instructions. Mothers stand clutching their toddlers. Fran has run to pick up Baby Doe, who's been living with her.

Sylvia King is standing on the back deck of her house, which is packed with people. Everyone living on the deck, and in the house, is outside staring at the fire. Jeannie and Zeke are there too, both of them pale and barefoot, gripping the remnant railing, leaning forward.

"Don't you even—." Sylvia snaps at them. Something in her is opening up: It's as if she's never seen fire before. Not *this* fire. What is happening now has never been part of her visions. It's uncharted territory. She feels weirdly liberated, even though she's scared and confused, like everyone else. She takes her eyes off the twins and stares out across

Tent City, which glows orange at the far edges. *Telling me to start over. It's a signal.* Somebody screams on the far side of the yard. The fire has reached the first tent, but no one on the deck knows that. Sylvia looks back toward Jeannie and Zeke, but both are gone. "No!" she yells. She jumps down the steps to the yard and plunges into Tent City to find her children. She wishes desperately that Carson were there, and hates him for bailing on them, for saving *himself* first.

As the fire laps at the tents, it unleashes an acrid black smoke—burning plastic—that grows like a demon emerging from hell. The garden hose doesn't stand a chance against the hungry firestorm. Dozens, then hundreds, of tenters begin scrambling to grab their children and whatever belongings they can carry. The tents are packed close together, and the ubiquitous barrels, garbage cans, lawn chairs, laundry lines, and other obstacles further prevent there from being any clear or direct route of escape. People are choking now, the fire is racing through the tents, and the smoke obscures a clear line of site to the curb, the street, the outskirts of Tent City. Big clumps of people pushed close together are trying to run, to stay ahead of the heat and fire itself, and get out as quickly as possible. Sylvia is trying to run against the tide of people. She's calling for Jeannie and Zeke, but her voice is lost. She is convinced now that she need not leave here alone. *Now they will come with me. Now that it's over, we'll leave together.* She'll scoop up her children, and then together, they'll find Carson and they'll all escape. They will find somewhere where they can all change, adjust, establish new ground rules, and figure out how to look ahead, as they used to. *I will learn how to begin again, how to look forward. We all will.*

When you crowd enough people together in a defined space, the crowd itself becomes a living organism. It has energy, a rhythm; it moves and breathes; it cannot remain still. The crowd in Tent City is a restless beast, anxious to break out of its pen. A series of explosions sends jets of fire into the air, along with jagged bits of metal that rain down like military-grade flak. Aerosol cans, lighter fluid, anything flammable that anyone squirreled away in a tent to barter or use explodes on contact with the fast-moving fire. A shard of metal embeds itself in Joe Wenkowicz's skull and he falls to the ground dead before he knows what happened. A three-year-old screams when a shard gashes her arm.

The explosions are frequent but random—terrifying the crowd and ratcheting up the energy to escape. An explosion rocks a tent a few feet from where Sylvia is trying to push forward. The force of the blast, coupled with the whoosh of the fire, pushes her off her feet as the crowd redoubles its effort to mass forward. She is on the ground, with no room to get up, as people treat her like an obstacle to be gotten over or through. Feet pummel Sylvia's ribs, her calves, her stomach. A large man holding two children steps on her head. She knows she must get up; she tries to propel herself, but every time she gets a palm planted on the ground so she can push, something solid presses her down again. She tries to shout, but her voice does not reach. She tries again and again to get up. Again and again, the waves of heavy feet, stumbling and surging forward, force her down. Her nose and scalp are bleeding. She finds it difficult to breathe now. Two ribs are cracked and the chemical smoke combines with the yard's thick, dry dust to form a toxic layer that hugs the ground. A fresh explosion pumps new energy into the crowd. Someone steps on Sylvia's windpipe, crushing it. She looks up and sees herself on the deck of the house. She's looking out from the deck into the yard, watching the twins running through the garden hose in the grass on a hot summer day, a day she remembers because she sold three houses.

Part IV

The Fourth Spring

Chapter Thirty-Nine

AP—The U.S. unemployment rate continues to rise with no moderating trend in sight. The latest seasonally adjusted unemployment data from the Bureau of Labor Statistics indicates that both state- and metropolitan-level unemployment rates have reached their highest levels in nearly a century. So-called "bread lines" are an increasingly common sight in cities and towns across the United States. In Willing, PA, where the economic collapse is now entering its fourth year, the municipal government has been disbanded and the population of Willing itself has declined by 62 percent, while Remington County as a whole has suffered commercial and residential property foreclosure rates nearly triple those of the national average.

Farrah has been trying to skip a stone for more than an hour now, and she still can't quite get the hang of it. *Almost!* She yells into the wind, as one stone after another glances edgewise onto the water before sinking. Farrah looks like a flag blowing wildly in the wind. Her long woolen sweater coat billows against her thighs. She plants her black rubber fisherman's boots on the stony shore like poles. A baseball cap filled with skipping stones—gray and brown stones worn flat and smooth by a millennium spent tossing in the waves—sits on the stony shore next to her. Zeke and Geronimo are sitting on low beach chairs nearby, watching her, and laughing until they are both in tears. It's only April and it's still freezing, but the sun is shining, and the outdoors finally seems like a possibility again after eight months of mostly dark and cold.

"Life is beautiful," Geronimo says, as if continuing a conversation that had already begun. Zeke ruffles Geronimo's silky, angled hair and smiles. His sense are all one sense: sightsmellsoundtaste. The ocean, the wind, the waves, the salt on the brisk air. Zeke is still learning what peace feels like. He's bathing in it, even though he suspects the feeling cannot last much longer. Every hour feels provisional. He still wakes in the middle of the night at least once a month, shaking with nightmares. *Not such a tough guy now, are you?* Farrah gives up and walks over to them.

"My arm is sore," she says. "What am I doing wrong?" She hugs her sweater and squints out across the Atlantic Ocean, her eyes tracking a pair of seagulls coasting on the wind above the shore. She is in the moment, yet she stands with a lean, coiled tension that suggests she's ready to strike out, ready to try something new all over again.

"You're pathetic," Geronimo says, still laughing.

"I can't help it if I'm still new at this—living by the ocean," she says, not remotely offended, as amused by her incompetent stone-skipping as they are.

"I'll show you again," Geronimo says. He gives Zeke's good hand a quick squeeze and hauls his long body up from the low chair. "Two things," he tells Farrah as they walk back to the cap of stones. "The angle of your wrist and you gotta keep the stone level before you flick it out." Their voices trail away from Zeke, carried by the wind. He sinks back in his chair and closes his eyes. Resting still feels so good—like a privilege or a rare art form. He hadn't realized the full extent to which "rest" had been eliminated from his daily life throughout all those months in Tent City until he was completely removed from it. *Look at me: I'm an old man.* With eyes closed, he rubs beach stones between his fingers; smooth and cool to the touch, the stones are soothing. He hovers between waking and sleeping, the surf drumming rhythmically, hypnotically.

"I found her!" Jeannie is shaking Zeke's shoulder. He jerks back to consciousness, shoves her, looks wildly around. "Whoa, whoa, easy Zeke Eel! It's just me."

"I thought—"

"I know. I'm sorry. I shouldn't have—"

"Don't *ever*—"

"I won't," Jeannie says. "No sneaking up. That was stupid. I'm an idiot. I should've known—"

"Don't beat yourself up, Jeel. You're supposed to be lightening up, remember?" he says.

"I found her, Zeke!"

"Found who?" With adrenaline still flooding his body, Zeke thinks, for an instant, maybe Jeannie found Sylvia, selling real estate in some beautiful town somewhere...but no...that's impossible. *Mom's gone. Really gone.* "Oh," he says out loud, as a fresh wave of finality hits him.

"What?" Jeannie asks.

"Who'd you find?"

"Gina! I saw her on YouTube, giving a speech at a huge immigration rally in Tucson! Isn't that incredible?" She doesn't tell him that she's been spending several hours a day researching the web, in hopes of finding Gina. She didn't want Zeke telling her not to get her hopes up. She knows he still worries about her.

"What are you going to do?" Zeke asks. Jeannie pauses. "Jeel?"

"We already talked. It was amazing to hear her voice. She's so strong, Zeke. Not like me." Jeannie's eyes fill. "Shit. I really need to toughen up."

"You're doing fine," Zeke says to her. "You're okay. Really, you are. And you're incredibly strong, Jeannie. Maybe stronger than all of us." She shakes her head. She knows he is looking at the dark circles that seem to have taken up permanent residence under her eyes. The twins are just turning 20, yet both have patches of gray in their hair and fine lines creeping around their eyes.

"Anyway," she says, wiping her nose, "Gina's working for a group in Phoenix that helps families at the borders, protecting their rights, making sure their kids are safe. I almost can't believe it. We talked about this in high school, and now, like, here it is. She says if I can get out there she can find me some work with these people. I mean, it's a real thing." She does not tell him that Gina is living in a makeshift group home and it's all provisionally hand-to-mouth. This is the new normal and it doesn't matter to Gina or to her. In fact, it's beside the point.

"Jeannie," Zeke says quietly, "I'm not Mom. I'm not gonna give you a million reasons why you shouldn't do this." He smiles. "It's good to see you get this excited about something." Jeannie is thinking how much her brother has changed. Less like their dad, and more like a friend. A twin, even. "Whatever you need," he says. "I owe you."

While Tent City was burning to the ground, Zeke knew it was time to execute the emergency plan that he and Farrah and Geronimo had put in place just days before he was assaulted. They already knew Tent City was getting hot for them; they couldn't find enough Enforcers to keep the escalating violence in check. It was probably only a matter of time before they themselves became conspicuous—not by choice. They were right. As Zeke was laid up in bed recovering, the others pulled their drug stash out of the white tent and brought all the small house safes filled with cash to the Cavern. They stuffed all the money into sturdy canvas duffle bags they'd bought at Linton Crossing on an earlier supply run. The night of the fire, Zeke gave Jeannie a burner phone; he always had several on hand, for business reasons. He had two in his pants pocket the night he was assaulted, and Farrah and Geronimo made sure they were still on him when they brought him up to the house, unconscious. Zeke told his sister not to lose the phone, under any circumstances, and not to erase the number he'd pre-programmed.

As the fire grew, Zeke hobbled away from the deck railing and waded into the chaotic crowd. Because he was traveling with them, not against them like his mother, he had an easier time getting to the edge of the yard, and out to the street, where the others were waiting for him in Geronimo's old Cadillac. Zeke was focused on the plan. He had to be; he couldn't screw it up with the others depending on him. He trusted that his family could fend for itself. His mother and his sister would look out for each other; his father, well, he was off doing his own thing, anyway. Zeke figured that Carson would learn soon enough that his absence came at a cost, whatever that might be. The three friends drove all night and when they reached the small, non-touristy little coastal town of Stonycliff, Maine, they stopped. The sun was rising over the Atlantic Ocean. They parked and watched the sun dance on the water, their eyes red from smoke and exhaustion.

"This is it, then," Geronimo said, turning off the motor. They all nodded. The air was fresh and cool, and for the first time in many months, they each felt they could take a long, honest breath. They slept in the car. By the end of their first day, they managed to rent a dilapidated shack in this depressed fishing village that was the opposite of picture-postcard Maine. Only a handful of elite restaurants around the country were still offering lobster on the menu, and lobster was the foundation of Stonycliff's economy. The local fishing families went about their business grimly, accustomed to boom-and-bust cycles. They took their boats out at dawn, as usual, and economized at home, as always, waiting for the economic tides to turn their way once more. No one could say how long the wait would be this time.

The three Tent City entrepreneurs, now homeless refugees themselves, piled the duffels under a thick seaman's tarpaulin in a corner of the little shack. There wasn't much to it: gray-weathered boards, a dusty oak floor, a black pot-bellied stove, and a modest wall kitchen. But after months and months of sleepless nights, bodies on high alert at all hours, the shack felt luxurious. They spent the first few days curled up on two mattresses left behind by previous tenants, spooning, making love slowly, unfurling their bodies and their minds amid the unaccustomed velvety quiet that surrounded them. They ate soup and baked beans out of cans left in a cabinet. They shared a complete lack of urgency—about anything. During their time in Tent City, they'd amassed $40,000 in cash—more money than anyone in Stonycliff had seen in three years running. They found a little store in town that sold sturdy padlocks amid a jumble of fishing supplies; they bought four and attached them to the door and windows of the shack. The sleepy little town posed no obvious threat, but the three could not quite let their guard down.

On the fourth day of their respite in Stonycliff, when they were all spending most of the day in bed, Zeke's burner phone rang. It was Jeannie. It took her awhile to get the story out. She could only tell it in pieces. And it took Zeke days more to get it straight in his own mind. Nothing made sense, at the end. He transferred money to her phone. She got on a bus, and then another bus, and by the time Zeke picked her up in Bangor, she really did look like someone who had only just escaped the Nazis. She was even clutching a torn tote bag that held little beside the old family menorah that she had vowed to keep, though she still could not say why. It was almost the only thing she grabbed from her tent as she fled. Zeke tapped into his inner contractor and with help from the other two, they put up some makeshift walls so that Jeannie could have her own little room. Zeke put Jeannie to bed and refused to let her leave the shack for several weeks, feeding her spoonsful of soup every few hours as if she were a baby bird.

The four of them hunkered down as fall turned to winter, taking turns to run out for essentials, mainly food and blankets and wood for the pot-bellied stove. They kept themselves apart from the town, as much as possible, striving for not just a low profile, but no profile. The three partners didn't sell drugs. They didn't work any angles. They splurged on new laptops, their only luxury—setting Jeannie on her quest to find Gina.

Jeannie has no idea how much money her brother has stashed away. She doesn't like to think about money. She hates it, in fact, and wants only the smallest possible quantities to pass through her hands, just enough to keep body and soul together. She tells Zeke she'll take Greyhound out to Arizona, and that she'll pay him back as soon as she can.

"Forget it," he says. "I'll buy you a plane ticket." They argue, but Jeannie gives in, suppressing the urge to thread the needle as narrowly as possible, just this once. There will be time, she hopes, to shrink her own footprint as her capacity for service, to be of use, grows once again. *Something has to matter*.

Jeannie leaves in early May. Zeke drives her to the airport in the old Cadillac. They barely speak. When either of them will see their father again is a gaping wound of a question, one they are not ready or willing to discuss. Their mother is so present within them and between them, there is no need to speak of her at all—not yet. When they will see each *other* again they also leave hanging, unanswerable. Zeke drops his sister at the curb. She's bringing almost nothing with her, as she has virtually nothing to bring. He tells her to say hi to Gina for him. She says she will. They embrace—with real warmth, like adults who know that life is conditional.

Zeke, Farrah, and Geronimo continue living where they landed the summer before. They live frugally, willing the money to last as long as possible. They do not discuss the future. They don't have any words for it. They came of age at a time when all the usual signposts—how to get ahead, find your place, build something—were being toppled, leaving the way forward unmarked. There are no rules to follow, so they make them up as they go along. Maybe they'll invent something new. Maybe they won't. They don't have expectations because there is no one around holding out expectations for them to meet. No bar has been set; no hurdle presented as something to be gotten over, so they can move on and make something of themselves, as the saying used to go—a saying they have never really heard anyone say out loud. For Zeke and Farrah and Geronimo, time does not bring progress; time is not money. All of their earlier hustle was driven by a dire need to survive—to not starve, to not give up indoor plumbing. Zeke's entrepreneurial zeal has leached out of him. Whether he'll ever feel like hustling again, whether he'll relish the chase and the challenge, he couldn't say. For right now, the three of them will take each day as it comes. They don't see the point in living any other way. They are casualties of a war not of their making, yet their lives are already shaped by its consequences.

CHAPTER FORTY

Carson's joints are stiff with cold and he feels a century older than he did yesterday. He slowly extracts himself from his sleeping bag. His lower back is a mess after months spent sleeping on a hard floor, but he ignores the pain. The unpainted window frames in the room that now constitutes the main perimeter of his life still bear decals of the window manufacturer. The interior drywall is unadorned; the nails still show. From the outside, panels of peeling Tyvek are concerning, and Carson knows he'll have to figure out what to do about it. But for right now, he needs to perform his daily survey from roof, which he reaches by means of an extension ladder propped up against this Willing Enclave house—the house that was intended to bring all the skittish buyers out of the proverbial woodwork.

Carson balances on the roof in his disintegrating work boots. From up here, there isn't that much to see: some open land, some thin woods, and his legacy: two more partially constructed houses and three ragged foundations that are silting up, arrayed along a modest swell of land where a half-built road peters out in a bed of gravel. But Carson wills himself to pull back the curtain of reality and envision a future that can still unfold—and will, if he keeps chipping away at it. Just because everything and everyone around him has downshifted does not mean he must also. He does not dwell on "why," preferring to focus on "next." He doesn't read the news; he doesn't have to. He knows what he knows. He suspects the Willing Chamber of Commerce was disbanded long ago, but he doesn't need or want anyone to confirm it. And good riddance. He hopes that Sandy Tipper has been knocked down a peg or three. The great unravelling, as he has come to think of it, cannot go on forever. *For every action, there is an opposite and equal reaction.* And after everything that's happened, he feels a "rebalancing" is approaching. It must be. His vision for Willing Enclave will emerge from dormancy and bloom back into reality, like the dandelions just now poking up from the April soil.

He watches and waits. He envisions Sylvia in her lavender coat with the pretty buttons walking up to the front door of the very house he is standing on. She's hosting an Open House. The new road fills with cars. Parents with young children stream into the house. They poke and prod through every room like a swarm of happy ants. This happy, happy home. The kind of home where he and Sylvia might have settled with the kids, in another lifetime. Life as it is meant to be. As it was. As it will be again...Sylvia pushing her brown curls away from her face as she pours over deal sheets at the kitchen table. The children are in bed. They make love on the living room couch, half-empty brandy classes beside them on the coffee table. There is no room in his imagination—in *their* imagination—for scorched earth. It just isn't meant to happen. Certainly not to them.

He stands on the roof of a house that is not a home as a cold spring wind slices through him, taxing his balance. He sees that some of the roof shingles already show signs of wear. He cannot prevent his mind from searching again for the moment when he was meant to intervene, to divert the course of events leading up to this moment. *The time is out of joint.* An eerie sensation ripples through him, not for the first time: *I am living someone else's life.* He forces himself to recall random moments that *did* happen, were always *meant* to happen: Meeting Sylvia in high school. Scraping together enough money with Darius and Vin to buy their first tear-down, and the giddy feeling that they were about to remake the world in their own image. Watching the twins jump over the water arcing from the garden hose—little dancing sprites on the vast green lawn that was their calling card to the world, that put the world on notice. *We are here. We have arrived. And we're not stopping.*

And then there is everything that never should have happened. *I* *should have...*echoes in Carson's brain like an endless recitation of the rosary. Not prayerful, but accusatory. And alongside the recriminations are the images he resents for taking up residence in his mind's eye, when they never should have been there in the first place...

Staggering out of the Baker building, choking and gasping for breath, covered in soot the night the heat lightning struck like a vengeful god. He stood in the dark, empty Main Street and watched the roof collapse as fire consumed the entire structure. By the time the Remington Fire Department responded—anemically staffed and equipped, as though saving downtown Willing hardly seemed worth the expenditure of dwindling resources—the fire had leapt to the roofs on either side. By daybreak, most of the historic city block resembled a ruined stone castle and Carson's last gambling hand was lost. He was uninsured. That was part of the gamble, too.

He made his way home, somehow, coughing as though he would puke up his lungs. Yet as he turned the corner, home was not where it belonged. In its place was a burned out hulk of a wreck. And through that smoking wreck Carson had an x-ray view of Tent City reduced to an ashy, smoldering, stinking wasteland—like the battlefield at Ypres minus the trenches. His whole body began shaking. He'd lost his phone in the fire downtown. He didn't know where any of his family were. He wanted desperately to grab them by the shoulders and tell them that everything he'd done, he'd done for *them,* to secure *their* future, to find a way out of the vortex—*that's what Sylvia called it. But I couldn't be in both places at once. You must understand...*

The soles of his boots lapped up the heat as he walked into the remains of his house, calling out names, one after the other, as if Sylvia or Zeke or Jeannie would bound downstairs for the pizza he'd just brought home after a long day. He didn't think about the burned rafters that might crash down on him, or the weakened flooring that could collapse beneath him. He didn't care, at that moment, one way or the other. He was met with silence, but for the hiss of hot wood and the shifting energy of broken and melted materials. Tarnished zippers flashed here and there: all that was left of tenters' abandoned sleeping bags, as they climbed over each other to get out. The glass deck doorway was still partially framed. He walked out onto the sliver of deck still standing, shards of glass crunching underfoot. The sun was shining, which seemed all wrong. He looked out across the land as he had done hundreds of times before—always reassured by the calm expanse that was both protective and declarative. This time, the view did not compute. The fire took everything all the way back to the stream. Here and there, across the blackened ground now wet from the rains that finally came, big chunks of debris stuck up at odd angles. He stepped down to the ground, his soles burning, and he realized, with a lurch of horror, that the debris was bodies, burned beyond recognition. He stopped moving. *No, no, no, no. Not this. Not them. Not me. Not us.*

Carson walked the grounds of Tent City for two hours before he saw what he was trying very hard not to find: Sylvia's wedding ring, affixed to a burned corpse…

He wobbles on the roof of the Willing Enclave house. He heads back down the ladder, feeling sick, crawls through the window, and sinks onto his sleeping bag. He forces himself to visualize poker hands, to keep an entire poker game straight in his head, every hand, until he wins. Finally, he hears what he's been waiting for: three pick-up trucks pull up the drive to Willing Enclave, one after the other, the tires crunching loudly on loose gravel. This isn't a dream; this is real. Carson puts his head out of the unadorned window and looks down on Vin Palmer wearing an unmistakable WPC cap, as well as Nick French and Bruno Fernandez. They stand away from one another as they approach the house, heads down, feet scuffling as if they're half-ashamed to be there. But Carson can practically hear the gears turning in their brains, as they separately assess the pros and cons—and alternatives, if they have any. They'll have to pool meager resources. Beg, borrow, and steal, if need be. He smiles. *Now we begin.*

Chapter Forty-One

NO TRESPASSING!

```
Main Street is closed to the public until
further notice between Berkley Street
and Compound Street on the north end and
Irongmonger Way and Martini Street on the
south end. Violators will be fined up to
$1,000 and 30 days in jail.
```

Nobody comes downtown anymore to buy anything. Or do anything. Or to have fun. The thinning herd of cars and trucks traveling Route 12 almost never takes the Willing exit. And if they do, it's usually because they don't know the area. They think, mistakenly, they'll find a diner or a coffee shop or even just a place to buy aspirin. But they won't find anything like that until they reach Linton Crossing, which has just experienced its first downtown failure—a home goods store where people like Betty and Barnaby Bachman buy mid-century modern furniture and exquisite tableware.

What is downtown, anyway? In Detroit, it's to the south. In Cleveland, it's to the north. In St. Louis, downtown is east. And in Pittsburgh, it's west. But in Willing, it's pretty much just an idea, at this point, like the Tong River itself. The Baker Block and its neighbors look like a row of decaying corpses, collapsing in on themselves. Amid the ashy blocks of stone, charred wood, and twisted metal, a light dusting of late-winter snow lingers in the cold shadows of April's weak sunlight. The county lacks the capacity to clear it all away, and there's no pressure to do so, anyway. No outraged calls from the Chamber of Commerce. No indignant editorials about the eyesore's negative effect on local businesses. No complaints from taxpayers about wasted tax dollars. There is no one left here to complain about such things, and no one to complain to.

The Sudsy is gone.

The tobacconist's is gone.

The used bookstore is gone.

The dry cleaner's is gone.

Dean's Bric-a-Brac is gone.

Cyn's is long, long gone.

The 7-Eleven on the outskirts of town, once the favorite of budget-conscious workers like Bruno and Jorge, sells a hot dog or a slice of pizza for 59 cents now, because that's all anyone has in their pockets at any one time. The Dunkin' Donuts where Sylvia stopped only if she couldn't get to Cyn's left six months ago. They couldn't make a go of selling doughnuts for 10 cents apiece. And for many people, sugar is a luxury they ration now, anyway. The hot dog usually comes first.

The ShopFine is still open, but all the registers are self-checkout-only and most of the shelves are stocked with open boxes, from which shoppers must pluck their own items. The store employs just one full-time manager and two part-timers who stock shelves. None of them would dream of living anywhere near downtown Willing. None of them can recite a single PLU code like Winnie Suggs used to, either. A forgotten art, and one that required some investment, after all.

But Willing is not truly empty. There is an abundance of illegal shelter to be had, if you can stand the as-is condition of these places. The Cavern, for instance, like many other buildings still in one piece, has been repurposed. It's been requisitioned for a use much closer to the original one: it's home again, in a way. But the occupants this time are not a close-knit family of immigrants earning their living from the shop below, striving to adapt to America's commercial rhythms, its frenetic pull-yourself-up-by-your-bootstraps mentality. The small rooms this time around are little more than basic shelter. Without electricity or heat, in rooms with peeling cabbage-rose wallpaper and cracked plaster, no one is comfortable. And the over-crowding makes everyone irritable—fights are fairly common. Stealing property (what little anyone has) is also common, as are accusations of theft, whether real or imagined. The less anyone has, the more jealously they guard it. The Cavern is turning into a miniature Tent City. A tenement, in fact. Dottie Crandall, who's among the dozen refugees squatting in the cramped warren of rooms (with a single toilet), is trying single-handedly to reconstitute a team of Enforcers, which she intends to lead. Surely, people will pay *something* for protection, in a place like this. People like Alison Hart, whom Dottie thinks won't make it to 25 without her services, can surely find a way to make it worth Dottie's while.

No, Willing is not empty. It's not a ghost town. It is a holding pen, a purgatory, a way station. Everyone in Willing today knows very well where they came *from,* how they started out, and where they used to think they were going. All of them believed there was a shape to their lives, some purpose revealed or at least forthcoming. But tomorrow, and the next day, and the day after that stretch before them now as one long, terrifying blank. They find themselves on the losing end of a bargain they didn't realize they'd made, or when. The future used to be worth its weight in gold. Now, it's penniless.

THE END

www.ingramcontent.com/pod-product-compliance
Lightning Source LLC
LaVergne TN
LVHW030919080826
845145LV00013B/2961

* 9 7 8 1 9 4 8 5 9 8 9 1 0 *